SCARY MODSTERS

... and Creepy Freaks

DIANE RINELLA

Copyright (C) 2014 Diane Rinella
Cover art copyright (C) 2015 Diane Rinella
Cover art and design by Heidi "Azurylipfe" Darras
http://azurylipfe.daportfolio.com/
with Diane Rinella

ISBN: 0615984045
ISBN-13: 978-0615984049

Dedicated to the ones I love...

For Maria: Because she understands.
"Birds of a Feather" - Paul Revere and the Raiders

For Brian: The song of our first dance still fits.
"Wonderful World" - Joey Ramone

For Trishalana: I adore you.
"Trishalana" - Paul Revere & the Raiders

For Steve: Even though you are stuck with me, you never
complain. Amazing.
"Waterloo Sunset" - The Kinks

For Andrea: Because only a true friend would tolerate me for so
long.
"Thank You For Being A Friend" - Cynthia Fee (The Golden
Girls version)

For Frank & Alice Rinella and Tony & Jean Rinella:
I miss you more each day.
"Memories Are Made Of This" - Dean Martin

For Joshua: Simply said, "I Remember You" - The Ramones

Acknowledgements

How do you even begin to acknowledge people you will never meet, let alone tell them how much they mean to you?

To my readers: Thank you for allowing my words into your heart. When I published *Love's Forbidden Flower* I never expected how many wonderful people would share their thoughts and stories. If you read my Forbidden Flower series and are now allowing me into your heart again, you truly are a gift. If you are new to my work, thank you for taking a chance on me.

To my beta readers, Miranda Johnson from Mommy's a Book Whore, Julie Barman, and N. Stevenson Jennette III. Thank you for telling it like it was and putting up with my crazy questions.

Thank you Jennifer Theriot, whose fantastic novel, *Out Of the Box*, is mentioned within these pages.

To the World's Greatest Stalker, Darla Roybal. Thank you for motivating me when my inner spirit fails.

My long-time friend Steve Stone, with whom I could banter about music for days on end and never grow weary. Those conversations inspired much of this book.

Last, and in no way least, my husband, Brian Preston, and our daughter, Trishalana Rinella Preston. Thank you for tolerating the madness that is me.

Introduction

Rock and roll isn't about the Beatles. It is about them playing The Cavern Club—that cramped, musty, brick cellar where England's greatest entertained bored, working class youth. It's about kids who dreamed big as they spent every hard-earned penny recording demos. Some of those bands went on to top the national charts. Fast forward a few decades and a lot of those hits are lost because corporate big wigs choose what should be remembered.

Rosalyn's real life counterparts seek what time has forgotten. That being said, to have any realism in *Scary Modsters* I could not stick to mentioning only the bands people are told to know, no matter how fabulous they may be. I've done my best to keep the number of references some may find obscure to a minimum and to never rely on them to imply meaning without explanation. It's not the song that's important to Rosalyn; it's the effect it has on her.

A playlist, comprised of each chapter title and the artists whose song it represents, is at the end of this book. It can also be found on YouTube.

As for Peter's tale, while all of the events depicted in this book are fictitious, rock history books are loaded with similar horror stories. Some of his real-life contemporaries had interesting rides.

For those who do not catch the references in the title:

Mod - A British subculture, focused on music and fashion, that originated in the nineteen sixties.

Mobster - A participant in organized crime.

Scary Monsters [and Super Creeps] - A David Bowie album.

Happy discovering!

Have a Cigar

Peter

May 13, 1966 was a day most wouldn't give a turnip over. Take a look at this picture. You see that guy? The smarmy, dark-haired, young businessman sitting behind that big, wood desk? That's Ben Stoddard, or as he likes to call himself, Big Ben. I refer to him as Mr. BS. He's the one who took me. I mean he took everything—my career, my happiness, the girl I loved, and my life.

Now look to those four young lads sitting across from him—the ones that seem as if they've never had a penny to their names. The ones eager to sign on that dotted line. That handsome devil with the sandy blonde hair and the stupid grin—that's me, Peter Lane; singer, guitarist, huge chump, and idiot extraordinaire. I was on top of the world at that moment. We all were. You know that witticism about how you have to be careful you don't sign your life away? It's no joke, because that's exactly what I was doing.

We had just been given a new car, a swanky apartment, and unlimited credit at all the fancy boutiques on Carnaby Street. You've heard of Carnaby, right? The place where every self-respecting mod paid too much for clothes he couldn't afford, even if they had been offered at fair prices. We were told to dress like we owned the world because we soon would. A tour was being planned so we could conquer America, just like The Beatles. All we had to do was sign on that little piece of paper you see on Mr. BS's desk. We signed it in blue ink from a fountain pen—but had we known whom we were dealing with we would have pricked ourselves and used blood.

Two years later I was hovering above my casket, watching people lower my body into a dark, dirt hole, and cringing at

1

how the once beautiful man had become broken, burnt to a crisp, and about to be devoured by worms.

Everyone thought it was an accident.

Then and there I vowed revenge. Plotting it was easy, but finding my way back was another story.

Friday on My Mind

Rosalyn

A brunette, a raven-haired beauty, and a girl looking like a peacock all walk into a bar. No, it's not a joke; it's my not-so-mundane life that generally feels like the setup for a wisecrack.

No matter how many times my friends and I claim we are going to do something new, every Friday night we find our tushes planted at Mulligan's. However, today our weekly Friday night venture truly seemed out of the cards since my friends were originally too tired from their workweeks to consider anything short of collapsing. When you are in your early thirties and single you should be embracing life, not rotting on a sofa. Thus, when my friends bailed, I detoured into Warped Records which is both a second home and how I envision my little corner of Heaven. Some would call the smell of old album covers a dank stench, but to me it's a musky perfume that seeps into my pores and comforts me with the knowledge that no matter what fails me I always have my sanctuary.

Among the bins of paradise and the blaring Siouxsie, the perfect gem captured my gaze and held it for ransom. Before me was a pair of eyes so unlike any other that they were nearly indescribable.

Piercing? No. That implies they shot through my skin and reached my heart; however, these somehow reached my soul. Captivating? Again, that was misleading. While they did hold my attention they also kept me at bay. Perhaps haunting? Yes, they did indeed haunt me. They also seemed to follow me to wherever I stood. A true description was so elusive that the color wasn't easily defined. They were deep blue, yet also flannel grey with a hint of green. In a certain light they seemed black with specks of gold.

All of these emotions and colors were brought forth by just one picture—a picture on an album that had been slipped into plastic and unceremoniously tacked to the wall, yet somehow it jumped out at me and begged for worship.

"Who are those guys?" I asked Shane, the store's clerk. Shane's tight black pants, white Split Enz T-shirt, black suspenders, and short, curly, brown hair made him look like a skinny, nineteen eighties teenager in a forty-something-year-old's body. His hot pink English Beat button sold the outfit. In an odd way our obsessions make us kindred spirits. It may be like we are third cousins, twice removed, but kindred nonetheless.

"Not a clue." Shane absent-mindedly tapped a pencil on a note pad while his hazel eyes sat on a ragged copy of *Rolling Stone* that was decades out of date. "How is it you don't know? You're the super genius no one can stump." He sighed, conceding to the call of duty. "I suppose you want me to halt my important work and show it to you."

"If it's not too much of a bother to pull yourself away from that fascinating article on INXS that is so old it will soon disintegrate, then yes, please. I would appreciate your struggle of removing the tack for a lady."

With the flick of his wrist, Shane sent the magazine spinning across the counter. "Geez, you practically live here, so I thought you would be more at home yanking the thing off yourself."

"Glad to see that chivalry is alive and well at Warped Records."

The album was presented with a bow. "Milady, as per your request." Shane's smugness made me grin. "Anyway, it arrived with some other records from a recent estate sale. Rob seemed to know who they were."

My eyes honed in on the price tag. "Six dollars? That's a lot for a potentially crappy band no one has heard of."

Shane's view floated from the magazine to the notepad.

"Yep. Six bucks is what this says. I hung it next to the two hundred dollar, Jagger-signed, *Goat's Head Soup* to be funny."

Four men, who were partially obscured by a golden overlay of paisleys and swirls, stared back at me. Their clothes were colorful, slightly Edwardian, and accented with fur. It was all very fashionable for the nineteen sixty-eight copyright printed on the back of the cover that held no liner notes. Three of the men felt so insignificant that they were but mere blurs. All I noticed was the cute one with the sandy blonde hair and magnetic eyes whose signature started with the letter P.

My fingers glided over the autograph. The ink felt as if it were luxurious azure velvet. It also gave off an energy that put a beat in my head. What really caught my attention was a spot of what appeared to be dried blood. When I touched it, a fuzz, reminiscent of the thrill I get when hearing a vintage guitar effects pedal, vibrated through. I had to have that album!

My purchase consisted of a modest haul of a single, three CDs, and the mysterious album I could not let out of my clutches. I got into my ninety-seven Mustang and headed home. The plastic bag of music sat in the passenger seat and taunted me to dive into it. I popped in a CD and cranked The Seeds' sixties garage rock classic, *A Web of Sound*. Its dated-sounding, tinny fuzz and groovy beat had me dancing in my seat. Strange looks were drawn from two cute guys in a vaporwave-exuding, black Mercedes as we sat at a stoplight with our windows down. I waved. They snickered.

Although my only external reaction was a shrug, internally my heart frowned into my stomach. I've tried to be like them and embrace something trendy. But in being part of the in crowd I found I was betraying myself. My heart only sings when I'm truthful about my passions for clothes and music of the past. I really hope those guys are genuinely experiencing joys I can't find in the current times instead of hiding from themselves like I once did.

Once home, it was straight to the family room stereo to listen to The Stones and crack a beer while dancing to *Exile*

On Main Street. I had to shove aside stacks of albums I had taken out of the oversized, shutter-door closet the night before for reorganizing. With the signed album propped on the sofa as if it were an audience, I shed my alter ego by ripping off my tailored suit coat. The liberation of no longer feeling dressed for a corporate costume party brought me back to life. The flick of my neck with each shoulder roll sent my deep-auburn, iron-pressed locks flying. My hips ground while I stared at the record. I kicked my stilettos across the room (nearly landing them in the stone fireplace) before shimmying out of my skirt. My butt plopped onto the sofa with me wearing nothing but my blouse and panties. The man on the album with the engaging eyes pulled my attention to him. "Who are you?"

From my cell phone I typed "Deep Trance" into Wikipedia before taking a swig of beer. As the details appeared the malty liquid was nearly sprayed out of my mouth before being choked back. Clearly Rob, the shop's owner, had no clue as to the value of the album. Easily it was worth six hundred, not the six I thought I foolishly paid.

Deep Trance was the third album by the legendary band Love Machine and marked a departure from their usual pop sound. The album lacked label support causing some to believe it was intended to fail in order to offset the financial gains of other bands. The original cover was to depict the band behind an opaque veil of psychedelic swirls, but management rejected it, claiming that the photo made the band unrecognizable. A test run of the rejected cover produced a handful of copies that were likely destroyed.

Love Machine! "Holy St. Elvis!" The infamous, chart-topping, UK band that barely caught a break in America? That had to mean—

I grabbed the album while still a little dizzy from my revelation. "This is signed by Peter Lane!" In a grand master flash I was standing on the sofa, bouncing and squealing at the top of my lungs, "Oh, my God, Peter Lane! Peter freaking Lane!" It was a proud fangirl moment—the flipping out over the scribbling of a dead legend that sat in my hands. My only embarrassment was over how I ever missed who the guy was. Thankfully Rob missed it too. With a jump I flipped my legs out from under me and landed my butt on the sofa. "Well, Peter Lane, I certainly never expected to meet you, such as it is."

My deep-brown eyes were more drawn into the image than ever. Peter's impish gaze seemed so deep and powerful. His eyes were now a solid black, and my mind started slipping into their void while haze clouded my peripheral vision.

The sudden screech blaring from my phone brought my hand to my heart and snapped me back into the present. One Direction blasted through the air, clashing with The Stones. Darla was calling. Sometimes my friends' taste in music scares me.

"Hey," I answered. My voice sounded oddly detached.

"Drinks! Twenty minutes! Mulligan's! Meet us there!" came screaming into my ear.

"What happened to being too tired?"

"Don't know. Don't care. I just got a burst of energy. Must mean we are not meant to be at home tonight. Get on it!"

I've Just Seen a Face

August 1966

Peter

My personal playland awaited, or so I tried to convince myself as a cute little bird held my door open so I could strut into the hive known as Klein Photography Studios on a balmy London morning. Truthfully, I was utterly clueless as what I was to do. *Rave Magazine* claimed that I was the face of the mod generation and actually desired my mug on their cover. Whoever could have imagined me, poverty-born Peter Lane, on the cover of a pop magazine? Darling little girls were going to pin my picture to their walls. It was hardly the musical accolades I desired. Still, it was bloody amazing.

My kingdom fluttered with the chaos of minions rushing in and out of doorways in various states of undress. A waif of a girl gave me a snooty up-down as she passed. Without all of her typical paint, I hardly recognized top fashion model Gloria Smythe. She was cute but looked nothing like she did when dolled up and half-naked, enticing me to buy a product that faded into the background compared to the creamy skin she flaunted. Makeup really does seem to be magical, and it made me slightly concerned for what they were about to do to my lovely mug.

The bird ushered me to meet with the photographer inside a room with a big, white screen and loads of blinding lights. "So, this is the flip side of glamour," I mused.

A man, not much older than I, wearing a ratty old cotton shirt, frayed jeans, and the kind of sandals that made floppy noises as he walked, talked me through the plans for the shoot. Clearly the guy wasn't one of us—the ones with unlimited credit on Carnaby Street. The situation made me feel rather elite.

Basically, I was to sit, keep my trap shut, and, of course, look good. I'd be instructed when to smile and when to look thoughtful. "There's an art to it," he told me. "You have to look like you're a little on the bored side, but if you look truly bored, the girlies will think you're not real."

What did that mean? Nothing seemed real in that place where faces were hidden under layers of paint that made people resemble matching porcelain dolls.

Next, the little bird ushered me off to the makeup room. Compared to the sterile studio and the hall lined with framed prints of fashion ads, the makeup room was inviting and homey. Sketches of people and places unknown to me were tacked about with care. They seemed to represent things incredibly significant to someone. When I saw exactly whom that someone was, my eyes transfixed on the lovely, straw-blonde crumpet with a makeup kit. I glanced away as she looked at me. It was an automatic reaction, and I'd no idea why I was shying from this gorgeous creature even though my body screamed for me to dive in.

The little bird introduced me to the makeup girl as if she was a piece of furniture. "That's Jane MacFadden. She'll do your makeup."

Irish? Damn. I could hear Mum nagging already.

Jane's smile warmed me like I'd just downed a pot of freshly steeped tea. Still, I couldn't quite bring myself to fully look at her. I also couldn't figure out what it was about her that made me so shy. She invited me to sit in her chair, and the lights around the mirror turned blinding when she flicked on the switch. I groaned sharply. "Sorry," she said with a reserved, guilty smile. "I always forget to warn people."

Jane turned to dig into her makeup kit, and I was able to face her backside without issue. It was a very lovely backside, leaving me to wonder how it looked without the pesky cover of a skirt.

She approached with an armful of little containers of

foundation in an array of English pasty white. She held each up to my cheek, set a few aside, and then meticulously returned the rest to the box. Her whispery voice that requested I look at her didn't have the slightest trace of an Irish accent nor was she a native Londoner.

My face rotated in her direction, and I finally sank in a full, delicious view. She was absolutely gorgeous. Again my eyes hooded as I let her examine my mug. That girl was bringing out all kinds of odd emotions and twisting my insides to knots.

She returned to her makeup box, and my eyes landed squarely on her body. Jane reminded me of a classic portrait done by one of those Italian painters you see in the fancy museums. I wanted to slide my hands up those curves and paint her with my fingers.

Again I shied away at her glance, and then felt her gentle touch to my chin as she drew it towards her. My breath stilled as her orbs of blue sunlight captivated me. She hesitated. Was she just examining my face or was she experiencing the same magic I was?

Jane stepped back, but our eyes remained locked. No longer were we subject and artist. A little spark had turned us into the quintessential man and woman. Danger of it flaring into a huge fire seemed to loom.

I couldn't let this moment pass. Returning later to slip my number to the makeup girl would be a cocky rock star move. My flaring and ebbing pulse screamed she deserved better.

She started applying the foundation, and my lips fumbled to find words. I wanted to make a nice impression and not sound like one of the other blokes who came in day after day and expected her to fall at his feet. The dolling up couldn't take long, so fast action was of the essence. "Do you like dogs?"

Jane put down her makeup applicator. When she cocked her head the dazzle in her eyes turned my heart's rhythmic beat into a fluttering harp. "You know, Peter, all day long I chat with people in that chair, and they come up with the craziest small talk, but never have I been asked such an icebreaking question. Why do you ask?"

"When I was little we had this old hound named Fred. The thing was absolutely huge." I chuckled at the memory as Jane resumed her work. "Seemed to take up the entire flat. Fred had been passed around through the family and wound up with us because we were the only ones who lived where he was allowed. He had belonged to my uncle who died during the war. Fred became kind of a badge of honor, or at least that's what Dad said publicly. Privately he grumbled about being stuck with the poor guy. Fred was my best friend. I cried for weeks after he passed."

Jane brushed some rosy powder on me. Despite my moderate concern that I was being blushed up like a girl, I carried on. "With all that's going on in my life right now I have to wonder what else there is to get excited about. Two hot singles, an album racing up the charts, tours being planned, and now I'm on the cover of a magazine. What's left? Of all the things the future could possibly hold, the two things I want most are to make music and have a nice house in the country with another hound dog. So, I guess what I'm really asking is, Jane MacFadden, what do you want out of life?"

Jane stared at her brush like it held a distant memory. When she took a seat on the makeup counter, the bright lights that made so many others look ugly unless they had stuff caked onto their face only enhanced her natural radiance.

"Earnest died when I was seven. I was completely broken-hearted as well. My parents offered to get another, but I didn't want any dog other than him. Now I'm wishing I had. I'm never going to pass on the opportunity to have something special again, no matter what it is. I was afraid of gaining love and then losing it. What are you afraid of?"

The question knocked my noggin and made me take pause. My mind saw my parents, struggling day after day with nothing to leave behind in the world but a son. "Fading away. I'm scared to death that someday I'll look at my life and find it amounted to nothing."

A glow came about her that made my heart puddle out from inside my body and goo up on the floor. "I don't think you'll have that problem, Peter. Something tells me the time you have here will be one hell of a ride." The door opened and the girl from before came in to nab me.

My eyes locked on Jane's. In the silence so much was said. Emotions rang like bells in my ears.

"I want to be with you again."

"I want to know everything about you."

It was like we were each pleading to the other while standing in total silence. "May I take you to dinner tonight?" I asked.

A glorious smile crossed her face. "Yes, I'd like that very much."

"Will you be here when I'm done? I'll come back and we'll arrange it?"

"Absolutely," she said, and my heart flew off into Heaven.

Spill The Wine

Rosalyn

Mulligan's used to be a quaint, neighborhood bar with pool tables and a dartboard, until the area was redeveloped. Now the place resembles a gorgeous saloon from the end of the Victorian era, complete with faux-stained glass windows and tables of cherry wood. While I absolutely swoon over the decor, Mulligan's new management seems to be doing all it can to turn it into a pick-up spot. The new clientele makes me feel like I'm on an auction block. Sometimes I find myself hunched over my drink, barely peering up in fear that judges are strolling by with rulers while making sure one of my ears isn't a millimeter higher than the other.

Why is finding a decent guy so difficult? I have five basic requirements; a good heart, a respectable level of intelligence, is able to love me for who I am, has quirks of his own that he is happy with, and the ever-elusive "makes my heart light up". Ideally, he will also complement me musically because, well, I have a few hang-ups. Dad nicknamed me Rox, a twist on the term rock and roll, for a reason. You see, there is my Golden Rule: Guitars almost always need to be electric, and call me crazy, but singers have to be able to sing. Then there is my extremist side: Whoever invented the drum machine should be executed along with the creator of Auto-Tune.

Now I know that sounds a bit harsh, but these are values that my dad tried to instill in me while I was in the womb; thus, a huge chunk of what I listen to existed before I did. All of this used to make me feel pathetic, but years of being teased has brought me to accept it takes courage to be quirky, much like the strength the peacock sitting across the table from me possesses.

"What will we drink to?" Darla asks. Her layered hair of greens and blues, complementing her deep green eyes and pale skin, sways as she tosses it aside to clear her view. Although Darla and I now work under the same roof, she, Jacqueline, and I have been buddies since high school.

Jacqueline is the true definition of best friend forever. She's also my housemate. Two years ago, tragedy blinded me to the possibility of ever seeing good in the world again. Jacqueline saved my sanity by insisting that I move into the house her parents gave her as a college graduation present. Like me, she hates the single life. Guys fall all over her due to her trim figure, gorgeous crystal-blue eyes, and raven hair. However, when they realize she's worthy of respect, they flee to the security of a mindless bimbo. This, coupled with the fact that she works in a man's world as a marketing head for a sports TV network, explains a lot about Jacqueline.

"To my devious plan of stealing the purple and pink floral go-go dress Rox is wearing!" Jacqueline says, seriously jealous before teasing, "Gran would have gone nuts over it."

Okay, so my taste in music may not actually be my biggest obstacle with men. Truth be told, if I could jump into a time machine, my first stop would be Gran's closet, circa nineteen sixty-six. "You're just jealous that Darla and I are bold enough to show our true colors."

"Damn right I am!" Jacqueline flashes her lovely smile while raising her glass. "I don't know how you two do it," she adds with sincerity.

With the *clink* of our glasses my head flings back and the tequila burns a trail down my throat. The fire leads the way to my little quiver. Upon my head's forward return, my eyes land on a piece of art in a well-tailored, deep brown suit with a retro tie of pink, green, and yellow paisleys that would make a nineteen sixties mod jealous. His medium-length hair is slightly tossed about and gives him the air of being a fashion model who just got out of bed. However, his face looks determined. It screams he and his comrade are pawns playing a game of corporate chess.

"And round two is in celebration of ..." Darla's words draw me back into reality. Grabbing my second shot I raise it to meet those of my friends. "Okay, Rox, what's he look like?"

"Huh?"

"The guy you've been checking out," Jacqueline adds. "I see you drooling at whoever is over my shoulder."

Busted.

Warmth comes to my cheeks as Jacqueline subtly twists her head. Her eyes meet his, and he replies to her with a little nod and a smile. It's far more than I've gotten out of him. Typical Rosalyn luck strikes again.

Darla is all too fast to let her eyes drink him in as well. She then darts her head back around and whips up her glass. "To the fact that tonight Rox is finally going to get assertive and give that guy her number!"

A chorus of *clanks* and *woos* follow. What the hell. I've nothing to lose. Many would say I've already lost my dignity by the way I'm dressed. Maybe tonight I'll finally turn into a slut. At least then I might see him in the morning and maybe that will lead to another night. If I don't, certainly I'll be back at Mulligan's tomorrow, or worse, home alone playing with my, um, cat.

Yeah ... I don't own a cat. I also couldn't sleep with a guy I just met if my life depended on it.

With the downing of my shot, my view flips back to the guy who sits across the room at the bar. Even though he doesn't look like an outdoorsman his skin is gently bronzed. He's a far cry from the pale rocker type I've spent the last few years drooling over. Long hair, tight pants, and a wicked smirk always get me, which is probably why I'm sitting in a singles bar.

Mr. So Freaking Cute catches my peering and gives me a slip of a smile before returning his eyes to his associate. Now I'm slightly embarrassed, but the alcohol is kicking in, so I dare hold my ground until his eyes float back to me. He raises his glass, and I return his grin before shying away. Frankly, that's the farthest I've gotten with somebody in a long time. The glow that has blushed its way onto my cheeks is brought on more by embarrassment than alcohol.

"Twirl your hair," Darla whispers.

"What? Why are you whispering?"

"Just do it," she says, continuing her hushed tone while slapping at my arm.

Once again I catch his gaze, then twirl my hair only to shy away because I feel like an idiot. His expression of seriousness dissipates. The dark eyes of his business partner give me a cold glare. I must be infringing upon his sales pitch. My courage fades even more. "Don't let that stuffy guy stop you! The cute one is totally checking you out. Go for it!"

It's funny how encouragement can come out as assertiveness. Just a few weeks ago, on the night Darla met her new boyfriend, she was as sheepish as I am. "How?"

"Use one of the cheesy lines they use on us."

"No!" Jacqueline's hand smacks the table. We really should get some food to go with this alcohol. "Women can't complain about men then do the same things they do. You need to get creative."

"And how do you propose I do that?"

Darla downs the rest of her drink and laughs. "If she knew, she'd have gotten all kinds of creative on the scary guy over there in the flannel shirt. Come on, Jacs, we all know you wanna be his baby mama."

Jacqueline gives Darla the "I'm gonna kick your ass" look as she yells, "Don't call me that!" but midway through she breaks into a laugh and a brief giggle fest ensues before they stop and stare at me, totally deadpanned. In unison they nod to the hottie. It's kind of creepy.

Out of desperation I try a strategy that I thought of long ago but never felt compelled to actually implement. I make a show of faking my phone is dead, and then tell the girls, "Shake your heads like I've asked you a question." They play along as I shoot the device a look of disgust while making sure

I have the attention of Mr. Sexy Tie. Looking completely disgruntled, and feeling like a dork, I go on the prowl. I'm sure to moisten and part my lips, soften my eyes, and sway my hips gently while slightly pushing out my chest. I'm surprised I can actually walk this way. "Excuse me. My phone died. May I borrow yours? I just need to make a quick call."

He hands it to me with a smile. His friend seems aghast. Please, buddy, Marilyn Monroe and I nearly share measurements—but you guys only think that's what you want. When it's standing right in front of you, you miss it entirely.

Oh, yeah, I almost forgot. I'm wearing dayglo. I stand by that self-conscious, alcohol and stress-induced statement though.

My number gets entered, and then I put his phone to my ear just long enough for mine to vibrate in my purse before handing his back. "Thanks."

"That was fast. Didn't your call go through?"

"I got what I needed." With a little wave and curve of my lips I return to my friends. I'm wide-eyed, giggling, and slowly wiggling. I must be the world's biggest doofuss. Self-doubt again gets shoved into the wind as we all huddle around my phone. My fingers are so jittery I mistype the message three times before finally hitting send.

Hello, my name is Rosalyn. Would you like to share a smile?

Darla is all a flutter. "Oh, my, God! I can't believe you're doing this. It is so unlike you."

Jacqueline squeezes my hand, thus endorsing my courage. Our heads all turn to the hottie as he reads the text. His head ticks and a little grin blooms. Yay! Interest! Sucking it up and putting myself out there may have—

He then pops the phone back into his pocket and ignores me like I don't exist.

Sympathetic pouts come from across the table and help soothe my crushed heart. What can I do but raise my glass and shrug? The girls do exactly as female friends should; they call him a jerk who doesn't know what he's missing. It's pathetic, but my gaze returns to the man. I hope to find something that will ease the rejection, but with the exception of chatting up the waitress while his buddy is in the john, he's back to being all business.

Maybe I'm the jerk. After all, I did interrupt his meeting.

Yeah, and he could have bothered to look at me. No more excuses for his behavior.

I nudge my chair a little to the right so that we are out of each other's line-of-sight, and the night forges on. Groups burst out in laughter around us. One drunken guy bumps into another and drinks fly behind my back. They lament over their spilt whisky before heading to the bar for more. Us girls gossip about nothing of merit because we just want a good time. Out of nowhere, a round of Blueberry Lemon Drops arrives at our table—a gift from someone who wants to remain anonymous.

Jacqueline peers over her shoulder. "Maybe Mr. Holier-Than-Thou is slipping in an apology for the brush off."

Darla is less than helpful. "Or maybe they are from the scary guy in the corner who's been drooling over Jacqueline all night."

We raise our glasses and drink to the guy with the unkempt beard, plaid flannel shirt, ratty jeans, and Berkinstocks while Mr. Can't-Be-Bothered stays focused on his business associate. The luscious cocktail slides down, and it's time to walk home before the self-loathing I've kept at bay kicks in. It's not easy to be me, and as much as I love who I am, sometimes my resolve falters.

I begin to stand. "Well, it's been a long week. I'm off to—" My heel hits a splash of whisky from the earlier incident and twists under me, sending me downward. I'm barely able to break my fall by slamming my hands onto the table. I nearly take it down with me.

Nope. I'm not embarrassed. Not at all.

My hands smooth the beautiful fabric of my dress as I struggle to find dignity. With my head held high, I stroll past the hot man and head for the door. His mouth is slightly agape, his friend is snickering, and my pride is outwardly swelling while inwardly crumbling. I wish I could bring myself to stop trying so hard, but I can't stop striving for happier days.

I'm Not Like Everybody Else

Rosalyn

Insomnia sucks. Our family room is a disaster from my last bout of 3 A.M. boredom that I fought by starting to clean the closet. The coffee table is covered in vinyl, and I can barely make it to the stone mantle across the room to set down my glass of water. While the section of the floor between the sofa and the entertainment center is scarcely visible, I know that buried in the stacks of records is my renewed spirit that will soon spring forth. Bar Guy's shine off was a little much.

The Chocolate Watchband's cover of "I'm Not Like Everybody Else" blasts through the room, and its essence renews my spirit. Ray Davies may have written it, but David Aguilar's plea for acceptance cloaked in impassioned defiance sells me on the credo. Yeah, with the right surroundings I knew it wouldn't take long to bounce back from tonight's earlier embarrassment. Who I am is just dandy, even if my resolve does get wobbly at times.

Needing to rectify the haphazard state of the closet I pull out a huge stack of board games that nearly knocks me over. It gets plopped on the floor next to some homeless albums of which *Deep Trance* sits on top. A monopoly game that crowns the stack tips into Peter's image. Crap! I can't let that treasure get ruined!

I move the pile to the safety of the coffee table before heading back to the closet. Tomorrow that album gets framed and displayed near the other stuff I would be quick to save in a fire; family photos, my Dad's favorite guitar, and a signed copy of David Cassidy's autobiography. That book may be easily replaceable via eBay, but I ran through four blocks of

L.A. traffic, chasing his limo from stoplight to stoplight to get that thing signed, and damn it, I'm going to be buried with it!

The song selection switches to The Fat Man singing, "Ain't That a Shame," and another stack of games gets pulled into my arms and then placed on the floor. It's back to the closet then—

Wait...

Abruptly I spin back. A Ouija board, which I haven't used since my last childhood slumber party, crowns the first stack of games with Monopoly now sitting next to it. "What the? Didn't I just put ...?"

I really thought I left Monopoly on top. Weird ...

I shrug off a case of the creeps and go for another stack of games. While setting them down my eyes catch sight of the album and I gasp. Slowly I stand with my eyes locked on the cover as if it's a spider I fear will flee before getting stomped. The album has rotated so that Peter Lane now faces the Ouija board. I scan the room for the non-existent eyes I feel are beckoning me to take action. Was there an intoxicant other than vodka in that Blueberry Lemon Drop?

The touch of my fingers to the planchette proves that my mind has been fried. Why did this album seem to hunt me down? Why do I have an overwhelming urge to contact a shattered soul who died young, broken, and unappreciated while I'm just braving to peek out from under shelter after barely surviving my own storm?

The memories of my past bring a clench to my stomach. I'm not ready to relive them. My eyes close in an attempt to shut them out while forcing in thoughts of the curious man who signed this album. It's better this way.

Minutes pass with my calling into silence without even a vibration in return. Refusing to give up, I again reach out. "Peter, are you there? Is anyone there?"

Silence.

Nope, no one is here but me—the sorry sack who needs a

life.

Is it the crazy romantic inside me who whispers that the album holds mysteries? Am I just a nutty fangirl? Or is my desire to escape reality greater than I realize?

The part of me who longs for romance digs deep down inside, and instead of sending my energy into the universe I try pulling its energy in.

Heavy sadness creeps forth and shrouds the entire room, yet a part of me that has been long disturbed seems to find peace.

"Peter? Peter, if you're there, please say something, even if it's to tell me to get lost."

Abruptly the music stops, and the planchette moves without my touch. It zips through letters to tell me, *trapped - no see - yes hear - help*.

With a gasp I jump up and away from the board. A flick of the light switch shows I'm still alone and that everything in the room is exactly as remembered. While that's a relief, the whole incident is still freaky as hell! I'd actually feel saner if something around here were different. Did I imagine all of that?

Quickly the board is stashed away. I've really got to get some sleep.

"Goodnight, Peter, wherever you are."

Marc Bolan's head rest on my cotton-covered chest while I'm deep under the cover of a pink, satin comforter. Colors glow from my dad's old TV that sits upon a nineteen forties, oak and walnut dresser. This is at least the tenth time I've watched *Beyond The Valley of the Dolls*. Somehow the zaniness of the cult classic is always the perfect accompaniment to the madness of my world.

My cell phone chimes in receipt of a text that is probably from Jacqueline and The Peacock. The cozy bed gets abandoned so I can grab the phone from my vanity and respond promptly, else my drunken friends may call the police in fear that I've been kidnapped.

Not that they would actually do that. They seemed to have learned their lesson last time.

From an unknown number a text reads, *I'm sorry about how I acted.*

Wait. What?

No way.

Seriously? Bar Guy?

My breath hitches with a shock of excitement before I remember what a prick he had been. Then again, I had interrupted his work ... and he did send over drinks. At least we all hoped it was him.

Who is this? I send in an attempt to play it cool.

The phone chimes. *Niles. You borrowed my phone tonight at Mulligan's. I'm the one in the suit.*

Rox, sometimes you really step into it.

He probably assumes that little stunt was an everyday occurrence, and that I'm a whore who parades my number around town.

The phone chimes again. *Never mind. I'm sure you're busy. Sorry to have bothered you.*

Great. He really does think I give my number to anything with legs and a schlong. *Sorry,* I type with my fingers racing. The guy is giving me stomach butterflies. *I rarely give out my number. I'm just a little sensitive and a whole lot embarrassed.* I hit send then bite my nail.

Why am I biting my nail? Because I fear some guy who brushed me off sees me as a slut?

Yeah, that's exactly why.

Why are you embarrassed?

I think I gave you the wrong impression. The second I hit send, my eyes squint as if shutting out my stupidity. I was supposed to be in the game, not confessing. Truthfully, I suck at dating games and would rather go for honesty. No wonder why I am single.

My bad. I thought you were inviting me to call you. Sorry if I misunderstood.

Now I've come off as a whore *and* a tease, not to mention he probably thinks I'm totally freaking insane. *Sorry. That's not what I meant. I'm not used to giving out my number. The whole dating thing is overrated. I wish there were a better way to meet people.* With a sigh I sit on the bed. Honesty is one thing, but I'm surprised by my display of vulnerability. It's been a while for so many things for me.

Me too. I have incredibly bad luck when it comes to meeting people. How is it people get to have friends at all?

I totally understand and am grateful for what seems to be a heart-felt reply, so I do the same. *Meeting people seems impossible, especially someone I could have anything in common with at all.* More vulnerability? Rox, what are you doing?

Sounds like you and I have something in common. That and we both text in complete sentences. :) Would you join me for brunch tomorrow?

My eyes bug out a bit, and I reread the text, twice. My fingers start jittering like I've suddenly forgotten how to type. I should slow down, but I fear if I do, I will take too long and the forces of evil will come and yank my phone away. *Yes. Brunch sounds great. Where should I meet you?*

How about I play the gentleman and pick you up? Is that too weird? Does 11 AM work?

Sounds great. No, actually it sounds wildly perfect! I can't freaking wait to tell the girls. They are never going to believe this!

Biff Bang Pow!

September 1966

Peter

The four of us cackled like fools while walking into the office of our manager. Our first two singles had shot up the charts with a bang, and our newly released album was doing exceedingly well. We were on the covers of magazines on every news rack from Manchester to South London, and were unable to walk down the street without being noticed. Part of that had to do with our music; part of it had to do with our clothes.

Practically every day I wore a new shirt, trousers, jacket, and accessories. Apparently it was bad for our image to be seen wearing the same thing twice. My friends were some of the best dressed as well. After all, my closet only held so much, and the clothes had to go somewhere. I'd an entourage catering to my every whim so they could get a piece of the discarded fortune.

Being at the peak of fashion was a surrealistic dream come true for this lad who grew up in war-torn East London. My father worked in a steel mill, and I was expected to follow suit and scrape for pennies like he always had. Happening upon a discarded guitar with a big crack in the wood and no strings had been a stroke of luck. After that my life propelled forward, bringing me from tattered old jeans with barely an arse left on them, to pressed stovepipe trousers.

White shoes were all the rage. Their high price and ability to easily scuff made them an unthinkable luxury a few months before. If they were the least bit dirty, it was an unforgivable strike against you. The soles barely got scraped before the white was scuffed, and I was told to purchase a new pair.

The four of us took seats across from Mr. BS's enormous desk and were excited as hell for payday. We were also about to discuss what we had been told were "tactics" for the new record. When Mr. BS finally bothered to show, he and his swanky suit plopped across from us while looking like he was the cat that just had quadruple helpings of Canaries. "Well, lads. How are we doing today?"

We were all smiles—on top of the ever-loving world; however, our grins quickly faded when Mr. BS started doling out the cash. We were anticipating big, fat checks, but our hopes were misguided. Instead, we were handed about half of what was expected. "Where is the rest?" I asked, rather put off.

Stoddard looked taken aback by my question, like I was utterly ridiculous and had insulted his integrity. I explained that *New Musical Express* reported we had sold nearly nine hundred thousand singles at three for a quid. It was only logical we should expect more than the little under a thousand pounds each we were just handed. Mr. BS seemed surprised that this underprivileged, snot-nosed boy could do basic math. He went into a lecture on how finances work. "After all lads, you know what those Beatles say about the taxman."

I didn't buy it and pressed on.

"You're all wearing it," Stoddard said. He seemed unaffected by the silliness of his statement. "The charge accounts on Carnaby are running up the bills. Even though you're getting those clothes at a steep discount they still cost an absolute fortune."

It seemed hard to believe that we were wearing over one hundred thousand quid worth of clothing, and I wondered if the name Stoddard meant liar in another language. All I knew was I was going to be a lot more careful with my white shoes.

Mr. BS was ecstatic at the success of our last album but was also somewhat concerned about our present efforts. Our peers were allowed to experiment in the studio and find unique sounds. However, we weren't to have that privilege.

"Lads, what you're doing sounds great. I think we have several more hits on our hands. However, boys, you might want to step back from the booth a bit. In fact, we insist on it. Also, I know Abbey Road is loaded with an instrument closet to drive talented young men such as yourselves wild, and those Beatles have been goofing around, but we don't have their budget, so don't get any crazy ideas."

"Wait a minute," Johnny, our drummer, said, but BS cut him off.

"Well, it's not my fault. It's the engineer's. He thinks you'll be a bigger success if he's able to put his magic touch on everything. You're all aware of what Phil Spector's done in America. What George Martin's done for The Beatles. We're working on doing that for you."

That was bollocks and he knew it. Martin's success with The Beatles came from helping with the orchestral arrangements, not running the show to the minute detail. He never would have slapped McCartney's hand. They were the ones dominating studio two for months on end, recording and rerecording, dubbing and overdubbing, yet this yob wanted us to pull our music out of the vending machine and make it sound like all the other mindless pop dribble.

"What it comes down to, boys, is I want you to keep doing what you're doing but relax a bit. Enjoy yourselves in the studio more—just don't do it in the booth, and don't go raiding the equipment."

The four of us left the office feeling like we'd been run over with a lorry. How was it we were so good yet also so bad? Something told me we were about to find out. Frankly, it gave me the willies.

While driving down the road, the disc jockey announced the release of our latest hit. I turned up the volume and the shock of my life infiltrated my ears in the form of a song I barely recognized. I was pretty sure it was us playing and my voice singing, but it didn't sound like anything we'd ever done.

So that was what it was all coming down to. They wanted to manipulate our songs—our fantastic, well-written songs with a soulful drive—beautiful English R&B—and turn them into pop rubbish. We might as well have been writing children's lullabies for all that did for me. We had to get away from that asshole.

I'm Into Something Good

Rosalyn

Stepping out of Jacqueline's walk-in closet, I enter her room and twirl as if I'm a princess on her way to the ball. Her simple, blue, A-line dress that is still a tad big when she is bloated fits me perfectly.

It also makes me feel completely ridiculous.

"How do I look?"

"Freakishly normal. Are you okay?"

"No." I sigh at my image in her mirror. "I'm tired of walking out of here knowing I look great and then coming home feeling like a great looking schmuck. I'm trying reverse psychology. If I leave feeling I look like an idiot, maybe—"

Jacqueline's eyes flutter, and her face contorts as she gags. "Rosalyn, that is absolutely ridiculous. Do you have any idea how jealous I am you can do the vintage clothing and makeup thing? Anything vintage looks like a Halloween costume on me. With you it's stylish, albeit accented with a smidgen of quirky."

"Okay, truthfully, I just don't want my wardrobe to be the focus. I thought I'd try something different. You know I do that once in a while."

Jacqueline cocks an eyebrow and scrutinizes me. "Yes, but your timing is suspicious. If those guys got to you so much, why are you going out with one of them?"

"Come on, Jacqueline, we both know I try not to let my insecurities get in the way. Besides, I may have misjudged Niles, and I've nothing better to do today than give him the benefit of the doubt. Sure I could lounge around, read old issues of *16 Magazine* that have pictures of your *grandfather*, or

I could pull out one of the counter culture movies that I'm always watching. Oh! How about I plop in front of the TV for a *Here Come The Brides* marathon? Yeah, that's totally new. Wait, I need to think bigger. I'll go for something more modern, like from the eighties. *Sanchez of Bel Air!* I mean, just because it sucked so hard it failed before the first episode finished airing doesn't mean it's not worth wasting time on."

Jacqueline cringes so deeply on the inside her disgust seeps out of her pores and into the room, yet her outward drive is steady and determined. She's my rock. I can always count on her when I flail. "What would you be most comfortable in today?"

"A satin lined casket."

"That's it! When you start reminding me of my mom, I tune you out. Come on." Jacqueline pushes me down the hall and into my room. There is something in seeing my prized Standells poster with them in their hip, garage rock glory that instantly puts me mentally and physically in a better space. Sometimes the littlest things ground me.

Jacqueline flings open my closet and rummages through my clothes. "The only choice you get is jeans or a dress. Pick one. Hey, do you own any jeans that aren't black?"

"I have a pair of pink, leopard skin pants from the eighties in the bottom of that drawer over there. You know I can't coordinate anything. So either everything is black or if there's any color it has to be a dress. If it's a dress, I wear either black stilettos or white boots." Jacqueline drops her arms, shooting me a "you've got to be kidding" look, and I defend myself. "Hey, it makes life easy. I actually have a pair of hot pink boots, but I never know what to wear with them. Too bad, they're totally cool."

"Okay, we both know that you are majorly exaggerating." A new pair of black jeans and a long-sleeved black blouse with a corset-style midsection are tossed at me. "Here. Wear this. It hugs your curves perfectly and doesn't make you look like a tramp. And it's in your favorite color—deceased." Her steps ring with determination as she invades my jewelry box and hands me a black choker.

"Really?"

"I got that Bobby Sherman TV marathon reference earlier, and he always wore chokers. This way if the date sucks, you can realize that your alternative was dreaming about a once cute guy that is now in his seventies. Put it on along with some black boots." As I slip off the dress, Jacqueline calls to me, "Make sure your heels aren't too tall. His boots had Cuban heels so he probably has some kind of height complex."

"Cuban heels? Really? How'd I miss that? Seriously, I'm slipping. I mean—"

"You were probably too busy drooling over his paisley tie and sleek suit."

"I sure was—until I pictured it off of him." Yeah, that's how I missed the shoes.

"That's my girl!" Jacqueline hollers back while digging into my jewelry box for some earrings. "Do you think he wears boxers or briefs?"

"Probably boxers since his pants were a little formfitting and I didn't notice a seam." Yeah, I was too distracted to notice the shoes. "Maybe he wears those funky boxer briefs that remind me of a male version of Spanx. Poor guy. Clearly he needs a woman to break him of his ridiculous habits."

"Welcome back to reality, Rox! Now go get dressed. You don't have much time."

The clock strikes eleven, and the doorbell chimes almost as if Niles had been waiting for precisely the right moment to announce his arrival. He looks amazing, standing there in tan skinny-jeans, a black turtleneck, a deep grey blazer, and not just Cuban heels, but Beatle boots! (Why, yes. Mentally I am fanning myself over the Roger McGuinn, circa nineteen sixty-five, ensemble.) Niles truly put some thought into his outfit instead of just rolling out of bed and throwing on a pair of jeans along with yesterday's pre-cologned T-shirt. Sadly, I consider this to be impressive.

It also makes me all kinds of bouncy inside that he dressed up for our date!

With a charming curl of the lips he steps back, touches his hand to his chin and sums me up. "Huh, a bit of the Goth look. Not quite what I expected." And now I'm back to not being able to win with this guy. "You know, black really becomes you. I appreciate a creative dresser."

The overly sensitive part of me that fears being hurt again debates the meaning of the term *creative dresser* as we walk to his car. It seemed respectful, yet was a bit of a zinger, so I reciprocate in a way I feel is equally iffy. "Huh, a new Camaro. Funny, I had you pegged as an Audi man."

"Ouch!" With eyes pleading me not to wound him further, Niles touches his hand to his heart and then winks while opening the passenger door. I'm taken aback. The gesture speaks volumes with me. I'm one of those girls who may be independent, but also adores old-world, male chivalry.

The instant the engine starts I wonder how I missed the dual exhaust on the back of this thing, because I am clearly hearing it. Interesting … The classic look of a muscle car along with some fun accessories, not a bad combination for a man who has put together two retro outfits, let alone is being a gentleman. Dare I be hopeful?

The E Street Band plays over the satellite radio, which is tuned to the all Springsteen station. Niles is already a huge improvement over the last guy I went out with who had never heard of Led Zeppelin. How people like that can manage to function scares me.

"What do you think of the new Camaro?" I ask.

"Eh. They're kind of poser fodder. I mean, it's a fantastic car, but I prefer the real deal. I've been working on one for the last couple of years whenever I visit my mom. It's kind of the thing I do when life doesn't go right. When I step back and see progress life seems okay again."

Hmm… Vintage Camaros were kind of girly for a muscle car. "What year?"

"Sixty-nine with the rare, four twenty-seven engine. My

mom didn't want it anymore, but I couldn't let her get rid of that thing since I practically grew up in it. It'll be a beast when I'm done. You a car girl?"

Okay, I retract that girlie car thought. "A little. Mostly I appreciate anything classic. I'm driving a newer model Mustang, and while I absolutely love the little thing, it's just not the same as being surrounded by a real hunk of metal." My eyes come off of the man and onto the road ahead. Suddenly I become aware of the existence of my heart. My right hand presses into my leg as we head into a turn next to an embankment. While I'm grateful for the handling power of a new Camaro versus a classic one, my voice strains to remain calm. "Engines are referred to in terms of horsepower for a reason, and I've yet to find a horse with a built in computer." My right hand slips to my side to conceal that I am gripping my pants with a tight fist. I freaking hate embankments or getting anywhere near the edge of a road. It's not one of my more endearing quirks.

The corners of his lips rise so high it brings crinkles to his eyes. "So you'd rather have something that roars versus something that whines like a cheap jet engine?"

My hand relaxes as we come out of the turn, and I'm back in the moment. "Exactly. I love the deep roar of a classic engine."

His face enlivens. His glow brings me from tense to tingly. "I couldn't agree with you more."

Niles has all the marks of a well-raised gentleman; opening doors for me, helping me with my chair, and awaiting me to take my napkin before grabbing his own. He folds his into a neat triangle and places it in his lap with the fold facing him before smoothing it. It's really charming.

"Man, this all looks so good," he says of the menu. "Sadly, part of me just wants a big tub of fries to soak up some of the residual effects of the alcohol from last night. What are you leaning towards?"

"As much as I know I shouldn't, I'm going for the Caramelized Banana Waffle." Yep, I'm going to risk looking like a pig, because well, I've been honest about who I am so far, and the food looks too damn good for me to eat a salad that I can make in my sleep.

Niles's mouth and eyes widen in disbelief. "Oh my God, they have that? That sounds incredible!" His eyes dart to the menu. Wow. Their lime green color almost glows. "You're really going for it?"

"Yeah, either that or the Brandied Cherries French Toast."

"God, that looks amazing!" He tucks his hand under his chin, and a cluster of golden-brown locks skids across his brow with the tilt of his head. His eyes peer at the ceiling. Adorable. "I still think I need fries."

"Tell you what, if it will make you feel better, I'll share."

His face brightens, reminding me of a little boy. "And I'll get the Cherry French Toast and we'll go halfsies?"

Oh, my God. That was so cute.

Relaxation travels through my nervous system. It's reminiscent of when you take a few sips of vodka on an empty stomach and its effects first course through your veins. "Sure."

Niles places our order and tacks on two sides of hot fudge. He's brilliant! The fudge with the cherries and caramel will be absolutely epic.

And … And now I'm menu less, meaning it's time for that awkward moment when people succumb to small talk. I've no idea where to start.

"So, what type of music do you listen to?" he asks.

Glad to see Niles saved me by going for the jugular. My insides get all twisty. I *love* talking music, but this question usually goes the way of what I suspect would happen if the earth stopped moving at the same moment that gravity failed. There are few people I've ever really been able to talk music with; my dad when he was alive, Jacqueline's family, and the guys at the record store. So, do I tell Niles the truth and risk looking even more like a dork than I did last night, or should I cower? "I'll try just about anything. It all depends on my mood and surroundings." Well, it's not a lie. I will try anything once. It's just the odds of me liking something that most people my age have heard of are slim.

Niles has that look—the one where people slightly pull back because you so convincingly told them you were Cleopatra in a former life they want to believe you but can't. "Really? Last night I kind of had you pegged as a 'Cinderella Sunshine' type." My eyes go all circular at the mention of the song about a free spirit who wears clothes from outside of her time. It's one I have always identified with. "Sorry, that's a reference nobody would understand. I do that a lot. I'm really trying not to, but it's hard to stop being who you are."

Speech fails me. The waitress arrives with our food as I process the words Niles just smacked me with. "Are you talking about the song by Paul Revere and the Raiders?" I casually pop a fry into my mouth, but in reality I'm stunned—and dammed freaking giddy! Holy St. Hendrix!

Niles's face freezes mid-bite. "How do you know—"

"It was a single off of *Hard n' Heavy*, which sold so few copies that after the mis-issued black-and-white cover sold out, the next issue with the proper cover seems nearly as rare. It's really sad because it contains some of the best fuzz guitar ever."

Niles's mouth drops open with part of a fry sticking to his lower lip. "Yeah, that's exactly what I meant." The fry falls. "Wait, how do you know about that? No. Better yet, which version do you prefer, the album track or the single, and what's the difference?"

My arms cross in mock confrontation as I *baulk* at him. "Are you challenging me? Please! The single version. There's no contest. The break in the album version is too flowery, and yes, you are right. It's hard to be somebody you're not. You nailed it with the 'Cinderella Sunshine' reference." While I keep my cool outward demeanor, inside my mind my arms are being thrown up in surrender to the truth I wish I could change. "As much as I love who I am, I feel completely out of place in this world."

Niles's expression freezes. I can almost see inside his mind as he takes a step back and digests my words. "I know what you mean. Some days I would give anything to fit in. It's not a lack of self-esteem; it's my reality." His words come forth with a disguised, heart-felt pain that tugs at my insides. Now I am so grateful I put myself out there last night with him. If I'm going to start taking risks again, I think I was guided to the right one.

Niles sighs deeply at the fry in his hand before dipping it in hot fudge and popping it in his mouth. Oh, that's just gross. Is he trying to break the sad turn the conversation took with levity or does he really eat that way? I try to conceal my repulsion while spreading fudge on the caramel-doused waffle. Niles's face goes blank. A beat later his eyes light as if it's the most ingenious idea ever. "Oh God, you're brilliant!" He dips a fry into my fudgy caramel sauce and goes to town on it. "This is phenomenal. You have to try this."

Ugh… No, I don't.

Okay, well, it can't be much different with fries than waffles since both are starches, right?

Niles awaits my reaction as I try his new obsession. The caramel sauce hits my tongue and tastes decadent. With the *crunch* of the fry an oil slick covers my mouth. The grease gets mixed into the caramel with each chew. I almost gag. It's like swallowing chunky motor oil. "Kind of gross," I say, bursting his bubble. In sympathy for the crazy man, I grab another fry and dip it in the cherry sauce. Niles's throat seems to be closing in on him as I pop it in my mouth and savor the cherry, and then—"Gah! I stand corrected. Fries and cherry sauce, *that* is gross!" My exaggerated look of gagging brings the most amazing smile to his face. He hands me his cup of coffee to wash down the vileness.

"Well, at least you tried. I had a feeling when I saw you last night you were a kindred spirit of sorts. I couldn't put my finger on it, but other than the outfit, something inside me said I needed to talk to you. Unfortunately, the timing was bad and I handled it poorly. I'm really sorry I blew you off."

"And I'm sorry that I interrupted you. I kind a got dared into it."

"I'm glad you did." Niles dumps some fudge on his plate and swirls a piece of the toast in it and the cherry sauce. "Do you like old movies?"

"Yeah, any era of film as long as the movie is good."

His head dips down a bit, and his eyes peer up. There's that boyish innocence again. "There is a silent film festival happening next weekend. Will you join me?" Oh, my God. So seriously cute!

Yes, I most definitely will, and with the added bonus of the quirkiness that is Niles, I'm excited for the unexpected.

The Job That Ate My Brain

Rosalyn

Do I love my job or hate it? The answer varies from moment to moment.

Endeara Candies, a "mom-and-pop" owned candy plant, specializes in chemically flavored jellybeans and those red and white peppermints you get at Christmas. The continued success of this antiquated company is even more surprising when you learn everything is still run as if it's nineteen forty. Given the choice between keeping the old equipment and paying a maintenance crew versus going top-of-the-line and breaking even financially in under five years, the owners opted to keep the loyal crew of mechanics that save our butts on a daily basis. Even our office computers are nearly obsolete.

In all honesty, being a Payroll Specialist is an epically brainless waste of my business degree. However, when your world flips around a few times, you need to be gentle on yourself.

My friend, Oliver, whom I met a few years back in an Internet forum for an obscure band, is not only responsible for this job landing in my lap but for Darla getting her job as well. Meeting Oliver in person was surrealistic because for years we had been familiar faces at various concerts. At the time I was with Joe, which makes Oliver one of the few people who knows what I've been through. Now he works just down the hall from me in the sales department.

Today, in true company fashion, I've been presented a stack of employee folders I should have been given a week ago for promotions processing. They come with a huge apology and a high-quality chocolate bar with ground up potato chips in it. Translation: I'm being begged for forgiveness with traitorous chocolate.

I sit huddled over my tan, metal desk in the warm office whose flat, white walls make it appear cold. I've done my best to pop life into it with some framed, old concert posters and spread about chatzkies, but I've failed to give it the hominess I'm shooting for.

Footsteps stop to my left while I moan over the files. The wafting smell of cigarettes tells me it's eleven forty-five on a Monday morning, and Oliver's rounding me up for our weekly lunch hangout. It's one of my two lunch rituals; hanging with Oliver on Mondays and on Fridays it's whatever food the boss has sent in so the entire crew can eat together as a family. That's what happens when you work at a place run by Italians. Same as with your own relatives, everybody at Endeara Candies is family—like it or not. Truthfully, Friday lunches and the sense of kinship they bring are one of the few things I love about this place.

With a sheepish grin I slowly rotate my head to face Oliver and mouth, "Sorry." There's no way I will get these processed in time if I don't bail.

His heels click on the tile floor as he tosses his head back. Every time Oliver gives a funny little grin I struggle to keep from laughing. It's bad enough that he's already got the name and the straight, blond hair, but something in his jovial nature reminds me of Cousin Oliver, the goofy kid who popped in during the last season of *The Brady Bunch*. Actually, with the way he and Darla tease each other, it's more like *Sesame Street* and I'm Bert working with two Ernies. "They finally got you those folders, huh?"

My head hangs as I whine. "I hate being destined to die by eating off of the roach coach. Save me, please." Oliver chuckles at my misery. His hands fly out at the sides, as if asking how. "I buy, you fly." He shrugs, and I smack a twenty in his palm before he can change his mind.

He tosses it back on my desk. "I got it. Looks like you need someone around here to be nice to you. The usual?"

I nod. "Thanks, Oliver."

While just crossing the threshold, one of the warehouse team leads smacks into Oliver. He apologizes, darts in, and drops a three-inch stack of time cards (that should have been here when I walked in this morning) on my desk. He flashes a smile before speeding off.

Sometimes this place makes me wish I could grow a beard and join the circus.

The Last Rock Show

Peter

Yet another day was spent in the studio where the band perfectly played the same riffs over and over while the engineers whacked off.

Excuse me. I meant they adjusted the console and perfected our sound.

How was it that we were to crank out tunes and hit everything flawlessly on each and every take while the engineers were allowed to piss away time perfecting things that sounded brilliant in the first place?

At 5 P.M. it was off to the pub for the engineers while the band left to play a date anywhere from Leeds to Portsmouth. Another day, another recording. Another night, another date. "You have to play to sell those records," our manager said, over and over again.

Jane jumped out of the car, and the stress of the day flew away with the bounce of her strawberry-blonde hair. Once on the road my lids fell, and all turned into a peaceful black until we arrived in Liverpool. We'd barely enough time for soundcheck before heading off to the pub for dinner. The brick of fish I raised felt weighted while my mouth opened to it with a yawn. Fans clamored as I raced through the club's back door with the last of my chips in hand. Jane pulled a napkin out of her bag and wiped my lips and greasy paws while I chewed. It was so sweet I wanted to halt everything and walk off alone with her, but the stage manager yelled for us to get on with it. Ah, glamour. And to think merely months before I was jealous of people like me.

A spark jolted me from the inside the moment my shoe hit the stage. I struck a chord, the crowd cheered, and my body's voltage surged. Before me the ladies screamed while their boyfriends raised their beers. These were the things I lived for. All the other stuff—the magazines, the records— they didn't matter. Despite the fact I was being run ragged, I was happy as hell.

Proud Mary

Rosalyn

For nearly two years insomnia has been a well-deserved hell that I suffer in penance for my sins. Since lack of sleep suits me better than the drug-induced haze slightly effective sleeping pills bring, I often suffer through it by staring at the ceiling, watching TV, or by playing with battery-operated boyfriends until a coma hits.

Inside my dark bedroom my fingers fumble through the nightstand's drawer and pull out the TV remote. How did that manage to infiltrate the sacred chamber reserved for my plastic dream men? It's flung aside, and the TV pops on as the remote *thunks* onto the floor. An infomercial for the CD compilation *Love's Greatest Rockers* blares. While sliding on my belly I stretch to retrieve the remote and nearly fall off of the bed. All the while I chant, "Got it. Got it," as the song snippets change.

I tap the remote's buttons but get zero response. My grumpy state brought on by a lack of sleep makes me whimper. "Why me?"

With the back plate off, I spin the batteries and hope that the trick that rarely works will play out in my favor. My chant of "Got it. Got it," continues as the songs in the infomercial fly past. When Peter Lane appears on my screen to sing one of Love Machine's biggest hits, my desire to change the channel skids to a halt. My heart flutters during the powerful love song that has always had a special effect on it. It is one that I can only liken to gliding your finger over the smooth surface of a diamond in revelry of the tender meaning the gem holds.

The song snippet ends, and the now-functioning remote

brings me to the same infomercial on another channel with a ten-second delay. Peter returns to my screen, and again a sense of longing draws me into the music. Behind my closed lids he flashes me a smile. I breathe in deeply as if trying to capture a whiff of him before he can escape my mind. The song snippet ends, and his image is replaced with that of the signed album that now sits among my treasures. I grab it and head downstairs.

Despite the temperature of the cozy family room tonight it feels cold and impersonal. In hopes of pumping in some life I turn on the satellite radio. A random pop station sends an *unce, unce, unce* bopping through the air. Peter's image stares at me with an accusatory, "Have you lost your bloody mind?" type glare.

"Hey, it never hurts to try something new, right?"

Peter's glare intensifies.

"You are totally right. I'll switch to The Underground Garage. They play *good* new music."

Peter's glare now protests.

"Really. They play great stuff." My hand pops up in salute like that of a Girl Scout. "Fangirl's honor."

Did he just shake his head in disbelief?

"Fine. I suppose you would enjoy some R&B." His eyes follow me as I reach for some Ike and Tina on vinyl. The reflection I see in the onyx gems is not my own but that of my father. Much like Peter Lane, Dad loved Ike and Tina.

Tina's voice like over-creamed coffee tells me about how she thinks I want to hear something nice and easy. Ike starts in with the bass-line vocals of *Proud Mary* that vibrate down into the depths of my spirit. As Tina eases me into the song, I close off the world and allow myself to get lost in a moment of floating peace that will soon change into an explosion of nuclear power. "You were right, Peter. This is the only way to go."

The horns burst in, and my long brown locks flail while my hips wildly shake. My private world is enlivened, yet the inability to escape the sensation I have company has me glancing over my shoulder with nearly every step. Finally my hands meet the air in surrender to the obvious fact that my marbles are long lost. Sure. I'll succumb to insanity and piss off the soul of some poor guy by bugging him through a Ouija board. God, just how bored am I?

Ike & Tina continue to serenade as I hold court in the same position as the night before. Images of Peter fill my mind; candid photos of him holding a ball nearly too high for his dog to jump, mischievous grins as he poses, videos where the striking of a power chord brings him into a bold stance with his arm raised above his guitar, almost as if in salute to it. All of these aid in my quest as I fear Jacqueline will walk in on the display and have me committed. Nothing happens.

Tina begins another song while more images invade my mind. They put a smile on my face and warm my heart. Still there's no word from Peter.

The album nears its end, and the overwhelming sadness from the night before slithers into the room and hangs in the air like smoke from a dying fire. Emotions lock in my lungs and smother both my oxygen and my desire to breathe. Slowly the planchette begins to vibrate as if it has a nearly indiscernible pulse. *Need help*, the board tells.

My eyes close as I try to get a hold on the emotions of love and fear of loss that begin assaulting me. The sensation starts in my chest and builds down into my gut and up into my brain. It brings the temperature of my hands from cool to a warm simmer. Suddenly a pressure hits them, pushing them onto the planchette and sending them skating across the board. My eyes pop open to catch a glow emitting from a second set of hands that appear to be merging with mine. My heart sprints into my throat.

"Ack!"

With my hasty shriek the presence disappears.

"Dear freaking God! What the hell was that?"

The scare puts me in a rush to stash the board in the closet and run upstairs to cower under the covers.

My body tosses onto its left side, and my hips become twisted all funny. I roll onto my right, but my neck is contorted, and I'm cold. My hands fluff the pillow, and then pull the sheet over my head. A little tension releases as the silly notion of hiding lessens my discomfort.

Peter's image hangs in my head along with memories of the planchette requesting help. The air under the covers thickens, so I yank down the sheet.

Determined to be comfortable I curl to my other side and repeatedly take in and release deep, slow breaths. Finally, my muscles feel as if they are melting into the bed. A peaceful image of Peter unwinding in a lounge chair paints its way into my mind. It's such a lovely sight of comfort and joy, yet I become edgy and fear the image will fade.

Insomnia is a cruel beast. It makes my mind do weird things.

Out of frustration I grab my sketchbook and begin to draw.

All Sold Out

November 1966

Peter

I hated parties where you were supposed to be on good behavior at all times—trying to impress everyone, never knowing if who you were talking to could be the one to help you escape the clutches of the pop machine and gain recognition for the brilliance pulsing inside you. I would much rather have avoided the mess and have arrived after the pompous suits left. Or better yet, be at home alone with my lovely Jane who stood across the room with a group of "girlfriends." She didn't belong with those girlfriend-for-the-next-few-nights easy lays. It was hard to find true friends in an industry where men go through women like toilet paper, but God love her, she tried.

For months Stoddard had been up my bum to ditch her. "Why would you want to get attached to one girl while so many others throw themselves at your feet? We need you to stay clear headed so you can put your best foot forward on the road and in the studio."

What he really meant was, "Don't let a woman distract you from being a slave to me. I need you busting your arse and bringing in money."

Screw him. If there was one thing I would defy that guy with it was my love for Jane. No matter what bollocks the world threw at me, no matter how many problems Stoddard caused, Jane comforted me each night and greeted me with joy in the morning. If I didn't love performing so much, I'd have left that circus.

Townsend was talking my bloody ear off and bragging

about how each member of The Who had been instructed to write at least two songs for their soon-to-be-released album, *A Quick One*. This meant they actually got to write every track, unlike how half of my songs got shelved. Jane grew weary of her surroundings, practically hugging herself in insecurity. She nudged toward a group of suits that were laughing and then nodded toward the other side of the room.

"Sorry, mate," I nearly said aloud, "but I'm all too happy to ditch you. Have Moonie call me for the real party later."

"Peter," Jane whispered. "I just overheard those men. Why are you being sold? Didn't you just finish a new album?"

"We're what? Who said that?" Was this what I'd been hoping for? I was tired of working for BS and having our brilliant songs manipulated into something completely unrecognizable.

Jane subtly nodded to the corner where BS laughed it up with some guy I'd never seen before. "Mr. Stoddard was rather clear about it to that other gentleman. You didn't know anything about this?"

Dare I become hopeful? Then again, who in the bloody hell would he sell us to? "Not a clue." If Stoddard wanted out, I'd gladly help him make the deal. I also knew who I wanted him to make it with. I practically dragged Jane across the room to meet an old chum. Stuffing his head full of tarts at the buffet was producer and manager Vincent Marsden and his wife, Sandra. Vince recognized talent and gave artists their space. Not only would I slaughter donkeys to work for Vince, Sandra would make a perfect friend for Jane.

I asked the ladies to gather us something from the bar before dragging Vince into the corner and speaking with a reserved voice. "Apparently Stoddard's selling us. Do you know anything about this?"

Vince's eyes enlivened. "Selling you? You guys are one of the hottest bands going. What's he thinking?"

I cleared my throat. "He and I have not exactly been seeing eye-to-eye lately."

"Peter, he screws over everyone. You must have really

gotten under his collar. Then again, with the way that man enjoys hearing himself talk, he may just be mouthing off. If you are truly for sale, I'll make him an offer he can't refuse."

I must have been glowing at the man with the incredible reputation for taking care of his artists. "If you get us away from that thief, you can have double your normal commission and the band will still come out ahead."

Vince shook my hand with the firmness of securing an engine in place. "You got a deal." As he headed off toward Stoddard his poker face disguised what I knew. Marsden was a bulldog ready for a sneak attack. The men disappeared to play let's make a deal.

Sandra and Jane returned with the drinks. The girls looked rather cute together. It seemed they could become the best of friends. Now I could really give Jane everything. Being signed by Vincent Marsden could turn all I touched to gold.

Time crawled along, and the ticking of my watch grew in my ears. My thumb tapped wildly against the side of my glass. My eyes constantly peered to the corner where Vince and Stoddard once stood. Like a kiddie planning his purchase before entering a sweets shop I was already thinking about what to record first.

A group of birds behind me chattered on about how The Small Faces had just entered the room. Screw them. With Vincent Marsden at the helm I could take down that jokester Marriott in a heartbeat.

Finally Vince returned. His hair was disheveled and his complexion rather ghostly. With barely a glance in my direction, he grabbed Sandra and shuttled her out while muttering, "Your contract is not worth getting hung upside down by my ankles off of a balcony. Sorry, Peter, I've a family to protect."

My gut churned. I faked a laugh as if Vince had just told me a joke while he dragged Sandra out the door. I put my arm around Jane and kissed her cheek. "I love you, darling."

"Peter?" Jane had that concerned look in her eyes ladies get when they know there is something you should share with them. She was no fool.

"Oh, look. The Stones have arrived. Let's go have a chat with Brian and Anita." I needed out of there, but there was no way I could leave directly after Vince and not have it look like we went out to talk. Something told me I was clueless as to the magnitude of what Stoddard had up his sleeve.

The following day a note arrived via special messenger, welcoming Love Machine to the managerial talents of Chadwick Gordon.

I Can't Control Myself

Rosalyn

Damn! How I love the growl of Reg Presley's voice! It just always makes me feel so sexy, as if no man in the world could resist my curves.

The Troggs blast as my grinding hips sway me through my bedroom. It's the Rosalyn alternative to nervous pacing. Jacqueline's not allowed to see me this way. We made a pact not to get worked up over a guy until after the third date. She never upholds her end either, but we try not to be obvious about it. That totally counts, right?

For the second time—okay, really the third—I peek in the mirror to verify my eyeliner hasn't smudged and my hair is still in a perfect Veronica Lake hairstyle that has nearly two-thirds of it swooped to the side with a huge wave over one eye. Yeah, I'm far too mental over Niles.

As The Troggs fade out, Tom Petty resumes his role as disk jockey. He nudges me back into curiosity over Peter Lane in the form of a song by Love Machine. Peter's soul-inspired guitar mastery and his driving vocals send me dancing around the room and pathetically wailing like a cat in heat. Despite the fact trying to contact him freaked me out big time the other day, I plop onto the bed and surf on the man who keeps making musical guest appearances in my personal reality show.

Yeah, I'm totally mental, and not just over Niles. I can't stay away from this guy, nor do I really want to. Peter doesn't just make me all fangirly; he's also got a firm grip on my curiosity.

Wikipedia tells me Peter's father worked in a steel mill

51

while his mother was a waitress in a local pub. Peter's twin brother, Steven, died of bronchial pneumonia at the age of seven. Throughout his life, Peter claimed that Steven's ghost would occasionally visit. The entire experience had a deep impact on Peter and gave him a "live for today" attitude.

As a teenager, Peter hijacked the school's PA system and played the air raid siren along with a recording of haunting sounds associated with UFOs. Meanwhile his friend and future band mate, Johnny Paxton, released helium-filled weather balloons from the football field.

God that would be awesome!

The driving, blue-eyed soul sound of Peter's voice fades out, and Ricky Nelson singing "Fools Rush In" takes over. Fewer than two bars in I've had enough. I'd much rather watch Peter serenade me on YouTube. His powerful, yet oh-so-gentle voice fills my ears with a seductive purr. My hips wiggle deeper into the softness of the bed while my body and mind get lost in peace. As I join him in song, the passion of Peter's words makes me desperate for his touch. Longing comes forth from the depths of my soul and compels me to touch Peter's face. My hand extends forward, caressing the screen while my heart aches for an intense love again. Though the screen is cool and flat I feel connected to the man's presence. It's not as if I am actually touching him but more like he is responding to my call.

Jacqueline's rap on my door to announce Niles just pulled up jars me back to reality. Excitement radiates off of me as I head back to the mirror for a quick examination of my hair that I so foolishly could have messed up while dancing. A good-looking guy who holds my doors open, dresses well, and shares my insane tastes has actually entered my life. The possibilities have me cautiously optimistic and as excited as when The Rascals reunited for the first time in forty years!

The awesomeness of my outfit and my desire to see Niles both have me eager to answer the door. It may not be a dress of the silent era, but my curvy, satin and lace number was made in the nineteen forties. It, along with my period appropriate makeup, looks damn sexy—if I do say so myself.

My heart revs at the sight of Niles. For once I feel the sane one as he stands before me in a well-tailored suit and a bowler.

Yes, a *bowler*!

A bouquet of brightly colored blooms conceals his face. His eyes pop up from above the flowers, and his gaze comically scans back and forth. He hands me the bouquet and reveals a Charlie Chaplin mustache.

Okay, seriously, a mustache?

He looks utterly ridiculous but also absolutely heart stealing!

NILES

This woman has a smile that is pure gold, but her eyes turning into jawbreakers reveal the mustache is too much. Niles, when it comes to pushing the limit you have a lead foot.

However, the joy on her face is encouraging. Maybe I have found someone like me.

Scratch that. No one is ever like me, and the reasons why are too depressing to ponder. Now pull off the mustache and tell Rosalyn how lovely she looks.

Rosalyn

Niles yanks off the mustache. A zip goes through my midsection as he winces. That was a lot of effort just to make me happy. "Rosalyn, you look absolutely amazing. Are you ready?"

Yeah, I'm ready. For what I'm not sure, but I can't wait to find out.

Kernel by kernel, Niles tosses popcorn into the air and arcs it into his mouth. His aim is only partially terrible. Half of what he tosses bounces off of his lap and spills onto the floor. His awkwardness is endearing, and for once I kind of wish he was a little less gentlemanly. Seriously, his lips are dreamily kissable.

A kernel bounces off of his cheek, and I catch it in my mouth. He laughs. "That was impressive." My shrug implies it was no big deal, but then a wink confesses my luck.

I pull a bag of M&M's out of my purse and offer him some. His forehead scrunches as he eyes them like they are diseased. "What? You said you like M&M's."

Niles resumes popping kernels into his mouth. "I love them. Thing is, I can't eat them in movie theaters."

"Why? Does the flickering film turn them to deadly poison?"

"Consider it one of my numerous, adorable quirks. So, you haven't told me much about you. What's your family like?"

Oy. Of all of the getting-to-know-you questions in the world why did he pick that one? No matter how old you are when you lose your parents it leaves you feeling as if you are a helpless orphan. For me it presents a false memory of being an infant, curled in a corner, abandoned and crying. The mental image always makes my throat lock and—

"Ooh, sorry. That expression tells me I asked a difficult question."

"Very." I divert my eyes from his sight and swallow deep in the back of my throat.

The sweetest expression of an innocent child looks at me in concern. Now I really can't face him. "Trust issues too?"

"Boy, you never ask anything easy, do you?"

NILES

No, because getting to know someone isn't easy when you always lose friends. It's just a few minutes into our date, and I already want to punch myself for overstepping. "Sorry. I hear being with me is a challenge. I'm rather fond of that, though I'm told it's not necessarily a compliment."

When Mom expresses understanding she does it with personal contact, so I touch Rosalyn's hand in a way that hopefully shows I'm here if she wants to talk, but also don't want to make a federal case out of it.

Rosalyn

Niles gives my hand a double pat as if gently saying, "There, there." The intended display of comfort provides a welcome distraction. He often makes little bits of contact but it's never anything that can be read into. A touch to the arm, a touch to the shoulder—all of them never long enough for me to get a vibe of interest beyond friendship. But this is only the second date, and the pace is refreshing. He's dead on with the trust issues. The thought of getting close to a man still freaks me out.

The houselights dim, and I push away the negative thoughts. I used to allow myself to be happy, and I will be like that again.

Niles and I sit in a café booth where he attempts to build a pyramid out of sugar packets. My thumb flicks the seam of the paper sleeve on my coffee cup as I reflect on his earlier mention of family. Where it can lead concerns me, but a cathartic conversation really would be nice. I want to trust again, and, in the metaphysical sense, Niles feels like he's always trying to be a good person. "So, you mentioned family earlier."

His eyes rise from his project. "Sorry. I probably shouldn't have asked that question. I'm still willing to go first if you're in."

"Sure. Why not?"

"How about we play bits and pieces? I'll tell you a little something then you tell me a little something. When either of us feels it's going too far, we quit. Sound good?"

"I can deal with that. You have to start though." I take a swig of coffee while hoping to swallow down my sudden case of jitters.

Niles grabs another sugar packet and shakes its contents

to the bottom. He then *bops* it on the table a few times so it will stand up on its end. "My grandparents mostly raised me. Your turn."

"My dad raised me. You mentioned your mom in the car the other day. What happened to her?" He places the sugar packet in a row next to two others.

"She was there. My grandparents were retired, so I stayed with them while Mom worked her ass off to get me the best education possible. I was what you could call a bit of a problem child. What happened to your mom?"

Problem child?

Upon completion of the first layer Niles smashes down a packet of sugar to smooth it. He then lays it across the top. Somehow the packages underneath remain perfectly stiff. Amazing.

Was the term problem child related to narcotics? Drug damage would explain a lot about his oddness. Then again, I'm not at all one who has the right to question the source of oddities. "Mom died when I was nine," I offer. "Your dad?"

"He bailed when I was four. I barely remember him. Actually, I think it's more that I choose to forget. What happened to your mom?"

"Lung cancer. Are your grandparents still alive?"

"Yeah, they moved here to help Mom when Dad left. Now they are back in Mill Valley where they belong. What about your dad? Where is he?" Niles places two more sugar packets on top of the crossbeam. Of course the whole thing crumbles. He snickers. "Yeah, I know. I often attempt the impossible because I like to believe I can overcome anything."

He seems to shrug off his words, but something in his eyes conveys a deeper meaning. I can't help but think he's encouraging me to overcome whatever it is that makes me not want to have this conversation. "Dad died from prostate cancer five years ago. Siblings?"

Niles plops his hands onto the table and twiddles his thumbs. He's completely lost after the collapse of his sugar tower. "Nope. Just me and Mom." I slide him the packet of

M&M's he declined before the movie. Gingerly he pours the contents onto the table so they won't roll off. "You?" he asks.

"None, although I don't think siblings could get much closer than Jacqueline and I."

"You're lucky." Niles places his index finger on a brown M&M and pushes it aside. He then guides a yellow one into a different area as he rotates through all the colors.

"Yeah, I suppose I am. Jacqueline's parents kind of adopted me when Dad passed away. We had already been close since we were kids." My hand darts across the table to snag a yellow M&M. "You have too many." Niles gives an appreciative smile. "Anyway, my dad was in a band with Jacqueline's dad when we were toddlers. With our dads being musicians and her grandfather being a world-renowned guitarist, music became my sanctuary. Jacqueline's grandfather and I can talk about music for hours. He's got all kinds of crazy, old knowledge."

Niles pops enough yellow M&M's in his mouth to even them down to match the amount of dark brown ones. Next he starts alternating between eating the two. "Her grandfather's famous? Anyone I may have heard of?"

"Yeah, I'm betting you have. George Quinn."

Niles abandons his candy-devouring mission and sits erect. "*The* George Quinn? From St. Mary Shelly's Revival? That's Jacqueline's grandfather?" I give a little nod as his lips part in awe. His eyes search the sky as he takes a moment to absorb my words. "Jacqueline Quinn ... That name doesn't really fit her."

Okay, that's nowhere near where I thought Niles would go with that one. "No, her name is Marsden."

Niles adds eating the green M&M's into his rotation. He's reducing them down so that he will have the same amount as he does light brown ones.

NILES

"Huh." Marsden. Jacqueline Marsden. Yeah, that's better. Wait. No way.

"Her dad is Dante Marsden? Are you serious? The session musician? The one who was raised by Vincent Marsden, the famous producer? The guy is connected to pretty much everyone I idolize."

Huh. If I rub a green M&M across the table with the tip of my finger it leaves a colored streak. Does Jacqueline know she's lucky, or do people with both parents accept that as a way of life? Do her parents fight or do they always make kissy faces? Are they more like The Conners or The Cunninghams? Does a yellow M&M smear color too?

The scrape of a yellow one across the table brings the same result. Cool.

Whatever happened to Chuck Cunningham? He went MIA, just like my dad. No one seemed to miss him. Did he also forget they existed?

Rosalyn

Niles looks to the M&M's whose color ratios are now balanced and begins dragging them, one at a time, under his finger along the textured, beige table. The coating smears off of the confections and leaves a bright trail, thus turning the table into a canvas. The beautiful scene begs for preservation, so I grab a sketchpad from my purse and start capturing Niles.

Niles's glance sheepishly rises. "Can I ask you one more question? You don't have to answer now, but if you would eventually, I'd really appreciate it."

I give him a little nod.

"What was it like to have a dad?"

Niles has no idea what he's just asked, or the impact it has on my heart, not because of what it means regarding my own father, but the chord it hits regarding the last two years. All children should have their parents to guide them through life. My father was there for me until the day he died and never missed a single moment of importance. Not only did he pick up the pieces for both of us when Mom died, but he shaped everything about me, starting with giving me my name and ending with final words that encouraged me to be myself.

Sometimes when my resolve in that area falters I try to blow off the pain like I am stronger and bigger than everyone else because it hurts just too damn much to disappoint him.

My eyes begin to water, and I swallow back sorrow. I miss my family. Even though she had long passed, I used to talk to Mom on my private telephone line to Heaven. When Dad died I would talk to him too. Then life changed, and it was easier to not think about family at all. I really wish I could bring myself to pick up that phone again and talk to the people I miss.

"Rosalyn? Are you okay? Did I take it too far?"

I dab away tears I hadn't been aware I was shedding. "No, Niles, I needed this conversation and didn't know it. How about we spend the rest of this evening making plans for our next adventure?"

His boyish grin returns, and everything inside me gets all glowy. Niles reminds me of the happiness of being a kid and the joy felt when making a new friend. If there is one thing I need, it's to remember the simple joys adults so easily ignore. Niles is already good for me.

I Wanna Take You Higher

Rosalyn

Through my earbuds, Sly and the Family Stone play a funky rhythm, wanting to take me higher. I hum along as I crawl into bed. Something about this sentiment makes me think of the amazing date I just had with Niles.

Actually, right now everything makes me think of Niles.

Hmm … Niles …

Niles is really cute.

The blankets cover me, bringing toasty warmth.

Niles has fun tastes.

My arms wrap around my pillow, making me wonder how it would be to snuggle next to him.

Niles is sweet.

My body cruises over the earth on a cloud.

Niles is quirky.

Mmm … I like quirky.

Niles is kind of hot.

Mmm … I love hot.

The iPod shuffles, and the soft, orchestral sounds of The Moody Blues bring heaviness to my eyelids as the world fades.

Clang!

The clash of cymbals propels my startled body forward. The iPod's shuffle, taking me from smooth melodies to a pounding drum line, kicks me awake so I can be enlivened by "Circles of Iron" by Love Machine.

My feet hit the carpet with my mind fully alert. The *bams* of my heart remind me of the sleepless night I tried to contact the man who just woke me. It's the same man in the unfinished drawing that sits on my battered desk over which my father wrote so many songs. Something about the drawing beckons me. While it stays perfectly still, I swear it's trying to flap itself off the desk and into my hands.

I grab it and stare. Why does it match my vision perfectly, yet feel so empty and lacking? I've a desire to add something to the eyes, but I always stop short of adjusting them. Those eyes call to me here just as they do on the album cover. They sound like a voice from within the walls of this silent house.

Impulsively I add wild flowers of pink and purple to the background. Now it looks right, but it feels as if it has already been hung and sits off-center. The sketch gets tacked over my desk next to the one of Niles at the café. As if I've slipped them into the perfect frame both drawings appear enhanced. Maybe Peter needed color to bring him to life. I pick up his album and stare at his image under the golden swirls. Why can't I let go of this man?

The faint sound of a bluesy piano seeps into the bedroom. That's odd. Why is Jacqueline up at this hour?

With the album still in hand, I head down the stairs and follow the sound toward the family room. Jacqueline is probably–

Oh, holy crap!

Inside the dark room, a stream of moonlight seeps between the curtains, acting like a spotlight illuminating where I have twice sat with the Ouija board. The music seems to emanate from the beam. That's it. I'm out of here!

I turn to flee, but the music grows louder, and the moonbeam brightens. Now it all hits me. I'm not the only one who has been doing the summoning. I, too, am being called.

A whisper-soft touch glides over my hand. It's startling, but instead of causing me to jump in fear it brings about peace. I take pause and listen intensely to the tune. What song is this? I'm gonna feel really stupid when I figure it out.

I have an inclination I'm being guided toward the closet. While humming I grab the Ouija board and set it up. My fingers tap along on the planchette. If I could just turn up the volume…

Oh, I'm not tapping the medley. I'm tapping the piano fill. This is totally Fats Domino.

Suddenly the planchette moves. *Saw with your eyes.*

Ohhhhh, crap. My hands jerk in fear. My voice comes out in a rapid whisper. "You saw with my eyes last time?"

Without a touch the planchette zooms.

Yes.

Uuuh … Is … Is he here? "I'm sorry. I got scared." Yeah, scared because I felt my body was being taken over, which is why I should have myself committed for saying, "Maybe we should try again."

A grip enrobes my hands and thrusts them onto the planchette.

Pull.

"What?"

The throbbing of my pulse increases in my temples, reminding me of a scratched record whose speed is set too high. Peter commands through the board, *Pull me to you.*

A surge of adrenaline hits as my mind reaches out and yanks. *Creaks* and *cracks* fill the air as if a large egg is breaking open and bringing a new creation to life. A pulsing, gold light ripples before me with a high-pitched wind whistling through the crack. It swirls into my hair and whips it back. My energy feeds off of the emerging force—a force that screams I need it. I become desperate for it, wanting it to engulf me. My focus intensifies, and the light blooms with a brightness that burns my eyes and forces them shut with the help of every muscle in my face.

I can't dig any deeper. I can't pull any harder. I can't—

My hair drapes back down and a tender energy replaces the winds of chaos. A whisper, laced with an East London accent, travels through the darkness. "Thank you."

My eyes creep open. "Peter?" I stand and step back, an automatic response of fear.

"You can see me? Really?"

I'm awestruck both by the ghost and by my idolatry. Holy Rock and Roll Heaven! "Yes, you're hazy, but you are here. How is this happening?"

"I've no idea. You must be some type of angel."

"Dear God!" I mutter while looking down at the board. What have I done? An urge to put it away, as if in doing so my actions will be undone, brings me to my knees.

"Well, I may be exquisite, but God is a little much for comparison." Peter chuckles while dusting off his blue, brocade jacket that covers a white shirt with ruffles on the breast that match those on the cuffs. "Seriously, how do I look?"

It's not the fact he's totally cute that gets me, it's those damn black, drainpipe trousers and boots. These little things make me just kind of go all freaky fangirl. "Exactly like you did when you died." The pace of my voice matches the racing of my feet as I make for the closet and tuck the board away. Now what? I peek back at the man and my heart goes haywire again. That's Peter Lane!

"That's awful! I was charred and peeling like a burnt sausage."

Finally, I force myself to get a solid look at the man. "No, you look like before you were barbecued."

"Without the bags under my eyes, I hope. I was terribly in need of sleep that day."

"No, actually your eyes look rather … magnetic." And hypnotizing. Not to mention something about them is putting both my heart and my hormones in a spin like I'm under attack by my boyfriend drawer come to life.

"How rude of me not to have asked your name." He steps forward, and I try not to gasp.

"It's—It's Rosalyn."

"Like The Pretty Things song?"

"No, the Bowie version." Peter seems confused. Duh! Of course he would be. "You knew him as David Jones."

" 'The Laughing Gnome', guy? You mean that tall, skinny, bloke actually amounted to something?"

"He kind of helped define an entire movement, but yeah, when you come right down to it, I was named after The Pretty Things song, especially since Bowie just ripped it off. Seriously, if you're going to cover something, why not have a little fun with it instead of going straight for the rip off? I mean—" Wait, why am I babbling about David Bowie to the *ghost* of Peter Lane?

Peter

There is something rather striking about this girl. Then again, she's the first being I've laid eyes on, living or dead, since I made the biggest decision of my existence—one that still seems barmy. How long has it been? Years? Decades? A century? Is there still time to complete my dastardly little deed, or has the whole mess been in vain?

"Peter, how is it possible you are here?"

A complicated question. The answer is still a bit of a mystery. The why of it better explains the situation. "I've unfinished business." If I got here because this girl thought of me, can I get to Jane by thinking of her?

It's time to thank the angel responsible for my release and embark on the journey for which I've waited so long. My devotion to Jane stops my lips just shy of giving Rosalyn's cheek a kiss of thanks. Who could blame me for wanting to though? I'd be a fool not to long to kiss the silken cheek of this beautiful creature.

Rosalyn

Peter looks perplexed, as if something about me brings forth questions. His hand extends towards my chin. While the caress lacks physical contact the sensation makes me swoon as if a hundred butterflies have fluttered out of my heart.

Peter's face hones in on mine, and the proximity of his lips puts a tingle onto my cheek, leaving me clamoring for more. Dear God! Peter Lane almost kissed me!

"Rosalyn?" Jacqueline's voice startles me.

Peter

A pretty, dark-haired girl in a slinky, blue nightie enters the room. She looks right at me yet misses me entirely. Pity. I certainly can't miss her.

My body flickers and slightly fades as I attempt to leave, yet my mind remains fully in the room. Again I try to force the fading. God, please take me to Jane.

My ability to fade slows and adds to the heaviness of my heart. Maybe I need to address business first. I summon my anger from within and focus every bit of hate on Stoddard. I'll get the bastard that wronged me. Maybe I didn't have the power when I was alive, but all the stories about ghosts who are hell-bent for revenge must have some merit. I haven't spent years surrounded by a black nothingness for no reason at all.

Finally my mind and body both float away. "Goodnight, Rosalyn."

Rosalyn

"Rox? Are you okay?"

"I'm fine, Jacqueline. I'm just suffering from boredom, insomniac style."

Peter's voice hangs in my head as if he were still here. My eyes scan the room one last time before I grab his album and follow Jacqueline off to bed.

Can't Find My Way Home

Peter

A huge, detached, brick home seated in the lush countryside fills my view. So much has changed since I was last on Earth I can't be certain where I am. The house sits in an exclusive area on a road called St. Marks. These hills reek of cash.

Have I made it? I'm pretty certain that girl's accent was American, so I had to go all the way across the pond. Is traveling really this easy? With a little focus, I find myself inside the house, standing in an office where that same smarminess that always filled my gut with sick whenever Stoddard entered the room looms in the air.

Behind an intimidating, wood desk hang gold records awarded to Benjamin Stoddard. The entire room is lined in riches—riches that he undoubtedly stole. Some type of camera is mounted in one corner. If I'm visible to whoever is on the other side of that thing, I'll soon know.

While I circle the room, my picture on one of the awards stops me dead in my tracks. It's a platinum certification of something called, *Love Machine—The Complete Masters,* awarded to Benjamin Stoddard. Platinum? I never knew of this album, and I've certainly never heard of a platinum designation.

A little silver disk has been placed inside where the album should be. My, records have gotten small. Where are the grooves? The date of the award says two thousand nine.

Two *thousand* nine? We were still selling in two thousand nine? What in the bloody hell year *is* this?

I dart to the desk in search of a calendar but only find a few gadgets. Have people done away with paper? All that is here are some plastic whatsits. One of them reminds me of the futuristic phones that were coming out in the sixties, but the thing is minuscule and has no handset or cord. A big, flat rectangle with wires coming out of it is propped up on a stand. A little device resembling a flat plastic orb sits next to some kind of typewriter without a place to put the paper. It reminds me of part of the consoles that accompany those big tape machine computers in the movies. Where has my bum landed?

The orb has the feeling of wet plaster as my hand drags through it and the desk it sits on. The same thing happens when I try to touch the rectangle on a stand. A *fizz* comes from it, and the box pops to life like a telly. Where are the knobs? Why can't I find a bloody calendar?

The knobless telly again fizzes and a calendar appears. Across the top it says, "April 2014."

Twenty-fourteen? I've been dead over forty years! Is that bastard Stoddard really still alive? Just how old would that geezer be now?

A pen sits on the desk. Now there is something I recognize. If I can transport my body I should be able to move other things. Mentally I attempt to lift the pen. Nothing happens. I try again while envisioning a zapping force sprouting from my brain. The faintest of movements occurs, though it's ever so slight that it may only be my imagination.

The doorknob flicks. Strolling into the room is an old guy who's nearly bald and the sparse hair that's left is gray. Although lines crinkle around his eyes and he moves a little slower than before there's no mistaking that this is the guy who ruined everything for me.

Stoddard heads straight for his desk, passing right through me. So it's April, two *thousand* and fourteen. I'm finally with Stoddard, and I can't do anything but barely rattle the pen on his desk. This is bloody ridiculous.

Anger pulses through me so heatedly that I perceive the room filling with steam. My hands grip around Stoddard's neck with the intent to strangle him, but they don't take hold. I'm all the more enraged. He loosens his shirt collar and clears his throat, all the while playing with the little plastic orb.

How dare he not feel my anger? That platinum record belongs to me. I'm the one who wrote the songs. I'm the one who slaved in the studio. All he did was steal my money. My hand goes through the record as I try to rip it off the wall. "You filthy bastard!"

Stoddard looks around the room. His back does a little shimmy before he resumes his work.

That's the best I can do? Slightly disturb this guy? I've got to find a better way.

With my mind I try to fling the record at him, but all it does is tip off center. Stoddard looks at it questioningly before strolling towards it and snickering, "Peter Lane, you are still a thorn in my side."

"No, Stoddard, I've only begun to cause you problems. Mark my words; somehow I will get you where it hurts most."

I can't stand to look at the bastard anymore so I storm for the door. I have no problems passing through the barrier. I've got to find Jane. Somehow I need to let her know I'm sorry for all the bad things that happened. Focusing on Stoddard brought me here, so focusing on Jane has to take me to her.

The memory of Jane's beautiful, blue eyes cools my anger. The tenderness of her touch. The softness of her voice. They are all so heavenly and all retained in my soul. How does she look now? Has time gotten to her like it did Stoddard, or is she still lovely? I bet my heavenly creature is still as glorious as a fragrant rose.

Calm swirls through me, and I feel transported to a brighter place. When my eyes open I'm back in the home of the Rosalyn girl. Bloody hell!

When I died the place we lived in was on fire. Did it get fixed and Jane stayed? I focus on the flat while remembering all of its little details before internalizing the emotions of my life with her. I open my eyes and find myself standing before it. At least I think I am. It looks completely different, yet I am certain this is the right place. Inside the home children laugh and a lady prepares a meal. Nowhere can I find an indicator Jane was ever here.

I shut my eyes and focus deeper on her beauty. I miss her touch, her scent—everything about her. When my eyes spring open I'm back at Rosalyn's.

I'm too late. I must be too late. Why else would I return to this room that contains a shop full of albums, some furniture, a fireplace, and ... and its mantle crowed with pictures.

My hair flips back as I stride toward the mantle. The snaps show Rosalyn and the girl who came into the room before I left along with other smiling faces. None of those faces belong to Jane or anyone I know to be related to her.

Wait. What is this?

A faded snap grabs my attention. It's of a couple I know all too well—my old friend Vincent Marsden and his wife. How the hell is Marsden tied in with all of this? I need to keep exploring this house.

Bless The Wings
(That Bring You Back)

Rosalyn

Being freaked out by summoning Peter continues to unsettle me as I try to find a comfortable spot on the mattress. The whole thing plays in my mind like the scene in *The Brady Bunch* where Marcia gets it in the nose with a football, over and over again.

In the darkness I yank open the nightstand drawer and reach for the nearest battery-operated boyfriend. What will it be? A loving romance, a one night stand, or shall I turn into a shameless groupie whore? In light of my agitation level the whore route sounds best.

My hand slinks down my leg and slides up my silky nightgown. The boy toy touches me in that oh-so-perfect spot that makes my very core gasp with delight. Yes, the groupie whore is what I need. It's nineteen eighty-four. He's got long, over-sprayed black hair, tight black pants, and hazel eyes. As the tip of the vibrator reaches its destination a liquid ache begins. It's time to turn the knob and—

"What do you know about Jane?"

Peter's voice sends my body jerking and flailing as my heart tries to smack itself out of my body. I try to mute my shriek so I don't freak out Jacqueline. "What the hell are you doing here? Jesus!"

Peter stands at my desk, staring out the window and toward the heavens. "I can't find her. I need to know what happened." His voice is so distant and lost his pain radiates into my throat.

So that's his unfinished business. Maybe I should stay

across the room because I have no idea what this man is like and he may hard-core flip out when he hears what happened. Oddly I do have a natural inclination to be close and offer comfort. Somehow I know that I am safer with him here than I've been in years. My hand slips through his body as I attempt to touch his shoulder, yet it makes direct contact with a vibration of despair. His pain makes my inner fangirl cave way to the woman with a broken heart.

"You don't need to say it. If she's not here she must be over there." His voice is soft and broken. "She was too young to die. I was too. My twin brother was younger still. I spent my days trying to enjoy life to the fullest because of his loss. It's unnatural to die young. You hold the answers as to what happened with Jane, don't you?"

"Maybe." I sit at my desk and open my laptop. Peter bends down with his head next to mine. His radiating sorrow reminds me of my own. The comfort of an understanding soul fills part of a void that has resided inside since I can first remember. My eyes get misty while feeling as if I've finally come face-to-face with the brick wall of reality.

Through my burning, blurry eyes, I type in the name Jane MacFadden Lane. Each image causes tears to form as if I've lost another person who's dear to me. Peter is undeniably right. No one should die as young as he did, let alone those we lost that barely got started.

On Peter's Wikipedia page sits all of the information; news of Jane's car going off the road and soaring down a hill, her death being ruled a suicide, and the conspiracy theory that after the crash somebody set the car ablaze. A witness said two men, covered in blood, were seen running away from the wreckage. "There is no way that Jane killed herself," Peter mutters through sniffles. "She was stronger than that. So, so much stronger."

"How do we find the truth?"

"I don't have to. I know she was meant to die in that fire with me because of my big mouth. Everything started coming together to shut me up while they made their plans to take us out. If we looked happy and perfect, people would focus on that instead of questioning why our lives had fallen apart. That's why they finally gave me some of the money I deserved. Keep suspicion low, and keep Peter Lane's trap shut. I'm certain that was the mantra."

"Your death wasn't an accident?"

His eyes press shut. "No," he whispers, firmly.

Peter

I can't look any longer. Though I have missed seeing her lovely face, thinking about the pain I caused Jane is unbearable.

The glow of the dastardly thing lights up numerous sketches of people and places tacked to the wall behind the desk. All of them are in black-and-white except for one of a young man with hope-filled eyes who sits in a café and plays with something on a colorfully streaked table. It strangely deepens my hurt. I continue looking for a new diversion and find another sparing use of color that sends my head spiraling—a portrait of me I thought long gone. How does *she* have *that* drawing? "Where did you get that?" That sketch is the reason I keep winding up here.

"I drew it," she tells rather nonchalantly.

My head snaps in her direction. "*You* did? When?"

"The night I first tried to reach you. I couldn't sleep, so I did that."

"What picture did you take it from? Did you find it on that computer thing?"

Her cheeks go a tad red. I seem to be embarrassing her. "It just came to me."

I take a closer look at the sketch and shrug off my outward excitement while inwardly acknowledging that if I weren't dead I'd fear a heart attack. "I guess I'm just surprised at the pose. Why did you put me in a garden at sunset?"

"I don't know. I just sort of had an image in my head and followed it."

My chest tightens as I recall the moment. "So you drew

me and the flowers from memory?"

"Yeah, I guess so."

And what a memory she has! The emotions galloping through me tell it is possible for a dead man to feel as if he has seen a ghost, because I am looking at one.

I've found her!

I've found Jane!

Freak of the Week

Peter

I'm in utter disbelief. We are reincarnated in groups that continuously travel in the same circle of friends and family, time and again. Thus, while it would make perfect sense to find Jane in a future life, I never expected to see her now.

Is this why a picture of my old friend, Vince Marsden, sits on the mantle downstairs? But Jane only met him briefly. Maybe it's me being brought back to him. If some of the people in my circle have already returned, who else might pop in for tea?

Rosalyn

Peter's eyes keep scanning the room then returning to the drawing as if it is the apparition. God, I wish he'd stop looking at it. My hands are totally fidgeting because I'm mortified he even knows I drew him. I must come off as some kind of pre-teeny-bopper who does nothing but lie on her bed and dream of teen idols. Peter's loss for words suits me because his staring makes me want to crawl under a rock. How can I get him to stop looking at the humiliating thing? "Peter, it's five in the morning. Even though it's Sunday, and I don't have to work today, I should probably get some sleep."

"I'm sorry. I must have woken you. That was rather rude of me. You know, whenever life got overwhelming Jane had trouble sleeping. I wrote a song to lull her off. Shall we give it a go?"

I crawl into bed and snuggle up to my pillow as Peter kneels beside me. He attempts a caress as if smoothing hair away from my face. Everything about him seems warm and adoring. It's as if we've loved each other for years. His lullaby soothes. My lids turn heavy as my mind slips into that sweet space between consciousness and sleep where your muscles seem to disappear. By the end of his serenade I'm drifting off on a cloud of bliss.

The brightness of the sun's rays stirs me awake while I'm enrobed in warmth beyond that of the sheets. My mind goes to Niles before I notice Peter wrapped around me like the wings of a guardian angel. It's really weird. The invitation to stay was never extended; however, I don't mind Peter's presence in the absolute least.

A sweet smile crosses his face. It matches mine. "Good morning," he says. "Sleep well?"

"Amazingly."

Jacqueline knocks on my door. She sticks her head in almost before I can say, "Come in." Her aura of happiness holds, but her brow scrunches quizzically. Oh, crap. Can she see Peter now?

"I thought I heard you on the phone. Were you talking to yourself?"

Whew.

Hold up. Is it really good only I see Peter? "I make the best company. No offense."

"None taken. Look what was just delivered to me," she sings while revealing a bouquet of red roses from behind her back.

"Who are those from?"

Her eyes twinkle as she plays with a petal. "Remember I told you about that cute guy who moved in up the street?"

Oh, this is going to be bad, but I play the game anyway. "You mean the guy with the business card with a fancy title and the even fancier address?"

"Yes!" she says, beaming. "The one with the gorgeous green eyes and a smile that damn near killed me."

"Nope. I don't remember him at all. Clearly you have

regressed to when you were eleven and are dreaming up imaginary boyfriends again."

"Well, my imaginary lover just sent me flowers before asking me out. You know what that means."

"Trou-ble!" we chime in unison.

"Yep." Jacqueline sighs while setting the bouquet on my dresser. "I can't trust him with the dishes let alone my heart."

"Sorry. That really sucks. I can't believe how some guys will wrap themselves in a red flag."

"He's totally telling me to wear my best underwear." Jacqueline bounces on the bed and scoots herself up so she is now lying on top of Peter. She stacks some pillows behind her and tries to settle in, then wiggles in an attempt to get comfortable and doesn't understand why she can't. Peter laughs and slides his hand up her leg, causing Jacqueline to quiver. "Geez, just thinking about it gives me the willies."

I bite the inside of my mouth to conceal my laughter at Peter's silly expression that shows he wants to lick Jacqueline over every bit of her body. A twinge sneaks its way into my heart as if saying, "Hey, what about me?"

"What's the matter, luv?" he asks. "A tad jealous?"

Peter straddles over me, drops to my other side, and nuzzles into my neck. My tingling spine makes him difficult to ignore.

"You know," Jacqueline says mischievously. "Maybe I'm misjudging Tom. I mean, there are nice guys out there, right? Niles brings you flowers and acts like a gentleman, yet he hasn't tried anything inappropriate, *has he?*" Jacqueline leers at me.

"Oh, please! I would've told you if he had."

"Is that the guy in the other drawing?" Peter asks.

"What's the matter, luv? A tad jealous?" I ask Peter. Unfortunately Jacqueline is clueless of the fact that my words are aimed elsewhere.

"You know it." Jacqueline stares off into space. She's got the look she gets when she doesn't want to give up but senses she should know better. "Rox, do you think I could be misjudging Tom? I mean, in all honesty, I kind of have a bad vibe about the whole thing, but I don't want to get so jaded that I always assume the worst in people."

I really feel for Jacqueline. She has a problem most girls would kill for, and it depresses the hell out of her. She's gorgeous. I don't mean pretty, or attractive, or even beautiful. She is, hands down, one of the most gorgeous women you will ever see. Every good looking guy who thinks he is only worthy of the prettiest bimbo hits on her mercilessly while the good ones assume she is out of their league. Several times I have watched her approach men only to have them think she's either a high-class prostitute trying to turn a trick or that their buddies put her up to it. As a result, her quest to find Mr. Right makes people think she's a finicky serial dater. The truth is she's lonely as hell.

"What does your gut say?"

She sighs. "Not to go, but my heart tells me I have the head of a bull. Want to double up? Safety in numbers, just like in horror movies."

I hate to tell her no, but I don't want to screw up with Niles either. "I don't know. Niles might think it's weird. We're still in that friend/getting-to-know-each-other phase."

"Still no kiss beyond the cheek?"

My no is disgruntled.

"What?" Peter asks. "The man must be gay."

Jacqueline stares off. She feels as lost in the world as I do but for different reasons. It breaks my heart. She has been so amazing to me that this is the least I can do for her. "Let's give it a shot and see what happens."

"Really?"

I nod and Jacqueline hugs me before swiping up her roses and making for her room. Peter's fingers glide over my arm. "Darling, I really don't like the sound of where this is going."

"Why, Peter, you are jealous!"

Peter leans in and whispers in my ear, sending beautiful tingles of fairy dust swirling around me. "Somehow I will find a way to show you a world so fabulous you could never dream it existed."

"And how do you propose to do that? You're a little on the dead side."

"No matter what that Niles guy has to offer, be sure to save your heart for me." His hand passes a caress through my chin. The resulting sensation coursing through my veins sends my heart thundering. Peter fades, yet the passion lingers on.

Wedding Ring

February 1967

Peter

Crazy as it was, four months into our relationship Jane and I officially decided to live together. Of course her parents were completely flipping their lids. As we all sat around the dining room table her father took the news so harshly the old geezer almost choked on his roast. He gulped down the meat and turned flaming red. He was ready to throttle me.

I panicked. This was my love we were talking about. The thought of being without her made me wish my body were devoid of blood. She adored her father, and I feared what his lack of acceptance could mean to us. My heart's words raced forth without my brain's consent. "Mr. MacFadden, I don't intend to shack up with your daughter. I plan to marry her. In fact, the reason I am here tonight is to ask for your daughter's hand."

My bold declaration surprised everyone, especially myself. However, even if I had planned the most romantic of proposals in the most opulent of spaces I could not have meant it more. From the moment I entered Jane's makeup room my mind turned all other women into shapeless mannequins.

With sheepish excitement I turned to Jane. Her tender lips I longed to kiss slowly parted while she internally questioned if I were serious. Marriage was to be down the road, yet my nod conveyed my words were for the now.

The tiny tears that formed in Jane's eyes told me she was more than fine with professing our love legally. The modern notion of taking your time before saying I do seemed crazy when you'd found the one who makes life worth living—the one who helps you find purpose in the mundane. That's exactly what I had found in Jane.

Jane's father turned to her. His voice was unmistakably stern. "Clearly you didn't know about this. How do you feel about this *matter*?" Matter was said like a filthy word reserved for trick turners in alleyways.

Jane smiled and my insides burst with joy. She answered by dashing around the table with her locks flapping in the breeze from her speed. I pushed back my chair, eager to run to her, but she plopped herself into my lap before I could rise. Her sweet lips made for the perfect dessert. "You're really serious, aren't you?"

My actions answered the question. I motioned her off of my lap with the intent of getting on one knee, but locks of her hair had flown across her face, and I didn't want even the slightest bit of her beauty concealed. As my fingers combed the locks away her eyes drew me in. I became so enchanted by them I lost track of formalities. Finally my left knee touched the ground.

"Jane MacFadden, the day we met you said you would never let another opportunity at happiness pass you by. You always put a smile on my face no matter how miserable I may be. How you manage to love me despite my quirks is completely without reason. Will you do me the incredible honor of spending the rest of our days together?"

"Yes!" she cried over and over again while bouncing at the knees. "Yes! Yes! Yes!" My lips met hers and the peace brought on by our decision was akin to finding comfort in front of a crackling fire. I didn't just have her in my arms. I now held all that was precious in the world.

Jane's mother sobbed, absolutely thrilled for her daughter. Jane's father, however, was silent except for his fingers that *thunked* rapidly on the table. "Daddy, are you okay with this?"

Her father groused, and I wanted to say something to plead my case to the judge but knew it was best to keep my yackety trap shut.

"Honey," Jane's mother addressed her husband, "I'd like to remind you that when we married we had been together fewer than six months. That was twenty-five years ago."

"Yes, but this is *my* daughter, and they've only been together *four* months."

"You're right, Daddy," Jane sighed remorsefully. Her smirk was concealed from all but me. I knew whatever she had cooked up would lead me into a whirlwind that I'd no desire to escape. "Peter, we have to wait until we reach the six-month mark. Meanwhile we'll live together as planned."

Mr. MacFadden seemed to be on the verge of having steam coming out of his reddening ears. "And just where do you plan to shack up with my daughter? I won't allow her to be in some rickety flat in London where the radiator never works and you're lucky if the plumbing does!"

Now this I was ready for; because while marriage is a formality, true happiness hinges on the dreams of the heart becoming a reality. "Actually, sir, that's a little surprise Jane's unaware of. Now that our second album was just released with a bullet I've secured a house in the country. We'll rent for now, but as soon as she decides it's where she wants to be, we'll buy it."

Jane squealed and gripped me tighter. Her father smacked his napkin onto the table as if it were a glass he wished to shatter. "Fine! Marry the man. You have my blessing but on one condition. None of this living together business. I don't care if you marry at the Registrar's Office. No daughter of mine lives in sin!"

Jane's eyes reminded me of diamonds in the sun. She knew my thoughts and didn't hesitate. "Well, Peter, what do you say? This weekend?"

"This weekend," I confirmed. Our lips met, and at that moment, as far as our hearts were concerned, Jane and I became one forever.

Oliver's Army

Rosalyn

"My God, who is that?" Inside the lobby at work I walk up to Darla as she stares out the window at a beautiful specimen. His deeply toned skin is so smooth it is jealousy inducing. "Damn, his cheekbones are as high as a skyscraper."

"Davion Pense," she says through a breathy sigh. "He applied for a job in the warehouse. You should get a good look at his lips. They are so kissable that I almost jumped across my desk and grabbed dessert. He's also single."

"How do you know that?"

"We had a nice chat while he waited for his interview. He lost his wife of nearly a decade last year and just moved here to start over. He's one of those striving-for-change, never-give-up types that we all try to be."

The smell of cigarettes coming from behind tells me the clicking of the heels I just heard belong to Oliver. "What are you two looking at?" All eyes remain locked on the target.

"Heaven," Darla says while sounding as if the man is a creature of her dreams.

I share in her revelry. "With the way he's built it's no wonder he applied to work in the warehouse. He would be perfect."

"Perfect for what?" Even though Oliver nudges my shoulder, it's Darla who gives his arm a playful smack. Here they go again.

"That's a nice thought, but he doesn't have the right forklift license. There's no time to train him, so they went with another guy."

"Bummer." I can't help but check out his ass as he walks

to his car. "It would be nice to have a little more eye candy around this place."

Darla rolls her eyes. "You mean *some* eye candy!"

"Hey, what am I?" Oliver protests.

Darla's eyes twinkle with mischief. "A thorn in my side who smokes too close to my lobby while yammering on his cell phone."

"I'd return the banter, but as a male member of the species I have learned not to fight. Instead I'll just put tape over the earpiece on your phone so you'll think you are growing old and losing your hearing."

"Well, I suppose it's not any worse than the time I used high-tac to stick your stapler to the ceiling." Darla tosses a copy of the dreamboat's résumé onto her desk. "I'm keeping this, just in case we ever need it."

I grab it for a once over. "Wow, he's got a lot of job stability and great letters of recommendation."

"Why can't all guys come with résumés and references?"

"Amen to that, sister!"

Oliver flails his arms. "Hey, hello! Guy standing right here, totally willing to be ogled instead of slammed for being male."

"Tell ya what, Oliver. You help Rox by grabbing this box one of the managers left on my credenza because he was too lazy to walk to the elevator, and I promise to watch as you do it."

"What? Are you serious?" I turn to find an overflowing Banker's Box of ratty folders. The ridiculousness just never ends around this place. "These are personnel folders." At least they're in a box this time.

"Yeah, he was gonna leave them for you in the break room but then he decided he shouldn't be so lazy and left them here."

How non-chivalrous, not to mention the fact those should always be under lock and key. How is it I know more about employee confidentiality than the managers? I've got to get out of this place.

Oliver takes the box from me as I start to head back to my

office. "Here, allow me. If I can't get ogled, at least I can be useful."

As he passes Darla's desk he stops and whispers to her, "Hey, thanks for covering for me the other day when I spaced on that meeting. You really saved my ass. Seriously, one slip and I could have lost my job. That would have lost me my kids as well."

Darla waves it off. However, the forty minutes she spent faking to the boss that Oliver was with a client while he was really off trying to patch things with his ex got pretty hair-raising. "No worries. You know I've always got your back."

"No, Darla, you've always got everyone's back. I owe you."

The Great Rock 'n' Roll Swindle

April 1967

Peter

I'd been waiting in Chadwick Gordon's lobby for over half an hour. He told me to haul it in because he had my check for the last album that hit the top of the charts two months before. Stop me if you've heard this one before, but to date, after all the expenses had been deducted the fact we had one of the hottest selling albums in all of the UK meant nothing financially—at least not in our pockets.

The secretary continuously eyed me. She must have thought I was a thieving delinquent who'd spring up from his chair and knife her. With a clearing of her throat she gingerly rolled her chair back from her desk, afraid to make a sudden movement. Cup in hand, she dashed out of the room. The sound of coffee pouring invaded my head, so I took advantage of my time alone by listening through the office door. From inside boomed not the voice of Gordon but that of Stoddard. Why was he there?

The click of the secretary's heels signaled it was time to slip back into my seat. On my way I grabbed a magazine so that it looked as if I had been up for a legitimate reason. Did BS know I was out there?

Finally the secretary got a call from the next room. Gordon's voice faintly came through the phone as he said it was time to cut my check. The door opened, and I kept my eyes to the magazine while wondering if BS would acknowledge me. The only greeting I got was a nose-itching whiff of his cologne and cigar smoke as he strode past.

The secretary flipped out the checkbook and started

writing. Once finished, she announced Mr. Gordon would see me and guided me into the office. As if she was eager to no longer have it in contact with her skin, the secretary slid the check across the desk for signature before slipping out of the room. Gordon scribbled on the thing and then came round and patted me on the back. It seemed he wished he had a knife to jab in. When I looked down at the check the knife I feared sat before me.

"Thirty-four hundred quid? What is this for? Are you requesting I pick up your dry cleaning?"

Gordon chuckled as he rocked back on his heels. I was being treated like a five-year-old whom had just been given some penny sweets. "Peter, I really must see you more often. I forget how entertaining that sense of humor of yours is."

"It seems you're the one with the sense of humor. You mean I spent what felt like an eternity in the studio recording that bloody album and I get this in return? I expect I'm to split this with the rest of the band. How are we supposed to eat?"

"No, Peter, that is all yours. I'm paying all of you individually. You're actually getting a bonus." He handed me a check for another thousand.

"What's this for?"

"You contribute far more than the other lads, so I thought you deserved a little surprise. You know, since you're so interested in the business aspects. I figure that means you understand how these things work, right, boy?"

Oh, yeah. I knew too well that piddly check was hush money. He wanted me to keep my trap shut because I was the one who'd been speaking out about the ridiculous sum of money we didn't make. I knew we were being screwed. I just couldn't figure out how.

Mr. Giant Arse gave me a grin coated in smarminess. He then picked up the phone and called his secretary. "Mrs. Saunders, would you please send in that gentleman friend of mine? I think Mr. Lane might like to talk to him."

Great. He'd just given her the code to send in the goons. With the checks in hand I headed out the door. "You'll be hearing from my lawyers." He and I both knew it was an empty threat. Something very shady was going on, which meant that no one his right mind would go up against the guy.

The secretary's eyes were fixated on her desk, and this dog that had just been given a bone could smell she was embarrassed. I took pity and wished her a nice day. With her eyes still to the desk I swear she mouthed, "I'm sorry, Peter."

The last place I wanted to do my wallowing was at home in front of Jane, so I decided to do it over a pint at the pub downstairs from Gordon's office. I tossed myself into a booth, pissed off as all hell. Even with those checks I'd barely a penny to my name. I had to wait too long between payments and the bills had piled. I hadn't a clue when more money would trickle in.

The booth's partition took my body's burden as I tried to find some semblance of peace within myself. Across the room a young man played darts. Each shot he took was a little jab to my soul. He looked hopeful and happy. I remembered looking like that as if it were yesterday. Actually, it pretty much had been.

Laughter burst from the next booth. Loud, jovial, maniacal laughter from a voice I recognized all too well. I should have known Stoddard would celebrate my misery at the closest pub. My head hung down to my beer as his words flowed through the partition and jabbed into me.

"To Mega Records," BS said, "and their partnership with Chadwick Gordon." Glasses clanked and beers were guzzled.

"It was a brilliant idea, boss," an unknown voice said. "Buying out the label and making a ridiculous deal with the manager for such a high percentage of sales is genius. Between that, selling the band and the masters of the new album, along with what you skimmed off the top and your commission, those guys are barely going to keep a dime."

Mr. BS cleared his throat. "Freddy, you need to learn the art of boasting. I wouldn't exactly call it skimming. It's a legitimate business deal. We just got a little creative with the numbers. It's like what we did with the clothing stores on

Carnaby by persuading them to give us products in exchange for publicity, yet adding the receipts to the ledger anyway."

It wasn't creative; it was damned brilliant. And yes, the art of boasting was indeed right. Stoddard was great at letting the world know he was an over-handed crook. People were so busy watching both their fronts and their backs that they didn't have time to mess with him.

"You know what though, Freddy? Money may mean everything to the ladies, but to guys like me, it's more of an insurance policy. No woman or rock star wants to be left in a rich man's dust."

I downed my beer with the intent of punching the guy. My foot hit the floor, and Jane's image coated my mind. I didn't want to cause her humiliation, so I slipped out the door before anyone could notice. All the while I vowed that I would get that man's head on a platter if it was the last thing I did.

Stupid Jerk

MILES

Rosalyn and I ride in the back of Tom's Mercedes. She looks incredible in a black, nineteen fifties' wiggle dress that hugs her figure and shows off her curves. The cleavage is nice as well.

Maybe a little too nice.

What caused this scratch in the leather on the back of Tom's seat? A brief case? Ski poles? A girl clawing to get away? A gentleman keeps his eyes on the seat; a pig keeps them on the cleavage.

Rosalyn's cleavage is a deep pool that I want to dive into.

Tom takes his sweet time getting out of the car. He whips out his phone and snickers while responding to a text before futzing with his sports coat. Does the guy not own a tie? Jacqueline waits, so I open her door along with Rosalyn's. "Sorry," Jacqueline whispers as she steps out.

Finally Tom makes his way around the car. "Thanks, man." He leans in and tells me on the sly, "Last night's hottie wants more lovin'. You know how it is." With a wink he takes Jacqueline's hand. What a scumbag.

Rosalyn shakes her head and stares at Tom as he strolls off. "I'll talk to Jacqueline inside," she groans.

Simple moments like this scare me, so Rosalyn is offered my arm. The layers of fabric that cover it remind me of Linus clinging to his security blanket. I'm an idiot for delaying the inevitable.

Rosalyn

I'm fully mortified. Tom needs to learn the definition of

the word whisper along with a few others, such as class and humility. Niles raises one side of his lips in awkward acknowledgement to the fact I'm hip to that asshole. He whispers in my ear, "I would *never* do that to you," then offers his arm. My heart melts as I'm reminded I'm on a date with a guy I'm getting to be pretty crazy over. However, the second we get in the restaurant I haul Jacqueline off to the restroom and fill her in on the ridiculousness.

"Looks like I'm buying my own dinner. Are guys ever going to prove us wrong?" The crack in her voice reveals vulnerability despite her strong words. At my offer to leave she raises her chin and locks her arm in mine. We do the Lavern and Shirley bounce and chant as we head back to the table.

Niles continues to be well mannered. He completely opens his napkin and sets it in his lap without the fold he used last time, yet still smoothing it down like before. Maybe he has some bizarre form of OCD. It's weird yet endearing.

Waiiit ... Didn't Miss Manners say at lunch you keep your napkin folded with the seam toward you while at dinner you open it fully? Niles isn't just polite; he's well-bred. Maybe that's how he was expensive to raise.

Okay, this is kind of odd. I mean, I know I'm odd, so I'm not judging. However, the math in the equation that is Niles is a little weird. He's well-bred and was expensive to raise, yet it sounded like his Mom didn't exactly have money to spend on a fancy boarding school. He did go to law school, and that's not cheap. Still, where did all these manners come from? His family must be a trip. I so want to meet them!

We all ogle over the menu. When the waitress arrives, Niles orders on my and his behalves. All eyes go to Tom who looks confused.

ΠILES

Did Tom really forget that his date told him not two minutes ago what she would like? He keeps trying to talk to me about sports and things in which I truly have no interest.

Instead he should concern himself with the beautiful woman across from him. Come on, Tom, you're an embarrassment to mankind.

"What do you do for a living, Niles?" Tom asks.

Did I misunderstand who my date is? Is Rosalyn a lesbian? We've never talked about this. "I work for Elliott, Asher, and Barton LLP. It's a law firm." Maybe Tom's just socially awkward. I can respect awkward, just not the rest of him.

Tom chuckles directly *at* me. "Yeah, one of the biggest in Los Angeles. What are you, coffee boy?"

He's got to be kidding. Tom gets an all-teeth grin and a deadpanned answer. "No, I'm a partner."

Again Tom chuckles like he's humoring me, but his grin dives when he realizes I'm serious. "Really? You? You must be a lot older than you look."

"I'm thirty-one. Does that matter?"

Tom resumes not believing a word I'm saying. "A partner in a prestigious law firm who is only thirty-one years old? Yeah, like that happens. Doesn't that take at least a decade or two after like seven years of college?"

I should probably tell him I was a Harvard man who was so bored out of his skull that he piled on classes. Graduating egregia cum laude loses its luster when you accomplish it because you had nothing better to do night after night than study. After a stint as a clerk for the Chief Justice of the United States Supreme Court, I headed home to Los Angeles and landed my current job.

Twice I saved my now partners' asses. First it was over the placement of a comma in what should have been standard fine print. That little faux pas equaled a multi-million dollar award for our client. Next the misfortune of one of the partners having a coronary attack threw me into a last-minute, second chair situation on a high-profile case. A nearly imperceptible mistake by the opposing counsel caught my eye, and I scored us a huge win on a case that we seemed destined to lose. My colleagues had no choice but to make me partner, else another firm would have swooped me up for significantly more money. Then the people whose butts I saved would be the ones under my scrutiny.

So yeah, I could put Tom in his place. Truthfully, I'd rather watch him sweat. Grandma always told me if somebody laughs over your accomplishments, you just smile at their jealousy, so that's what I do.

Tom chuckles uncomfortably. "Wow, you actually had me going."

Rosalyn shifts a bit in her seat like she's debating if she should defend me. She's so sweet.

"No." I place my business card before Tom. "I skated through law school because I'm an analytical thinker with excellent retention skills. Being a lawyer is easy for someone like me. It's people who have to shut off their emotions who have a hard time. You know what I mean, right? If you're emotionless it doesn't matter what happens, so you can spit stuff out without caring."

Rosalyn

I cringe while suppressing a laugh. Tom's been insulting, but Niles brings the sideshow to a whole new level. Jacqueline has kept to herself with the exception of smacking my arm under the table when Niles said he was a lawyer. I swear she screamed, "Why the hell didn't you tell me?" in my ear without uttering a peep. Now her teeth are grabbing her lip so she can't laugh.

The last salad arrives, and Niles takes my starting as his cue to begin. Silence blankets the table. Niles nods toward Jacqueline and gives me an "Is she okay?" look of concern. He touches a finger to the corner of his eye as if dabbing away a tear. My head shake reply is subtle, and I return the tear gesture thus confirming that she hurts.

With a glance at the breadbasket Niles snaps up his fork then stakes it into a roll. He stares at it like his brain has blanked out. "Hey, Rox, you remember that Charlie Chaplin film where he had the forks with the rolls at the end? Which one was that?"

Tom shakes his head and snickers as if calling Niles an idiot. "That was Johnny Depp."

"Kind of." Niles is unfazed by Tom's ignorance. "It came from a Chaplin film. I just can't remember which one."

"Johnny Depp did it in *Benny and Joon*, and Chaplin did it in *The Gold Rush*, but Fatty Arbuckle did a similar bit first in *The Rough House*."

"Ah! That's my girl." He winks. My insides get all gooey.

Niles holds his hand out in request of my dinner fork. He stabs it into another roll while staring at Tom like he's wishing it were a knife in Tom's heart. He hands it to me with a flashed smile.

Okay, that was a little scary, and very weird. "Dare I ask for some butter?"

Jacqueline properly passes it to me, and Tom gives her a smart-ass grin. "Too bad. I wanted to see what Niles was gonna do next. I expected him to saw the roll open and then tell her to go long while he flicked her some butter. His aim probably sucks, and it would land on the wig of the old fart at the next table."

Niles carries on as if Tom has failed to say a word. He picks up a piece of lettuce with his fingers and twists it so the dressing won't drip. All the while he stares like it's the most fascinating thing in the world. After he has Tom's attention he pops it into his mouth and resumes eating in normal-person fashion. Is he messing with Tom or is Niles being Niles?

"So," he asks Tom, "you never told us what you do for a living."

Tom looks like he was hoping to avoid this after Niles played his lawyer card. "I work for Citicorp." Tom's pride sounds forced.

"Are you a teller?" Niles asks with seemingly genuine innocence. I almost choke due to his delivery. Ah, now I get it. I'm witnessing Niles the Legal Eagle. If he can be this intimidating at dinner, he must be fierce in court.

"Hardly," Tom says. "I'm a Mortgage Loan Originator

with a degree in finance."

Niles relaxes back. His eyes take on the look of a little boy who's marveling with jealousy. "Wow, swanky title. You get to sit behind one of those big, bulletproof windows and hand out money. That's kind of cool."

Again Tom dares to chuckle at Niles, "No, only tellers get to do that."

"Bummer. I always wanted to sit behind one of those. It must be like working in a clear jail where you can mock people if they dare stand up to you. Bet it makes you sorry you're a loan officer and not a teller."

Jacqueline low fives me under the table then grabs my hand and squeezes as if saying, "I love this guy." As for me … Oh God, I'm screwed.

"Do you girls need to pick up anything on the way home, like say, for breakfast tomorrow?"

Is Tom really serious? That is the lamest hint ever! Let's see; we had a terrible conversation at dinner, Jacqueline and I insisted we split the check four ways, and we politely called the night short by saying we needed to get to sleep early. How could he possibly think that was code for something else?

When we reach our house, Jacqueline immediately sticks her key in the door. Sadly, Niles is the one who gets the hint. "Well, good night, ladies. Thank you for a wonderful evening." His kiss on my cheek is short and sweet. As much as I want more I'm really glad he has the class not to make a show in front of Tom, who needs no encouragement. "I always have a fantastic time with you. I'll call you in the morning."

Tom looks at Jacqueline who is already past the threshold and clearly not inviting him in. He moves forward to kiss her anyway, but I step between them and follow Jacqueline inside. She locks the door with lightning speed as I throw myself, face first, onto the leather sofa and groan, "That was the most hysterical disaster ever!"

"The worst!" Jacqueline dumps her purse and keys on the floor, then plops into the adjacent recliner and joins me in misery.

"When are guys going to learn splitting the check is our way of making it clear that we don't owe them a thing and the spot between our legs is closed for business?"

"I know, huh? If the date won't lead to anything more, I want to close things off politely, else I feel like a prostitute who's expected to have sex in exchange for the favor of buying me a meal. Once you start handing out sex for favors you'll be handing it over to every crossing guard in the county."

"Jacqueline, am I crazy for liking Niles?"

Her brow gets all scrunchy. "Are you kidding? Niles is incredible. You're a perfect match. And why didn't you tell me he's a *lawyer*?"

"He's kind of a nutcase. He's also far from being my perfect match. And I didn't know about the lawyer part."

"Why are you suddenly— Okay, Rox, we both know what this is really about. It's time to live again. And how did you not know he's a lawyer?"

Damn. She's on to me. "My insecurities have nothing to do with Niles's weirdness. We've never talked about our jobs. We always have more interesting things to chat about."

"No, but your insecurities have everything to do with your paranoia. Actually, let's work with this for a second." Jacqueline dashes to the kitchen and grabs a pad and pencil off of the counter. She flips aside the shopping list and plops back down on the chair. "We're going to make a list of reasons why Niles is absolutely perfect for you and a list of reasons why he's not."

"Noooo," I groan. "You're turning into your mother again."

"She only does this when she doesn't want to face the obvious. That description fits you beautifully right now.

Therefore, yes, I am being exactly like my mother. Don't worry, I'll hate you appropriately for it later."

"You know," I say, rolling over and facing the ceiling, "Niles was also raised by one parent. The other day he asked me what it was like to have a dad. It brought up a lot of pain, so I didn't want to talk about it. But it sounded like me asking what it was like to have a mom."

Jacqueline scribbles on her notepad. "Sounds like a pro to me. What else have you to share?"

"He was mostly raised by his grandparents. The situation reminds me of how much I love spending time with your grandfather."

"Another pro."

I crane my head to look at Jacqueline as she writes. "You know, this is kind of creepy. Not only do you look like your uncle the shrink, you're acting like him. In a strange way you two are freaks of nature like Niles and I."

Jacqueline continues her scribbling. "How many times do we have to tell you—"

"My uncle is a psychologist, not a shrink," we say in unison.

"Yeah, but your mom and I love calling him a shrink because of how it irritates the hell out of him."

"Okay, enough with your fascination about my uncle. Moving on."

Oh, but those chiseled features and bedroom eyes that I would love to drown in … "I can't help it. The man is totally hot."

"You do realize that sounds really weird considering how much my uncle and I look alike, sans his masculinity."

"Hey, you know, I never really thought about that. Since guys constantly give us so much trouble why don't we just turn into lesbians?"

Jacqueline stretches back and squiggles her butt deeper into the chair. "You've talked about this before. In fact, the last time I actually invited you to surprise me in the bedroom and you failed."

No way! Is she serious? "You did? How'd I miss that?"

Wait. Am I serious? Hmm …

"I said I wouldn't mind a young Eddie Van Halen paying me a visit. You totally ignored me."

"Look, just because I have a vibrator named Eddie Van Halen, circa nineteen eighty-five, that's no reason for me to have gotten that hint. You've got to be less subtle about these things if you want to sway me to cross over."

"Fine, do you have a boyfriend named Justin Timberlake?"

"Eew! No!" Now I have the willies. I mean, he's not bad but… Well, he's not exactly a bad boy. What good is having a vibrator that's not named after a bad boy?

"Guess tonight's not our lucky night. Back to Niles."

"Ooh, Niles." My voice sounds all dreamy. "He's really cute. I'm dying to know what's underneath those clothes. When I cuddled into his arm while walking back to the car tonight I noticed he has a nice build under there. Honestly though, it's been so long that I'm really more interested in knowing what's down below. Is that sick of me?"

"Wait, you haven't even touched him enough to know what's under his shirt? I'm not liking the sound of this."

"He's being a gentleman," I say with an air of dignity. "It's refreshing for once. Though it is freaking me out a little that he may not be interested in the way I hope he is."

"Has he made any advances at all?"

"No, but his eyes almost bugged out of his head when he saw my cleavage."

"His eyes were on your boobs half the night."

"Yeah, it was awesome!"

"Okay, back to this list. While you were babbling I noted how you two love the same music and can shockingly tolerate each other when it comes to movies and books. I don't know if you've noticed this, but it's hard for you to find somebody who can respect your eccentricities—and by eccentricities I mean weirdness. Face it. Niles is your perfect match, and it's possible you are the one who is not willing to take this to the next level."

Truthfully, my head accepted Niles as my perfect match the moment he made that "Cinderella Sunshine" reference and called me out on who I am. What scares me is I've been opening up to him. That means someday I will face what happened the last time I put trust in a man, back when—

Peter materializes in the corner with his arms crossed. Crap. This man's timing really sucks. "You know, Jacqueline, I'm beginning to think you're completely right."

"Admit it, Rox, you're hiding from reality."

Yeah, and I might be imagining an alternate one.

$\mathcal{A}$ Million Miles $\mathcal{A}$way

Rosalyn

I'm barely able to kick the door to my office open without dropping the stack of folders in my arms. The top ones go sliding and force me to twist and catch them with my upper arm. With that motion, the bottom ones almost slip out from underneath. Oliver comes bounding up just in time to heckle me. "You should have grabbed a box."

"Boy, the obvious never gets past you." The dock manager was supposed to be along with the rest of them and to assist me with the doors, but the only thing behind me is an empty hall. This is why nothing in this company ever gets done on time.

I start to drop the files on my desk but notice a gorgeous bouquet is about to be crushed. My speedy rescue maneuver causes the top of the stack to knock over my Betty Boop vampire statuette and bump my coffee cup. My hand spares the cup from tipping over, but coffee still splatters onto two employee folders. Poor Hector Garcia and Ken Jackson.

My hand races towards the card tucked into the bouquet.

I can't stop thinking about you. Saturday feels like it's A Million Miles Away – Niles.

"Who are the flowers from?" Oliver asks.

"Niles." Niles! Niles! Niles! And he made a Plimsouls reference! He's awesome!

Suddenly Oliver is accidentally shoved aside as the dock manager arrives with the rest of the files. "Here you go." They get dropped onto the first stack, and I manage to stop their slide towards my coffee cup to spare David Asher's pristine manila folder. The bouquet gets safely placed on my credenza between my Ringo Starr and H.R. Pufnstuf action figures.

"Is there a list of who gets what?" I ask the manager before he can walk off.

"Nope, that's why you have the files. They've got a pink Post-it if it's a three percent raise, a yellow one for a four percent, and I think there might be one blue one, which is five percent. Pretty self-explanatory."

"Is that actually written anywhere?"

"Nope, I just told you. Oh, and this batch doesn't take effect until next month, so you can shove them aside for now."

Lovely. "Here." I hand him a note pad and a pen. "In writing, please."

Oliver excuses himself, and I wish I could run away, too. File this in the stack of things I hate about this job.

Money Money

July 1967

Peter

By rock star standards our country home was modest. However, compared to the cramped East End flat I grew up in the place was enormous. The grounds were just big enough for the dogs to run freely, as dogs should.

As I lounged outside, basking in the cloud-obscured sun, Jane painted a landscape of our yard. It was a perfect replica until she added splashes of color to the lush green. "Why the flowers?" I asked.

"I'm painting our future. I threw some seeds around last week. Soon we will have lovely wild flowers."

"I suppose that next you'll pop in a few kiddies, too."

"Not yet." She sighed while putting down her brush so she could curl next to me. "I can't quite see that part yet. So much lies ahead, yet I'm waiting to learn what the next phase will be." Jane tucked her head into my shoulder in what seemed like a deliberate attempt to keep our eyes from meeting. "We're not going to be here much longer, are we?"

"What makes you say that?"

"Peter, I'm no idiot. You're not getting the money you deserve let alone the money we expected. I wish you would be okay with me going back to work. In fact, I insist on it."

She was right, and my ego hated it. I had a hard time admitting to her, let alone myself, the practicality in it. "You know perfectly well rock 'n roll wives are not supposed to work. They're supposed to enjoy their lives, travel with their husbands, and keep them on the straight. You saw what happened on the last tour when that singer was all over me.

The woman can't be trusted, and I'm only human. These package tours where you get lumped in with a bunch of other bands are dangerous."

I gave a wink, and Jane gave a playful shove. "Peter, really! There's no way you're touching her. Besides, if you do, it'll give me a great excuse to lob off her head. The woman drives me batty." Jane toyed with my shirt in that cute little way women do when they are trying to persuade you to succumb to their wiles. "Truthfully, I miss working. Being here alone all day isn't fulfilling. How about I see if I can go back part time so I can still go to dates with you and make sure that the grubby little girls keep their sticky, jam coated hands off of you?"

"Are you really unhappy?" I was concerned the conversation may have deeper meaning.

"*We* make me happy. No matter how glamorous it all seems, being in this big house by myself every day doesn't suit me."

"All right, darling. Whatever makes you happy." I pulled her deeper into my chest so that she couldn't see the relief on my face. Why God blessed me with such an angel was beyond reason.

Suddenly Jane jumped up and tugged at my hand. "Come on! Let's run!"

"Run?"

"Yes, I want to sketch you sitting right in that chair as the sun sets so we have to hurry. Let's chase the dogs around the yard and see how long it takes until they chase us. Ernestine! Fredericka!" she yelled as she ran off with me following behind. It was a metaphor for my life—chasing the dogs, knowing that in the end you are the one trying to get ahead. But if Jane was chasing with me I didn't care if I ever caught them.

Who Do You Love

Rosalyn

Jacqueline flashes through the living room in a sweet little black dress. The hints of blue and green in her smoky eye shadow adds depth to her sparkling eyes and make them appear to be aquamarine. "Ooh! Where are you going looking all gorgeous?"

"Dinner with Herman."

"The cute doctor with the bad name that you met at the market?"

"Herman Walappilee." Jacqueline looks to God. "Really? What kind of name is Walappilee?" When she recovers from her tizzy she scans my outfit—a purple scooter dress with a green jockey hat and matching belt along with bright pink accessories. "Did you steal that from the wardrobe department of *I Dream of Jeannie*? With your dark hair and wild makeup you kind of look like Jeannie's sister."

Best. Compliment. EVER! Squee! "Thanks! Seriously, how did she never get her own name?"

"Let me guess. Niles is on his way over."

"Yep! Dinner and a movie after a quick stop at Warped Records. It's a good thing House of Pies is open late. Undoubtedly we will make Shane stay while we search every bin. You can never trust those guys to keep the new arrivals segregated."

Headlights peek through the window as Niles pulls his Camaro into the driveway. "So, you've recovered from last week's momentary lapse of reason?"

"Unless he full-on shows he has no interest his lips are touching mine tonight."

"Rock on, sister. Slip me some skin."

After a low five, a skin slip, a hip bump, and a hug for good measure, it's date time.

Albums cover nearly every inch of grey, thus making the gloomy walls of Warped Records bloom with life. Bins of music form two long, narrow walkways leading to a wall of glass that imprisons stacks of unsorted jewels. The display always taunts me with dreams of what gems may reside within. However, today none of this charm holds my attention. Even that glorious smell of album covers that I can only liken to how some think of the tempting aroma of cookies is lost on me.

This never happens.

Never!

My mind is locked on Niles. He gazes at the rows with narrowed eyes. I bet he's wondering where all the good stuff is hidden. A double tug that matches the beat of the blasting punk/power pop sound of the Buzzcocks, jolts my arm. Shane drags me aside. "You're dating that guy? Really?"

My cheeky gleam confesses my happiness, but hey— "What's wrong with Niles?"

Shane's face gets all contorted. What's the deal? The question's neither insane nor complex. "He's a little ... odd around the edges."

I start to take offense but remember my own recent qualms. I kind of get it. Still— "I like guys who are a little odd around the edges. After all, some could say that about you and me as well. In fact, I seem to recall when I bought an Every Mother's Son album you said I had completely lost my mind."

"That's because it was the one without the hit. Even that album is marginal, and that's if I'm baked."

Instead of letting his baulk goad me into shame, I give him a playful tap on the arm and then do something completely uncharacteristic for my surroundings—pay more attention to a man than to the treasure trove around me. I snuggle my head into Niles's shoulder. "What are we in the mood for today?" My voice does not at all sound like I'm talking about music.

Niles glances down with a shadow of a smile. "Seemingly nothing these guys have."

"Hey, how is it we've never compared collections? How about we skip the movie and go back to your place so I can check out what you've got?" My teeth pinch the inside of my lip as I process how slutty that sounded.

NILES

Was her question straightforward? There are a million places my mind has dreamed of Rosalyn's hands touching. None of them have anything to do with my record collection. A beautiful woman at my house who is looking at records? It's weird, just like these New York Dolls albums. I mean, what twisted thing caused Buster Poindexter to emerge from the great David Johansen? The name referred to him and not a band, right? Since Buster Poindexter was an obviously fake name shouldn't his solo stuff be filed under Buster and not Poindexter? I'd file it under S for sucks.

Rosalyn's luscious lips form a beautiful smile. Speaking of things that suck, I wonder what those lips would have to say about Buster.

The house key feels weighted. What does Rosalyn expect of my home? Is she prepared for athletic gear and nudie mags? She might be a little disappointed in me.

Rosalyn

My foot hits a long wave patterned into a brick driveway— a tan on maroon version of the yellow-brick road. A small, well-manicured yard sits before the deep brown, shingled Craftsman home. Two small stained glass windows, with scenes reminiscent of waves, reside on each side of the chimney. They make me dream of what treasures the inside may hold. This is exciting. I've no clue what to expect.

We step inside and Holy Noel Coward! The nineteen twenties-style living room slays me. Art Deco furniture fills the room while an antique area rug covers the polished, hardwood floor. The furniture matches the deep-walnut bookcases that were built into the walls upon their construction. On each side of the sofa sit floor lamps with stained glass shades of maroon and cream. It's all very classic, masculine, and oh so freaking incredibly sexy!

Niles hangs my coat in the closet before taking me on a tour. I'm completely blown away by the kitchen. The refinished, original cabinets somehow blend with the modern, top-of-the-line appliances. "Wow. This kitchen makes me think you can cook. This is awesome!"

His shrug is just adorable. "I get bored sometimes, so when I can, I take random classes. Cooking has become quite the hobby."

"Yet somehow you've never cooked for me. Here I thought that you liked me enough to try to impress me a tiny bit." I nearly hold my breath while awaiting his reply. Will my hint get blown off? Niles cooking for me would be epic.

"Wanting to impress you is why I haven't cooked for you." He adds a wink before continuing our journey.

He wants to impress me?

He wants to impress me!

My insides squeal and bounce while clapping, then start Snoopy dancing!

Niles's bedroom contains numerous bookshelves and a desk. This house seems big enough to have space for an office. Why cram himself in here?

Three more doors attach to the hallway. Just past the bathroom I find pure nirvana. He's knocked out part of the wall between the two bedrooms and created a giant media room. It's lined with an impressive collection of posters from San Francisco's greatest concert halls and festivals; The Fillmore, Winterland, The Avalon Ballroom, The Trips

Festival. "Where did you get all of these?" Awe oozes through my voice and gives away the fact I'm totally on a high.

"My grandparents." He looks so cute and proud as he says it like he just damn adores them. "They used to go to these shows."

Niles slides open the door of one side of a room-width closet and gestures permission for me to peruse it. I'm so busy trying to take in my colorful surroundings I almost miss a framed piece of ripped out notebook paper with a poem scribbled on it.

"All I ever wanted was someone to smile with. Someday, when our worlds collide, my soul will be complete. Until then I await your simple hello and the colors of pink and purple that will forever flower my world."

"What's this?"

"It's from Peter Lane's notebook. You know, the guy from Love Machine. After he died his manager sold off the pages to fans. I found that one at a convention. It's not something I would normally buy, but a friend convinced me. Now I have a strange affinity toward it."

His voice makes it sound like it's no big deal, but his eyes await a reaction of idolatry over the sheaf. Normally I would flip out, but in light of recent events this is really, really weird, especially if the colors are in reference to the flowers Jane planted in the yard.

Hey, wait. This is dated July nineteen sixty-six. Peter told me he met Jane in August. "Is it real?" Shock resounds in my voice, and Niles smiles at what comes off as my inner fangirl.

"This room is the one place where I can count on honesty, which is why you and my mom are the only ones who've seen it." Niles grabs a remote off of a bookshelf and plops down on the floor. He lies back and hums Cheap Trick covering Fats Domino while tapping the remote in time to "Ain't That a Shame." I marvel over his enormous collection of vinyl. A beautiful kaleidoscope of colored spines stands before me.

"No CDs?"

He points to another mammoth closet across the room.

"Over there." His chuckle is more one of nervousness than musing. "They both hold so much weight that someday I'll come home and find they've completely collapsed and put giant holes in my floor."

"So, none of your friends have ever been in here?"

"Just you."

Why me? Does that mean …

A smile slips onto my face, and I try to conceal the fact that my cheeks have gone red. Have I become as special to him as he has to me?

In my excitement I randomly pick a shelf and pull out a treasure. "Hey, Quicksilver Messenger Service. I can't believe someone else my age actually knows who Quicksilver is."

The soft colors of the *Happy Trails* cover, a product of the artist and not of time, make the nice copy appear weathered. As the album slides out of its inner sleeve and into my hands a starburst reflects off of the surface.

Ah, the *bump*—that unmistakable sound of a needle hitting a record—followed by a short *hiss* that makes me want to bow before the turntable. Vinyl, how I love thee!

John Cipollina hits that first note on his guitar, and my emotions swirl as the sound soars over me. I take a place next to Niles on the floor. There's something about Cipollina and his own unique brand of playing. It's so signature to the psychedelic genre, as if he knew it was his responsibility to define it. "Have you ever been to San Francisco?"

"Just on my way to see my grandparents."

"So you've never really been there. There is nothing like walking among the magnificent Victorians—those beautifully painted ladies that stand majestically around you. San Francisco is art, history, and love all wrapped up into one amazing package."

NILES

Rosalyn's words regarding San Francisco perplex me. I respect the city's beauty, but Rosalyn speaks of an enchanted kingdom. "This music," she says, her voice filled with euphoria, "it sweeps me up and puts me back in the moment. I arguably wasted half a morning staring at the gorgeous Queen Anne Victorian the Grateful Dead lived in. This sound right here—this urban drumbeat, those raw vocals—even though it's nearly fifty years later the freedom of this music still fits the dream I feel in San Francisco's air."

How is it that putting the needle on the turntable can cause this type of emotional reaction? She hears a city filled with hopes, traffic, and art. I just hear phenomenal music.

"So, why am I the only one you've allowed in here?"

Pressure builds in my temples. Niles, you've got to start going there at some point. If there is one thing you and Rosalyn have in common, it's that you both understand how hard it is to be different. "I think you know it is not always easy to take risks. Sometimes people neglect sharing things for fear of the memories it will bring when they get hurt later."

"Wow." Rox sounds stunned like I was calling her out instead of confessing. "Jacqueline really was right. I had no idea it was that obvious. Is that why you're so reserved?"

Okay, so far, so good. "As unmanly as it sounds, scared is a much more appropriate word." I risk touching her chin and gently raise it so our gazes meet.

"Niles, I don't want to be scared anymore. What about you? Are you ready to move past your hurt?"

That's why she's been so patient—baggage. I wish it were so simple for me. Every other girl has been in this house for one reason—sex with a decent looking lawyer they picked up in a bar. But the girls worth keeping want love, and that's an emotion I can't fathom.

I bring my lips towards hers and then hesitate to look in her eyes and be certain she is ready for this. I should know better, because I can only pretend to give her what she needs.

Don't do this, Niles. You'll hurt her.

When our lips finally touch I hold back and let hers lead the way. It's a nice kiss, but will I actually know love if it ever hits me?

Rosalyn

Niles looks deep into my eyes, and I'm filled with anticipation over his beautiful lips touching mine. I've become so wrapped up in all that he is that this moment feels a lifetime in the making. As our lips touch, something inside my soul screams that this is what I have been waiting for, not just for the last few years but since the day I emerged from the womb.

I brace myself for the bursting of an emotional dam. The kiss is so tender, so perfect, that I could do it all night. It ends too soon, and I pull back in both surprise and relief. In some ways I had feared the sensation that comes with the first kiss—the one that gets you all wrapped up in a man. Jacqueline's right. My emotions must still be locked up. I was certain that the electricity between us would zap me off my feet. Instead, it was just a kiss—a nice, long, sexy kiss. I'm so filled with disappointment I actually hate myself right now. The man of my dreams is right here, yet I stupidly keep closing myself off because some jerk wronged me when I needed him most.

My eyes go to those of Niles, and I remember his words about being able to overcome anything. Despite the fact one part of my heart is holding me back, there is another part that want to shove forward even more. *Hey, Mom, Dad. It's your Rose. I think I may have found something special.*

With odd relief in somehow knowing the intimacy level for the night has peaked I cuddle into Niles's shoulder. He presses a few buttons on the remote, and while the ceiling lights fade, liquid lights color the darkness. This room is peaceful and absolutely glorious. It was meant for people like us. This incredible man who surprises me in so many ways really does seem to be akin to me. I just hope that I can appreciate him before he loses patience and gives up on me.

"Welcome back!" Jacqueline says as I come through the door. She plops herself on the sofa with a book while still dressed from her date. In addition to the plant that lives on the table where I drop my keys sits Jacqueline's extra wide curling iron and a carving knife. "Why are these—"

"I chased my date out with them."

"Yikes! So the good doctor—"

"You mean the wannabe gynecologist? When he didn't take no for an answer, I grabbed the curling iron and told him I was in for a game of proctologist. He got a creepy, turned-on look until I went for the knife."

"Geez!" I motion Jacqueline to move her legs aside so I can plant my butt on the sofa. Her eyes scan me while enlivening with the hope of hearing good news. "Relax. We both lost our stethoscopes. I'm great though. Really, really great. Baggage is another commonality, and it's comforting. I'm actually excited about possibilities now. You okay?"

She gives a half smirk to show she's less than thrilled but is trying to find the humor in it all. She then lofts her feet into my lap and lounges back. "We should have a first date rule not to wear stilettos so we can make fast getaways. If there is one thing horror movies have taught us, it's that falling is fatal."

"Well, if we are going to subscribe to that, we should only date brainy guys with street smarts since all of the handsome ones die."

Her tension fades. "Boy, we sure have learned a lot about dating from horror movies."

"Only what not to do. If they taught the good stuff, we wouldn't still be single."

Broke Down and Busted

September 1967

Peter

On a lovely summer afternoon, my back slammed against the backseat of a police car. My wince from the jabbing of my cuffed hands into my spine was muted in refusal of accepting defeat.

The cop in the driver's seat said to the one next to him, "I can't believe who we just picked up for trespassing. Mr. Big Time rock star stealing fruit off of trees!" He called back to me, "They were pretty happy to press charges over a few apples. What'd you do to piss them off? Bet you gave their daughter a right shagging!"

The prick officer didn't realize I often went to the orchard down the road from our old country home and grabbed fruit because it was one of the ways I was feeding Jane and I. That's what I got for acting the delinquent. A guy has a few barking dogs and a stereo that'll push the windows off the house a mile away, and the neighbors that don't like it sell him down the river. I thought for sure when the last record took off we'd soon have money in our pockets.

Idiots never learn.

The assholes at the police station were more ridiculous than the ones who'd brought me in. The laughter of the prick officers made me jump toward them while screaming my bloody head off. "Have you ever paid for one of my records? Do you know what happened to that little bit of cash you spent? Do you know how much I got? The band should've gotten thirty pence for every pound you forked over; instead, we were lucky to get a bob. You call yourselves officers of the

112

law, so put that power to use. Go after that yob who's been double and triple dipping. So much was skimmed off the top and pulled from the bottom that there were no royalties to be paid. I stole from my old neighbor's yard just to eat." The cops froze. Their smiles faded as they realized I was completely serious. My head dropped to my grumbling stomach. "If I go to jail and miss my dates, Jane's screwed."

From across the room, the cop who read me the riot act earlier got up from his desk and dragged me back to my seat. "Mr. Lane, you've been released. However, I strongly suggest that you speak of this to no one."

Only a fool would believe that I was being let off. This whole incident was a threat, telling me to shut up. I was more screwed than ever.

A few days later, the boys and I were called into Gordon's office. "Boys, I've got some bad news and some rather good news. 'Together With You' just hit the top forty on the American charts."

"We—We broke America?"

No. Really?

Dear God, we finally broke America!

"The bad news is those Beatles are killing the industry with that *Sgt. Pepper*. No one wants pop anymore. We're left with two options; put an end to Love Machine or try to give the kids something different. What do you say, boys? How about we give you a little creative leeway? I've got a nice little bonus for you if you can start tomorrow. When all is said and done, we'll shoot you off to America."

I don't know who was more foolish, that idiot for not seeing the light of day sooner or us for agreeing to his mad realizations. Regardless, we finally had creative control. I was on top of the blooming world.

Boris the Spider

Rosalyn

The golden glow of dawn breaks through the clouds as my car whooshes down the freeway. The exit for Niles's office approaches and I crane my neck in his direction. Thanks to another bout of insomnia, last night Google Maps served as this lazy stalker's greatest tool. The night would have been entirely sleepless had Peter not appeared. How is it that when he pops in, my body gets tied up in tingles and then I relax into blissful sleep?

My Mustang bounces as it hits the gravely pavement of work's driveway. For a Wednesday morning the lot in front of the mammoth building of steel and brick is surprisingly barren.

With each step toward the door I notice the rise and fall of my body, my hair bouncing in tandem. Days after our most recent date I'm more on a cloud than ever over Niles.

The front door flies open from barely a touch. I seem to have developed superhuman strength. How happy am I?

My fingers dance with a wave to greet Darla, who's already comfortably behind her reception desk and likely on her second cup of coffee. My cheeks almost hurt from the size of my smile. I expect Darla to wave back. Instead her hands smack onto the desk. "You are so not going to believe what Oliver did!"

Lord! With those two it could be anything.

"He gave me a present today." False sweetness drips from her voice. This is going to be bad, and by bad I mean ridiculous. Darla pulls out a grey plastic bag and extracts a Barbie-doll type figure dressed in a red jumpsuit. Jetting out from her back are four brown, sharply arched spears capped with single talons. Darla pulls out another piece with four of the same appendages and attaches it, then smacks the thing down on its front. I stare at the plastic girl with giant breasts and spindly legs growing out her back—spindly tarantula legs!

"What the hell is that?" shrieks out of me.

"Great question. I found the bag on my desk today. Clearly this is Oliver's revenge for me Krazy gluing his pens together."

I try to shake off the jitters the freaky thing gives me and catch sight of a bouquet of flowers on Darla's credenza. "Wow! Are those from the new boyfriend?"

"They came with the doll." She sounds embarrassed. I give her a look asking why until she stops being humble and fesses up. "A few days ago, his ex came here complaining about some random thing. Just as she was about to totally flip out I paged Oliver into a meeting. I then calmed her down by taking her into the break room for some coffee right as the warehouse guys were going in. We sat next to Charlie Lewis, who happens to be single. You can fill in the blanks from there."

"Look at you being all sly. Darla, you're brilliant!"

"Nah, it's just that no one really wants to be setup. It's best to let people find the magic on their own."

I love that sentiment. The world needs more magic. "The flowers were really sweet, but why would Oliver give you Arachnid Woman? Seriously, what is it with you two?"

Darla's smile of resignation also reeks of gratitude. "Oliver seems to be the only one who gets that I deserve better than being trapped at this desk. He's trying to get me a job in sales with him, but since I don't have a degree it seems to be a losing battle. Meanwhile, we antagonize each other so we can laugh despite our real issues." The doll gets tossed into her purse.

"Hey, Rosalyn," the plant manager calls from behind as he heads through the lobby and out the door. "I dropped off my share of the files for those promotions. There was no room

on your desk, so I dumped them on the floor. Thanks."
    With a whimper I head off to Hell.

The Threat

February 1968

Peter

Finally, an American tour!

In a hotel parking garage on a freezing, New York winter morning, Jane and I walked hand-in-hand to our rental car. We were eager to get in as much private sightseeing as we could before heading off for the show. When I reached down to open her door our road manager ran up and handed me a note with an address. "Mr. Gordon wants you to meet with his American representatives first thing this morning. He said to bring the little lady." I glared at him regarding his use of words. His hands went up. "Gordon's words, not mine."

With all the traffic, it took us nearly an hour to get to the address that was merely a few blocks away. When we finally arrived we found ourselves in front of an Italian deli. A free meal seemed right by me.

Nearly the moment I stepped inside a tall man who reminded me of a bulldozer in a suit recognized me. He guided Jane and I to an office in the back where we were asked to take seats in front of a barren desk. The room felt like a hospital version of a business—sparse, sterile, cold, windowless, and not at all inviting.

Another bulldozer strolled in and stood behind us, next to the man who had shown us in. Suddenly everything about the situation felt disturbing. Two meatballs with legs entered— really big guys who ate too many salami sandwiches and cannoli. Their designer suits were perfectly pressed and just stylish enough to make them exude importance but not be flashy. However, it was their pristine shoes that told the real story. The guys behind me though, the ones in the suits made a little loose for fighting, their shoes told a different tale. Highly polished loafers with scuffmarks complemented their scraped knuckles.

The two pristine meatballs sat behind the desk. Meatball One spoke as number two's eyes stayed locked on me. "Mr. Lane. Mrs. Lane. Welcome to the lovely state of New York. Do you know why we have called this meeting?"

"Mr. Gordon said you are overseeing the tour."

Meatball One smirked at Jane before returning his sights to me. "Do you know who I am, son?"

"No, sir. Mr. Gordon only said you are a colleague." Truthfully, I didn't know, but the condescending use of the word son and the company surrounding us was adding up to something sinister.

One of the guys from behind bent down and whispered, "Take a look again. I'm sure you have seen Mr. Suino along with his associate, Mr. Manzo, in the papers for their charitable work."

Charitable work, my arse. Of course I knew the names. Those men represented the two biggest crime families in the world. The only thing charitable they ever did was let people spend their lives in fear while running and hiding like hunted rabbits instead of offing them. I was screwed.

"We'll keep this simple," Meatball Suino said. "I'll be overseeing your affairs on the behalf of your manager, Mr. Gordon, while you enjoy your stay in America. I trust that so far the accommodations have been to your liking." A pause was given as if he had posed a question, not a statement.

"Yes, sir."

"Excellent!" He rubbed his hands together with the enthusiasm of a young scout eager to start a fire. "Now, about that album you're here to promote. I'm aware my associates over in your neck of the woods allowed you a bit of what you call creative control this go round, but let's not be hasty." His chubby fingers slapped a copy of the American version of our latest album, *Deep Trance,* onto the desk. The cover, designed by London's most innovative artist, was an eye-catching piece of art. "This album. It's good, but we don't really care much about that. What we care about are sales. I showed it to my fourteen-year-old daughter, and she said she wouldn't ask me to buy it for her because she didn't like the cover." With a single finger he slid the record toward me. All the while he was honed in on my impending reaction. "Don't you worry though. We worked out a deal a few weeks ago to use a photo from the same shoot as the last cover. It's one where your ugly mugs the teens find so attractive can get all girlie-like over and will want to throw cash at. That is, if that's okay with you." Again he paused.

It certainly wasn't! This was just a way to intimidate us, to show the band that we really had no control at all, yet I was without options. "It is fine, sir."

"You seem a little hesitant, Mr. Lane. Fortunately our team of artists have joined us today." He nodded to the muscle behind me. "Would you like a private meeting with them?"

In the silence, Jane's eyes screamed at me not to get cheeky. I shook my head. "No, sir. I see your point. Thank you." Damn! This was far worse than in England. I had such high hopes for America.

Meatball Manzo leaned onto the desk, and the muscle behind me nudged closer. "You will not discuss this issue with anyone. Not even each other, capisce?" His eyes flicked between Jane and I. The poor girl was scared rigid.

"Yes, sir." My eyes darted to Jane and begged her to agree.

She looked to both gentlemen and sharply nodded. "Yes, sirs." Her eyes then flipped to the guy behind me. She was absolutely terrified because he was reaching his hand into his coat like he was about to pistol-whip me to emphasize their point.

Meatball Suino looked to his goons. Though they stepped back, the sense of danger accompanying them remained hot on my back. "I've enjoyed our little chat. We hope you enjoy your stay."

Jane and I went on with our day. We tried to soak in the

sights of New York and forget about what happened. When we returned from the show that night we were certain to wait outside of the parking garage until others arrived. There was no way that we were foolish enough to get caught alone again. A sleepless night followed for us both, but Jane was so deeply shaken that it was only the beginning of many to come.

The next morning, my nervous jitters caused me to cut my chin while shaving. The jab of the blade seemed to release a part of my aggressions. I continued on while almost hoping for more pain. When I failed to cut myself again I bit down on my tongue. The pain helped clear my head. Upon exiting the loo, I found an album with the rejected cover had been slid under my door. Since it was the result of a test print only a few had been made. I didn't need to be a genius to know it was the one I had seen the day before and that it was put there as a reminder to behave.

Jane walked up and set her suitcase by the door in preparation to catch the tour bus. I questioned if I dared get Jane out of there and go on to the next stop in the rental car, or if us leaving on our own would cause a new set of problems. A drop of blood from the cut on my chin hit the album, and a chill rattled my spine. I felt I'd just witnessed an omen. The album was cast aside. "Let's go."

"But the bus doesn't leave for nearly thirty—"

"I'm taking you to the airport. I'll meet with the bus later."

In a flash, my toiletries were in my bag and we were heading out. "Don't you want this?" she asked of the album.

Indeed I did want it. It was the only work we had ever done that was a reflection of our true selves, but it had become nothing more than a reminder of the mess we'd been through. "It's rubbish. Leave it."

"Peter, you'll regret it later. You may not get another."

"No. It's rubbish." I grabbed the pen I always kept handy for autographs and signed the bloody thing before tossing it in the bin with the other trash. "That's the only version of us I will ever endorse. Maybe some fan will find it, and one person will get to experience the real Love Machine. Let's go."

Up in Her Room

Rosalyn

Niles and I lie on my bed in a heated, nearly animalistic, display of desire. Take a risk, my inner voice encourages. Start caving to your emotions.

Our tongues dance during tender, unrushed kisses while his hand glides up my arm oh-so-gently. The lack of pressure to surrender over my goods is turning my hormones into creamy butter and nearly has me begging for him to take me.

His lips venture down my neck, his breath hitting the sweet spot that always makes me ooze when it is tickled by a gentle kiss. My arousal intensifies and causes my grip on him to tighten, but to my heart the passion feels ... bland. Whenever Joe did that, love charged its way through me, and my heart would cave to his embrace. With Niles, my hormones are flying into a clenching frenzy that makes me want to pounce on him, but my should-be-buckling knees are stable and unyielding. Niles may not be super-charging my heart, but as his hand slides down my side and lands on the curve of my waist with such a firm yet delicate touch, I'll soon need to shed my underwear.

My breath turns baited as he pulls me in tighter. His fingers dig into my back just enough to thrill me. A wild need for him inside me overcomes, and I race to get his shirt unbuttoned. My hands slide up his warm, tight chest and then ...

Then I stop and cover my halting with a kiss, because for the first time ever making love with a guy would just be sex to me.

He shifts as his lips meet mine again, and the bulge in his

pants hits me oh so perfectly. The sensation is so good that I nearly gasp. Oh, yes, just sex would be wonderful, thank you. His hand slides up my arm and the staleness from before creeps back in. I don't get it.

Uncertainty dissipates, and undying love glows its way on to me and makes my heart feel like roses are blooming out from inside. My head flies back as Niles's lips touch the same spot as before. However, unlike the energizing sensation in my arm the kisses to my neck fall flat.

My eyes open and capture Peter standing beside us with his hand overlaying that of Niles. With a little wink Peter joins Niles on top of me. Niles shifts uncomfortably before resuming his work on my neck with his lips shadowed by Peter's. Everything about me goes ˡhaywire, and my heart turns into a magnetic field of passion that draws Peter in.

Niles slides his hand down my blouse. Peter shadows his actions in a twisted ménage a trois—Niles making technically perfect moves, Peter charging them with high doses of love, and me hating myself for allowing this moment. Oh God, how I want more.

I guide Niles's hand to the buttons on my blouse and his eyes lock on to mine, expressing hesitation as if he's divided between doing the gentlemanly thing by asking the lady if she is sure and going for the lay like his rock-hard erection is pleading him to do. His desire to shed my clothes wins, and I respond with a shuddered moan of pleasure. Peter's fingers travel up my thighs, causing my back to arch.

This is unfair. With my touch to Niles's hands he instantly pulls them away from my buttons. My hands cup his cheeks as my eyes search into his for answers. How can I care so much for him yet I need a ghost to make his touch complete? "It's okay, Rox. I'm fine with stopping."

"Niles, look at me. I need a moment of nothing but us." Peter sits and rests his non-existent hips on mine. My eyes hone in on those of Niles. I am open to love. I get it from Peter and it's yanking me towards Niles, yet I can't get a read on what emotions Niles has. "Niles, I need you to kiss me and show me how you really feel about me."

NILES

What the hell just happened?

I went from normal kisses, to sudden discomfort, to … to feeling strangely whole. Now that's gone and she wants me to show her emotion. This is bad.

Okay, just give it a go with the best kiss you can possibly muster and maybe it will pass. Else the jig is up.

My heart races in fear as my thumb traces her lower lip, baiting it as I moisten mine. All the while my eyes don't leave hers. I draw myself near and touch our lips together, softly at first and then slowly allowing the pressure to build. Gently my tongue begins exploring. Please, Lord, let me pull this off.

Rosalyn

Niles has me swooning over his flawless kiss—so tender and luscious, yet it fails to enrapture. Still, when he pulls away I draw his lips back onto mine. He lets out a nearly indiscernible sigh of relief as we begin another kiss. Warmth flows over me again, and the embrace grows passionate. Peter is back.

Peter

My flesh may no longer exist, but I can still show Jane love. If this is what it takes, then so be it—though I find it rather nasty to be here while this guy does the deed with my lady. Maybe if I continue long enough, I'll have proven a point and she will stop this madness. After all, she's got enough battery power in that toy drawer of hers to start a car. Between that and me it should be bloody well enough!

The Niles chap continues to kiss Jane and then goes back to groping her breast. The lucky bastard gets the thrill, and I have to play along with whatever direction he wants to take things. Or do I? Maybe I can do some fancy finger work so she will finish early and toss him.

He nudges down the cup of her bra and his lips go to her

tit. I follow along while Jane writhes. This sorry sod has no idea how lucky he is.

"What the hell?" asks a voice from above. Below me, Jane looks startled. I jump up, and the guy's eyes follow me. What the hell is right!

Rosalyn

Why is Niles looking in Peter's direction? "Niles, who are you talking to?"

Niles stands and looks down at Peter. "Him."

"You can see Peter?"

"Yes, I can see him," Niles says while sounding freakishly calm. Oh, thank God I'm not imagining him! "How was he on you and yet I couldn't feel him?"

Oh no!

No! No! No! No! No!

"Niles, this is Peter Lane. Peter, I believe you have strangely met Niles."

"The *dead* singer? The last anyone saw of him his skin was charred and flaking off like burnt Eczema."

Peter's expression grows indignant. "I looked a mess because I was in a fire. What's your excuse? And why are you so unfazed by my apparitional self?"

"I'm a lawyer. It takes a lot to faze me. Besides, when I was a kid not all of my so-called imaginary friends were nonexistent, but I'm betting even the fabricated ones could take out your scrawny little butt."

"Niles, I—I'm sorry. I want to explain, but I don't know I can."

Niles seems to have already figured out what transpired. He doesn't show the slightest trace of anger. I'd be pissed.

"It's fine, Rox," he says, solemnly. "I get it. This isn't the first time that— I should go." Niles grabs his coat and heads for the door.

"Niles, wait."

"It's okay, Rosalyn. You shouldn't care about me when it can only be one sided."

"What are you talking about?" One sided? Please tell me it's not what I'm thinking.

Niles takes his hand off of the doorknob and leans his weight against the wall. The scrunching of his eyes makes the hurt on his face redden. "I've been so dishonest with you that I don't know where to start." He gives himself a moment before the words fly out. "The night we met I was on a date."

My throat tightens. Facing Niles is the last thing I want, so my eyes focus on a dark piece of lint on the carpet. "I guess that explains a lot. You were waiting for someone and that's why you couldn't talk to me. But that should have nothing to do with now unless—unless you still love her." So that's his baggage. No wonder why I have been so hesitant with Niles. My heart already knew what my brain wished to ignore.

Niles forces a brave face. "No, Rosalyn, the guy was my date."

He's gay? I expect everything to hurt less, but it doesn't. "You mean that guy who looked like a business associate?" Wait, hard-ons don't lie. Unless he was just thinking about another guy while he was with me. If that is the case, I no longer feel bad about what I allowed Peter to do.

"Yeah."

The pain in my heart shoots deeper. "You could have fooled me. I thought he was trying to sell you something you didn't want."

"Actually, you're not far off. He was definitely trying to sell me on him, but I quickly found he wasn't what I wanted."

"So what you are telling me is that you can't love me because you are still in love with a former boyfriend." A metaphorical hand reaches out of my chest and pulls my heart back inside. I didn't realize how much I had put myself on the line.

NILES

How did we get here? How do I explain to Rosalyn this isn't her fault, and that for decades I've done all I possibly could to find a solution? Hell no, I'm not gay, but that was the last stone unturned, and I finally got the courage to flip it over and try. "Years ago my mom sat me down for a dose of the truth. From the look on her face I thought she was going to tell me someone had died. Instead she told me that I was already dead. I'm incapable of processing love. Hate and passion are on the list too."

"Oh, please, Niles. This is the worst spin on the, 'It's not you, it's me' thing I've ever heard."

Rosalyn's eyes look watery. When people cry you comfort them, but that means getting near her, and that's not what she wants. What do you do then? "Rosalyn, when my dad walked out his final words included calling me a sociopath. Mom has no idea that I remember. While it's far from true think about what just happened. You get nothing from me because I have nothing to give. Admit it, Rosalyn, when you touch me my response carries the emotional warmth of a wall."

Rosalyn

This is crap. It is, however, the most creative crap I've ever heard. Also, I *feel* his pain as if he's a radiator, and it burns. "How can you hurt and not love? And how can you be so calm about it?"

He simply shrugs, but his eyes reflect he's admitting a lack of self-understanding. "I have all the compassion in the world but none of the stuff that drives it. I only get by because while my mom worked her butt off to send me to doctors my grandparents made a point of teaching me what empathy is and programming responses into me. I'm a big hoax, Rosalyn. A hoax that is the product of sensitivity training and acting lessons. Some people are driven by love and hate to the point where they tune out all things standing in their way. I'm the exact opposite. It's like when my soul was built a few little details were left out."

"Well, I'll be ..." Peter mutters.

"Truth is, Rosalyn, I've never felt an emotional connection to anyone. You may have soft, warm skin, but the differences between you and a lamppost— Oh, God. I'm sorry. I almost said something really stupid." He says it so calm and matter-of-factly that not only does the burn of my own pain deepen, but now I hurt for him as well. So this is the impossibility he is trying to overcome. This poor man. How can you possibly fight a war when you don't have the tools?

"What are the odds?" Peter seems to be marveling over this scene. Right now I find him to be absolutely disgusting.

"Peter, will you please give us some privacy?" I shout. With a quaint nod he disappears.

"Rosalyn, I know kissing me is similar to the emotional equivalent of when you were twelve and practiced on your pillow, right?"

I give an embarrassed nod. Niles is perfectly putting words to what I haven't been able to describe. I'm seeing it now. His eyes are missing the light that shows his heart is alive. In them I've seen hope and boyish innocence, but never have I witnessed an expression of love—not for me, not for anything. "Niles, I really don't want to hurt you."

"Don't worry. I don't process hurt the way you do. Apparently, in order for that to happen you need passion. All you'll do by dumping me is toss me back into loneliness. That's okay. I'm used to it."

Niles heads out of the room. He rushes down the steps and out the front door with the urgency of fleeing a building of dreams that's crumbling behind. While I couldn't feel love off of him, his pain fills this room and digs deeply into my heart. Whether it is brought on by the truth of his words or by my personal sense of loss, another person I love is dead.

The Ghost Of Change

NILES

My most difficult moment was experiencing what the doctor called lesson one—understanding what I lacked. Next came acceptance, then learning right from wrong. Some would say I'm an absolute idiot for leaving Rosalyn, but if I stayed I'd eventually hurt her more. I'm surprised things worked out as long as they did.

The briefs on my desk have turned into one giant haze from my prolonged staring while the spot where Rosalyn's picture once sat continues to nag at me with loneliness.

Eyes and mind back to the briefs, Niles.

I stare towards the floor as if the drawer is open and I can see her photo that faces downward inside it. This is lame. After the yank of a metal knob I lift the corner of the frame so I can face the damage I've caused. I knew better, and I hurt her anyway.

Put the photo back, Niles, but … No, don't hesitate. Put away that part of your life.

The *slam* of the drawer shows the acceptance of my stupidity.

My computer screen *buzzes*, and my chest jerks at the sight of Peter Lane. "Got a case of the Monday blues?" he asks.

"Haven't you screwed things up enough already?"

"I was only trying to help you, mate. You're the halfwit who walked."

Interesting. This is the rubbing in of pain from one dead guy to another. If the dead can experience emotions, there's horrible irony in a corpse being more alive than I. "Peter, if you came here to see how I'm doing, the answer lies in the fact I've hurt my one true friend, and she was pretty rotten to me as well. Now, would you kindly leave so I can get caught up on work?"

Peter plops his butt down on my desk. Well, it's more like he hovers and then spins to sit cross-legged. His legs penetrate my paperwork. "Nice try. We both know you can't work when you're gutted, which is why I'm here to help."

What do I do next? Call Security? I can just imagine their reaction when I say they need to haul away a ghost. I'll probably get a free ride to the asylum. "What, like how you helped me before? Even if it didn't bother my ego, it's pretty awkward."

"Niles, old chum, you're misunderstanding the nature of my visit. Oh, silly me. I haven't told you yet. Is it my turn to talk?"

Can I scare him off? What could frighten a dead rock star? Maybe if I turn on some Yoko Ono.

No, Peter Lane loved soulful R&B. A dose of Auto-Tune laced hip-hop is the perfect insult. "Fine, Peter, go ahead. Say your piece." My feet lob onto my desk with my mind still on the contents of my drawer.

Peter

I'm astounded by how his words are testy yet his tone is relaxed. It's annoying. "You know, I can solve all of your problems. It's just going to cost a teensy bit of your time."

The sorry sod keeps his eyes fixated on his desk. "All of my problems? Buddy, no one's been able to fix any of them— not me, not my family, and not any shrink on the planet. I strongly doubt you have the solution."

Damn lawyers. A sales pitch is always necessary with them. "Oh, I've exactly the solution, and I understand your problem better than anyone. You see, you and I are split souls. When I allowed your creation, or rather, when *we* allowed your creation, I kept all the parts that will help me fix a little issue from our last life. Now I just need a smidgen of living, human help to carry out a teensy, little task. Once that is done I'm willing to fix your problem."

MILES

I've heard some crazy stories, but this one has got to take the cake.

Wait, is this apparition an apparition? Maybe I'm dreaming all of this. Why imagine Peter Lane of all people? Maybe I can get him to teach me a few guitar riffs. "You're telling me you're my soul mate? I know you don't need to use a door to leave but there's one right behind you."

"Don't be ridiculous! I am not your soul mate. Our soul is split. Search it out on that Internet thing you people can't seem to survive without. You and I were both Peter Lane. When it was time for us to reincarnate we split into two people. You got all of the pesky parts that would impair my ability to right things with Stoddard, like morality. We shared the rest. Well, actually I hoarded the bulk of hatred, love, and passion because it's my love for Jane that feeds my hatred for Ben Stoddard, and it is passion that fuels the desire to tidy things up. I wanted to keep all of each, but I couldn't be heartless."

I really wish people wouldn't raise their voices. I'm glad I don't have anger. People's anger gives me a headache. "Who's Jane?"

"Did I keep all the smarts, too? Rosalyn is Jane, or at least she was when we were married to her. After we were murdered someone rubbed her out too. Once you help me right some wrongs I can re-merge our soul. All that passion Rosalyn just felt for me, she will actually feel for you. You'll be normal."

I'm grateful that I'm propped back tightly into this chair else my ass would be on the floor. Married? I was married to Rosalyn? She loved me? If I were normal, would she love me again? Could I finally get this loneliness to go away?

This guy sounds completely crazy. I must be insane to give him a moment of my time, but his—what an idiot I am for thinking this—his illogical mumbo jumbo makes perfect sense. What if the reason I feel like half a person is because I am and it's all his fault? "So the reason I'm so screwed up inside is because of you? I've spent my life hurting people because I lack a full range of emotions just so you could get the balls to act on a grudge? I should throttle you."

Oh, that was wussy. I need to take more acting lessons.

Yeah, the acting lessons I wouldn't need if this bastard didn't rob me of a full range of emotions.

Peter

How calm Niles is during all of this is fascinating. With his words I would expect him to be on his feet and towering over me in threat. Instead he looks lost in thought. "Then why aren't you *throttling* me as you so eloquently put it? You've a very interesting way of thinking and emotions are pesky little beasts for most people. You used your gift and your curse to your advantage and became a lawyer."

Niles opens the drawer of his desk and peers down at the backside of a frame. So that's where his eyes have been staring this entire time. "That tiny bit of love you left me is hitting full force. What do I have to do?" he asks.

I don't allow the guy a second to reconsider before giving my sales pitch a go. "We're going to get Stoddard the way he got us. All you need to do is waltz in, sprinkle a little lighter fluid, and strike a match. You have to find a way to kill the surveillance system because—"

"Wait a minute. Are you saying somebody set that fire? According to legend you were wasted, hit a wall, and nodded off with a lit cigarette."

"You're really foolish enough to believe that? Didn't anybody ever stop to think how bloody hard you have to hit a wall, or how wasted you have to be to pass out so deeply you would miss a fire? If I had been that far gone, I doubt I'd have made it up the stairs. No, Stoddard had me taken out. Now I'm to return the favor. Since I seem to not be able to really touch anything, I just need a tad bit of living help."

"No way in hell. I'm not going to put blood on my hands with the offer of an empty promise."

I should have seen this coming. The old Peter Lane would never go for it either. The part of us that would allow it is small, and it's all within me. "Trust me, Niles, my promise is not empty. Remember the little episode we just had with Rosalyn? Help me achieve this, and she will welcome us with open arms."

"You really think I am stupid enough to fall for this trick?"

He's astoundingly calm. I'm going to have to play this boy. My disappearing act begins as I fade from his sight. "Fine. We'll see how your future unravels. I hope you're used to being alone because you certainly won't get anywhere with Rosalyn like this. You'll be in touch."

I Can Remember

Rosalyn

How did I allow that moment with Peter to happen? My cell phone gets tossed onto the nightstand before I turn out the lights for bed. Again I'm unable to bring myself to call Niles. For a girl who has never had a one-night stand I'm an unforgivable whore.

Warmth comes in next to me, and my pillow emits energy as if it has taken on life. How wrong is it that I can get so much love and comfort from a dead man but little from a living, breathing one? My head nuzzles into the softness of the pillow as Peter ropes his arms around me. "You all right, luv?" he whispers.

"No. I'm far from all right. What we did Saturday was unforgivable." Tears build in my eyes. I halt mid-reach for a tissue. I don't deserve its luxury for what I did to Niles.

"I was only trying to make you happy. You have to admit, you weren't exactly complaining."

Yes, I was all too happy and hate myself for it. I also hate myself for finding comfort now. "If you're here to try to talk me out of being with Niles again, don't waste your time. I seem to not have a choice in the matter."

"I really don't know what you see in that fake, gay vampire. And by fake I mean the gay part."

The back of my hand wipes the falling water away from my eyes. "Peter, crushing Niles has put me in no mood for joking."

"We've really crept our way into your heart, haven't we?"

God, this is like talking to my conscience. If the episode with the three of us didn't happen, I'd stand by my theory that my imagination has gotten the best of me. "How is it I can feel so much with you, and I want that with him, yet it just doesn't work out even though logic tells me it should? None of it makes sense when you put it down on paper, but when you put it all in my heart my emotions for you seem so right. I should feel that way for Niles, but when I'm with him it's all wrong. I think of him, and I have the feelings I have for you, but when I'm with him those emotions completely disappear. Then when I'm with you they reappear again." I grab a pillow and smash it down over my face. "Gah! My brain has turned into a bowl of clam chowder that's all crackers!"

"You know, luv, there's actually a very big reason for that. Though I have to warn you that the explanation sounds pretty daft."

I smack the pillow onto my hips and draw in a deep sniffle of remorse. "It can't be any crazier than what I just tried to describe. If you've got a solution, sock it to me."

Peter

With a little kiss on Rosalyn's forehead I reluctantly leave my position by her side. At her desk I point to the drawing she did of me. "Do you remember when I first saw this?"

"Yeah, your reaction was a little freaky."

With our new bodies come new brains, thus making us akin to amnesia victims. It's cruel. We all have a right to know who we were and the impact we had on others. "Jane used to draw as well. She did everything from beautiful landscapes to crazy swirls of color, but what she did best were portraits. You could never look at one of hers and not feel like you were being told a story. This sketch of me is a perfect replica of one Jane did—every last detail. It's as if you erased her name and signed your own. My expression, the lighting, the background, they're—" I choke back the pain that leaks out of my heart as I approach Rosalyn— "They're all the way she drew me on the day she said she knew we were on the verge of losing everything, yet she found a way to help me see the good in our lives."

I take a place on the bed. My hand's energy caresses Rosalyn's chin as I remember how I felt when I first professed my love to her. "I will never forget that moment in my existence, just like I will never forget you, Jane."

Rosalyn

His words stun me. Languidly my mind pieces together enough fragments of thoughts to process the moment. Why is he calling me Jane? It doesn't seem the least bit alien but more like a childhood nickname that has been long forgotten.

The energy from Peter's touch on my chin has me enraptured while he speaks of the day we met. At the mention of the sketches Jane had on her wall I look to my own and my breath locks in awe. Next he tells of the house they shared as if he were reminiscing with her and not relaying the story. Memories flash before me, coming from somewhere much deeper than the recesses of my brain. Smiles and chuckles burst forth at the recollection of happy moments I never experienced. At the mention of his proposal, tears of happiness seep into my eyes and my finger runs over where an engagement ring would be, expecting to touch a smooth stone. The comfort of acceptance runs up my spine. "Round cut," I say, "with a very smooth surface. Set in gold with little rubies on each side with diamonds next to those. Why rubies?"

Peter swallows hard as we both accept my knowledge that his words are true. "Because they were my mother's favorite. I wanted to give you and our children everything I never had growing up, and that was my way of saying I was going to see to it."

Finally part of my inner madness becomes clear. "This is why you make me feel the way you do. It's because I'm her. It's also why whenever I'm in a car and get near an embankment my body tenses." My spine locks with a bitter chill. My arms wrap around me while I recall the sensation of soaring and fear of hitting the ground. "Because I'm completely terrified of going over the edge."

Peter reaches out to pull me close, but the act is so futile it causes physical ache. My tears flow in mourning of the loss of my love decades before. "Here, luv," he says while lying where a scrunched up pillow sits. I curl against the pillow, and the tremors of sadness that have quaked through me quell. "Jane, would you take me back right now if I could find a way to be in the flesh?"

His tone is as bold as his words. The question seems silly. Would I take back a ghost from a part of my past that is so distant that it didn't exist in this lifetime, if he were alive? "I— I'm not sure."

"Let me guess," he says. "Niles."

"Yes," I utter while completely confused. Again I wonder how I can have such a mishmash of emotions for a man who doesn't exist and a man who's living but may somehow be half dead.

"Rosalyn, there's something you need to know about Niles and I."

Him Or Me
(What's It Gonna Be?)

Rosalyn

"You did what!" Oh, I so want to let Peter have it! "This whole thing with Niles and his emotions isn't just in his head, and it's all because of you? You creepy little bastard! How could you do that to him?"

Peter stands overtly erect to drive home the point that in his mind it was simply something that had to be done. "I didn't just do it to him. I did it to myself as well. Do you really think I enjoyed being locked away in blackness for all those decades simply because I sent Niles off on his own? Do you know how many drunken idiots tried to summon me without success?"

"Oh, pity for you. What about poor Niles? How could you steal a man's ability to love and still face yourself?" How dare he? And how dare I? I didn't think possible to feel more shame for what happened with the three of us, but now … I just can't see myself in any better of a light than I see Peter, a man who selfishly hoarded a person's most precious gift.

"I had no choice. Besides, Niles got to keep all the desire for the lovey, dovey stuff that gets in the way. Not that it's of much use to him."

I have to remind myself I am not a person of violence else I'm gonna ring his freaking neck! "Did you also get rid of that pesky little voice that tells you to act with logic and reason? If you hadn't been so foolish, you would've been reincarnated. Then, if you are my soul mate—like you claim—we would be together in a normal relationship. But no, you had to play the idiot male who wants revenge. You squandered away a great relationship for us, not that I'd have anything to do with you now anyway, and not to mention the fact you ruined life for Niles."

"I had to. His self-righteous morality wouldn't let me handle this."

"You mean your conscience wouldn't have allowed it."

"Boy, you really are my lovely, nagging wife. If you would just help me convince Niles to—"

Can I please go back to when I thought Peter was a figment of my imagination? "Are you out of your mind? Part of the reason I feel the way I do about him is because of who he is. You get him to play along, and I'll have nothing to do with either of you."

Peter

I should've known. Jane would've reacted exactly the same way. "But if you help me, Niles can be whole again."

"If you can magically fix this once that Stoddard guy is dead, you can magically fix it now. However, if you involve Niles in something dastardly, I won't have anything to do with either of you. Find a better way to help him, or you're both out of my life forever!"

If it were that easy, I would have done it the moment I realized Jane stood before me, but when you make a deal to have your soul split off, you can't easily merge it back. I had to do some serious convincing of The Big Guy's minions that I was the one to deal out Stoddard's karma. Now I have to get Stoddard to admit to my murder. Without that I don't get to merge back. If I don't finish before Stoddard dies, the deal is off—meaning Niles and I will be forever parted. If Jane learns it could be irreversible, she'll never forgive me.

I Don't Know How To Be Your Friend

Rosalyn

The law firm of Elliott, Asher, and Barton LLP is so immense that just their reception area, conference rooms, and executive offices dominate the top floor of one of Los Angeles's biggest buildings. Though the worst I've ever done is gotten a speeding ticket, knowing that I am surrounded by floor upon floor of lawyers is discomforting.

Actually, law has nothing to do with it. At this moment I am a guppy in an ocean of people who have true careers. I've got to pull my life together.

People whizzing by almost knock me over as I exit the elevator and head toward a bright-eyed, blonde receptionist. Her perfect features glow. She reminds me of a Hollywood starlet, meaning she looks a little ... pre-fabricated, yet I can't help but notice how comfortable she seems in her skin. "Can I help you?" she asks.

The could-be starlet has a figure designed to put girls like me in their places. She looks at my vintage, nineteen seventy-one ensemble, a lavender mini-skirt, white lace blouse, and gold chain belt like it's a joke. She then takes a second look as if she is questioning if I am the fashionable one and maybe she missed a memo somewhere. Next she tries to hide the fact that internally she is shaking her head, and that flash of awkwardness that hits me from time to time makes an appearance. Dad's words enter my ears as if he is standing next to me. "Always be true to the amazing person you are." Despite the fact my jealousy toward her self-assuredness is intimidating I force a smile of pride.

"Hi. Is Niles Barton in today?"

"Do you have an appointment?" As I open my mouth to answer, she interrupts. "Oh, you're the one in the photo. Rosalyn, right? His girlfriend. Lemme call Doris and see if he's in."

I'm taken aback. He actually thought of me as his girlfriend? Guilt over my actions with Peter flares again. After his big reveal three days ago I guess it's kind of obvious why Niles never made a declaration. I had reasons not to as well, yet in his own way Niles dared to move forward in hope. I wish I had his strength. Now I both hate myself and love him more than ever.

A woman of about fifty, with short brown, somewhat poofy, over-sprayed hair enters the lobby. She sports a maternal air that brings me instant comfort. "Rosalyn? Hi, I'm Doris. I guess you didn't know Niles decided to take today off. Can I leave a message?"

Pangs of guilt hit my stomach. He didn't answer the door when I swung by his house a few minutes ago. I don't blame him for being in full-on avoidance mode. I really did it this time. "No, I'm sorry to bother you," I say. My arms drop to my side, and I pick up a foot to leave with my tail between my legs, much like I feel my head is up my ass.

"Actually, Rosalyn. Can I speak with you for a moment please?" Doris's expression reminds me of whenever Dad needed to tell me something that was going to hurt. I nod and follow her. We pass numerous young people who flutter about. Many of them are pretty, young girls. Doris guides me into a private office and motions me past a sofa and coffee table. She invites me to sit behind a large, walnut desk with two cushy chairs before it. Though I'm kind of nervous over what this lady has to say, the funky splashes of green and purple in the tidy office put me a little at ease.

Doris takes a chair across from me. Her discomfort is reflected when she pauses to watch her twiddling thumbs. "Look, this is none of my business, but ..." Now I get a straight on look. "Niles is very special to me. He's usually sharp as a tack, but yesterday his brain was completely muddy, and he spent nearly the entire day staring at the walls. We even saw him talking to himself for a while. Notice how empty his desk is. Nothing ever sat on it that wasn't absolutely necessary for work. When you entered his life he started adding things that reminded him there was a world outside of this one. Yesterday morning he threw it all in the drawer. Rosalyn, before he met you, all he ever talked about was work and occasionally one of the classes he takes at night to fight off boredom. However, Niles talks about you every chance he gets. He's excited to have someone to share himself with. I know he struggles with some differences, but please, whatever it is that happened between the two of you, I hope you try to work it out."

My eyes can't stop circling the office. It's a far cry from his lively media room, which is the one place where he feels the truth lies. Does that mean he thinks the rest of his world represents a lie, or is his world so cruel he has to keep happiness confined to ensure that no one messes with the little good he feels he has? In some ways Niles is my polar opposite, yet he's exactly like me. I try to keep my happiness around me, but I do guard that which is most personal. It's like Niles and I are intertwined.

Doris puts on a show of crossing her legs and stroking her chin as if having a secret and profound thought. "Hmm … Anytime things go bad with Niles he visits his mom …"

"Doris, you wouldn't happen to have an address that I could accidentally find sitting around somewhere would you?"

"Well, since you just happen to come into the office, you might also just happen to stop by my desk, and his mom's address might just happen to be sitting out. Or at least it will be if you give me a thirty-second head start. It was really nice meeting you, Rosalyn. I hope to see you again soon."

A lady with green eyes and over-sprayed brown hair, dressed in jeans and a no-frills green blouse, answers the door of the Diamond Bar home. "Rosalyn!" she nearly squeals. She seems so happy that I swear her teeth are sparkling. Meanwhile I stand here like an idiot. Everybody Niles knows seems to recognize me, thus making the confusing love I feel for him deepen.

"Yes. Hi. I'm sorry to bother you, but Doris thought I might be able to find Niles here."

I didn't think it possible for her smile to grow brighter, but I stand corrected. "So he didn't call you? You're here on your own?"

Her excitement gives me the comfort of a short shoulder rub. It makes me feel that arriving unannounced wasn't as rude as I feared. "Yes, I'm sorry to be intrusive. Something kind of happened the other day, and … I know I should respect his privacy but …"

"Don't be silly, honey. You've done exactly the right thing." I'm welcomed into the house. Well, more like dragged through it and tossed out the back door while getting a quick pep talk. "I'm so glad you are here. My boy hasn't been this miserable in a long time."

My boy. Oh, that's just so sweet it almost hurts.

Just short of letting me out the door she stops and looks me dead in the eyes. "Rosalyn, what he told you is real. He's not dangerous. He just can't see the world as fully as we can. It causes him to do and say hurtful things sometimes. Trust me, he's a good man."

In the far corner of the lush yard lies a patch of dead grass topped by a nineteen sixty-nine Camaro with a pair of legs sticking out from underneath. The sound of a turning ratchet and an old boom box blaring Moby Grape both bring music to my ears. My heart smiles as I remember hearing how Niles's grandparents were hippies and thinking about the musical influence they obviously had. Hell, most people of the proper generation don't know of the legendary Skip Spence running around like a madman with a fire axe. Ah, the beauty of LSD and hotel rooms. Makes The Who look sad.

Peter

From behind the garage I peer at the pathetic sod. He looks pitiful under that car. All that moping and sighing shows he's weakening. Now might be an excellent time.

I start to hone in on my target when Rosalyn appears. Bugger! What is she doing here?

Rosalyn

My feet shuffle through the grass with hesitation over having no clue what to say, yet my heart races with anticipation over seeing Niles again. This man having few friends is senseless. I can't imagine anyone not loving Niles.

Through the hoses and wires attached to the car's engine I gaze upon his face. My emotions may still have moments of being pushed back into a haze by fear, but my feelings toward the situation are obvious. It sucks, and even though it's just been a few days I miss him so much I feel incomplete.

"Hey," I say loudly enough to be heard above the music. His ratcheting stops. Niles twists to look through the gap between the engine and the wall. His face softens in disbelief before he crawls out from underneath and squints up to me with the sun beaming down into his eyes. I step a little to the side so his face is shaded. He looks both surprised and as confused as I am. Plopping down next to him I rest my back against a tire. It's an opening signal that I want us to find common ground.

NILES

How in the world ... Doris. Doris must have called her. Depending on how this goes, Doris is either getting a raise or I'm calling her tonight with her new work address—the Unemployment Office. "Hi." I'm an absolute idiot for not knowing what more to add, but just like pretty much everything else involving Rosalyn, this has never happened before.

"The phone seemed such a horrible way to face you, so I went to your office today. When Doris wasn't looking I—"

"Looked down on her desk where she just happened to leave this address open." I chuckle not just because I'm happy, but also because it's what you do to show you are not mad. "Doris is both the best friend and the worst paralegal ever."

What does a guy do in a situation where a girl comes after him? What if she came here to explain and then leaves forever? Girls are strange. Sometimes they feel the need to overstate the obvious. They must feel guilty for telling the truth.

A whisper of "Guilty. Guilty. Guilty," plays in my head. That's from the movie *Head*, right? Or was it an episode of *The Monkees*? Rosalyn would know. "Hey—" I slam on the brakes. Is talking about *The Monkees* really appropriate right now?

Rosalyn

An awkward pause looms in the air. Both of us look at the sky, the car, and then our feet. I start to ask about the car then stop. Niles deserves the straight-up truth, so I let the words from my heart come forth. "Niles, what happened the other day wasn't my idea. Peter just kind of showed up and started doing that. I should have stopped it the second he started, but please understand that this is an odd situation for a lot of reasons. No one else has been able to see him, so what was I supposed to do, start screaming like a crazy person?"

My hands hold onto each other, then fidget into picking at my nails. That was a crappy thing to say. My eagerness to forget about the whole debacle is making me appear to be an insensitive bitch. "Niles, I'm doing a horrible job at saying I'm sorry. Not knowing how I should have handled the situation is no excuse for not owning up to my mistake. The truth is I'm scared because you really fill a void in my life. For some reason I don't understand myself, I trust you. Trusting someone is pretty much the biggest thing possible for me right now, and I'm a total coward who's not really ready for it. I'm also confused as hell over all the things that you said and don't know how to process them. This all scares the crap out of me, but—"

But as much as we obviously care about each other, the fact he can't seem to give me an enrapturing romance tells me I am setting us up for failure. I won't be so foolish as to think that I can change him, but I also don't want to lose out on what could be the most amazing thing to enter our lives.

Damn. For just once, why can't life be easy?

"Niles, would you be willing to accept my apology and forget the other night ever happened so we can go back to the way things were?"

He shakes his head, and the look of disbelief is not the little boy look I find to be so sweet. Instead it's one of self-disgust. "Really? With all I told you? Rosalyn, I was serious about that. It won't get better. You have no clue how much I want this, but sometimes a person has to accept reality." His head drops in annoyance with himself. God, I don't blame him. Not in the very least.

"Yeah, I—I know, but I wouldn't be true to myself if I didn't try. If you really do want this, let's just see where it takes us. Okay?"

"Yeah, it's more than okay, Rosalyn." The hopeful eyes of a little boy who won't give up return, and my heart seems light again.

"Great. I'll see you Saturday night. We'll go to the film festival as planned?"

"Pick you up at six for dinner first, okay?"

"Definitely okay." Niles follows me as I rise. "I should get going." We both stare at the ground, and then take turns peeking up at the other and wondering what to do next. Finally I open my arms and he does the same. My hug pours all kinds of love out to him, and I don't let myself think about what it lacks in return. More than ready to leave the incident behind us, I head off towards the gate.

Niles's mom stands inside the kitchen window. When I

shoot her a big smile and a little nod her hand touches her heart. She has touched mine, too. I take the universe's hint and head back to Niles. Peter's right. They have both worked their ways into my heart. "Remember when you asked what it was like to have a dad? It was probably just as amazing to have a mom. You know, even though I hardly remember her, I used to talk to Mom all the time. I'd tell her my problems as if she were really there. It somehow helped."

"Why don't you talk to her anymore?" He looks disappointed but not as much as I am in myself. I've let down all of those I have loved and have lost.

"I'm trying to. Something bad happened that changed me, and it's become too painful to think about death. Missing the people I love is like being without part of my soul. I'd give anything to be able to talk to them now. Anyway, I just thought I would share. I'll see you Saturday."

Peter

Bugger! I should have been more on top of this. Now she's giving him hope. With that, he'll never agree to what I need. I've got to fix this.

The Element: Fire
(Mrs. O'Leary's Cow)

April 10, 1968

Peter

Everyone thinks they know this story, but it's never been properly told until now.

Jane and I had been fighting like rabid animals for weeks. Although a check, large enough to cover all of our bills with a hefty little bonus, magically appeared a few days after the meeting of which we never spoke, the effects of our lives being threatened were far worse than those of our financial woes ever were.

One night we decided to live it up with some friends. The show we put on was so good our smiles had turned genuine and we no longer felt covered in muck. The flicker of the restaurant's candles only added to Jane's radiance. Her hand touched mine, and my heart skipped all over the place, just as it did the day we met. When she snuggled into my shoulder comfort eased my soul. As much as I loved the moment, our troubles had left me sleepless for so long that I was just bloody exhausted.

With studio obligations for the next day hanging over my head I kissed Jane goodnight and insisted she stay and enjoy the evening. After a cab ride home I downed a few sedatives and crawled into bed. I was already too tired to change out of my clothes. My lids turned heavy, and I drifted off in the heavenly peace of knowing that even if the rest of the world failed us Jane and I would make it.

A noise came from the front door. I tried to force my lids open to greet Jane, but I started drifting off again. Her footsteps hardly registered as she entered the bedroom, but the expected dip of the bed didn't follow. My eyes were barely able to crack open to find a big guy, who reminded me of Stoddard's goons, standing before me. Adrenaline forced me awake enough to attempt to stop him from spraying the floor and curtains with whisky, but I was so disoriented it was hard to stand. He backhanded me, sending my head slamming face-first into the wall. Stars sparked my vision, and I collapsed.

The goon laughed while I faded in and out. I was barely conscious enough to notice my skin tickling as a mist of hairspray rained down. If my face contorted, it would give away I was aware enough to know my only hope was to act down for the count.

The crackle of his fag was a terrifying portent. The cigarette was placed in my hand and the cuff of my shirtsleeve lifted, thus moving my hand close to the curtain. The *click* of a lighter resounded, and my body went rigid as he set the curtains ablaze. Blood pulsed in my ears, and my heart pounded so fast I swear I could hear my heart valves fluxing. As soon as he was gone I would make a break for it by heading toward the window at the other end of the flat where I could wait until he had driven off. Jumping into the bushes would break my fall.

Another strike of the lighter and my hair crackled as the flames burst to life. Knowing it was but a brief moment until the fire hit my scalp, my insides clenched. The pain seared as my skin peeled away from the heat, and I jerked. Panic, sleeping pills, and alcohol were fighting to cripple me. My clothes started going up, and I thrashed about in scorching pain. When the smell of my burning flesh crawled through my sinuses, a scream reverberated in my ears and all went black.

As quickly as it arrived the blackness dissipated. I found myself hovering above my body and watching as it burned. My spirit continued screaming as if still suffering from the intense pain. I resisted floating away while sirens from heroes coming to my rescue wailed in the distance, but it was long too late.

Beautiful Child

Peter

Women are fascinating creatures who deserve respect for the beauty and desire for peace that they bring to the world; however, they would forget their brains if they weren't sealed inside their heads. They call men unorganized, yet they need to make fifty-thousand trips to the bathroom, or to the car, or kitchen, only to forget why they walked there in the first place. Thank God for it though because now I've the perfect opportunity to stir up trouble.

Oh, to have a closet like Rosalyn's again. One that reveals that you own far more clothes than any sane person should. Rosalyn's wardrobe reminds me of Jane's old one—at least the one side that is so wild it looks like Peter Max had a splatter fest with his leftover paint does. The other side must be reserved for funeral clothing. How many dead people does Rosalyn know?

While I need to give Niles the courtesy of knowing he isn't alone, why spoil the surprise with a gentle entrance? I make my sudden appearance on a box near his feet, located under a very enticing lingerie collection. "This really grabs ya by the old crotch, eh?"

NILES

Peter's voice causes me to jump as if I am a little girl with a rodent running around her feet. Well, at least the rodent part of the description is accurate. Why can't I be one of the lucky ones who can't see this guy?

"Rosalyn's downstairs in ridiculous shoes that look awesome but make taking stairs nearly impossible, so I'm up here trying to find her purple hat. Geez, which one? There are three."

"Maybe it's the one above here." Peter insistently points to some mighty revealing corsets. His call for attention isn't necessary. It's impossible to miss that Rox has a collection of lingerie that is rather ... stimulating.

Eyes on the prize, Niles, not on the fantasy.

"Kind of grabs you by the crotch and strokes you toward it like you've died and gone to a horny man's torture chamber."

The man is gross.

Damn, that black corset must look amaz—

"Stop it, Peter. I'm here for a hat."

Peter leans against the wall and eyes his nails. "Yes, but maybe if you do a little exploring, you'll learn what tickles her fancy. It'll buy you time while solving the rest."

What an arrogant ass. I have emotional issues, thanks to him, yet he makes me sound impotent. "Peter, there is no solution. Don't try to convince me elsewise. I'm already on eggshells tonight with trying not to screw up."

"Who's to say we can't find a workaround? However, if you lose her in the meantime ..."

Damn. The guy's got a point. Pleasing women has been the only way to get them to come back. What's the harm in taking a little peek in hopes of getting a few ideas?

My hands dash to flip through the sheer delights. It's been awhile, and right now even the silky padding on the hangers gets my mind reeling. She's got something for just about every fantasy; a black satin nightgown, a skimpy maid costume, a little sleep set of a shorty gown and matching panties with bright swirls of color that make my head spin. Then there are the corsets; purple satin with black lace, black satin with silver studs, pink lace with sheer lining. Dear God in Heaven!

Peter

Excellent. Knowing Jane she's given up on waiting and is about to tackle the stairs. Time to speed it up. "Dare I even begin to imagine what is in the box underneath the wet dream-worthy garments in this den of sin and beauty? Maybe she's got a toy arsenal that will reveal a secret fetish."

"No, Peter. This has already gone too far. I won't invade her privacy anymore."

Niles grabs the hats. Damn him! I need him in that box, now! "Are you sure? You may not have another chance."

"Positive. She trusts me, and I've already violated that enough."

Bollocks! "Well, I am sure when Rosalyn has a little more time to digest how you can never give her the enrapturing love she craves you'll wish for this opportunity back."

"No way."

Niles starts to leave. With every bit of anger I can raise, I will the box to slide in front of him and smack against the closet's wall, causing the top to pop up.

Well, imagine that. I must be getting stronger.

NILES

Peter is a pesky little menace. This crap about us being the same person can't be true. Just slam the lid back on and slide the box back.

But if he's right about ...

No. Put the box back!

As the lid is about to go into place a birth announcement for Joseph Charles Lighten, son of Rosalyn Chambers and Joseph Lighten Sr., dated just under two years ago, conquers my quest to respect privacy. It sits on top of some blue and white infant-sized onesies along with a blue, crocheted blanket. All of it has maybe been washed once.

Rox has a kid? Will she let me meet him? Kids are so cool. I want a do-over on my childhood. Now I know how not to do things that get you ostracized by kids, but adults are just jerks.

Suddenly Rox appears before me. "What the hell are you doing?" She sounds like her scream is trying to choke her and is almost succeeding. Is the horror in her eyes brought on by what I found or the fact that I found it? Damn it, Peter!

When you are caught, tell the truth. People see through lies when there is no sincerity to help you cover.

No, better yet, you show you care. "It was an accident and... Rox, what are you doing with all of these baby clothes? Is this what troubles you sometimes?" Was that right? I was never conditioned for this scenario.

Rosalyn

Tremors quake through my body, starting with a rumble at the pit of my stomach and radiating to the point where my hands are trembling. Before me lies a never-ending nightmare whose pain constantly resurfaces despite how hard I try to smother it back down. If I burst out with a lie, maybe this will go away. "My cousin left them in my car, and I haven't had the time to drive to San Diego. It's kind of crazy, huh? I mean, what's she going to do with them unless she has more kids, which she'll probably never do."

Dear God, why can't this horror disappear? I know I screwed up, but how many ways do I need to pay for my sin? Seeing the often innocent boy-like Niles sitting among the blue onesies deepens the poignancy of the moment and sends my heart tearing.

Niles lowers his eyes and raises a birth announcement. "I found this too," he softly confesses, thus calling me out on not only being a horrible mother but also a terrible liar. "I'm sorry. Please believe I was just searching for a way to get closer to you."

I can't divert my eyes or swallow back the thickening in my throat fast enough. I need to get out of here and fly off to some faraway land and live in a cave of shame. But I'll never be able to leave the agony of my stupidity behind. Somewhere there has to be a drop of relief. Someone has to be able to help me find some semblance of good among the disaster.

I look back at Niles as I prepare myself to tell him it's a story for another time and that we are going to be late for our movie, but his eyes seem to beg me to show him the trust I need to find in someone. If I want to build a relationship with him, I have to trust him like he did with me when he revealed his secret.

I bring myself to kneel in front of the box, and the clusters of blue clothes surround me in an ocean of tiny reminders that the hope I once held begs to drown me.

God, I'm going to face this. Please let me find peace and absolve me of my sins.

"Joe and I had been dating for about a year when I got pregnant. I wasn't even sure that he was the one. Part of me really wished he would propose while the fact that there was no ring on my finger was comforting. I know that doesn't make any sense at all. I was a big ball of confusion when it came to him. Frankly, I still am."

The water in my eyes turns the clothes on the ground into a nauseating haze. I try to calm my stomach by focusing on one thing, so my eyes go to a blue, crocheted blanket made by Jacqueline's mom. It's the only thing she's ever crocheted, and I let her down.

"The entire time I was pregnant, Joe was the dutiful non-husband, no matter how tired he was. When Joseph was born, Joe insisted that we had waited long enough. Though I feared the prospect of saying I do, a part of me really agreed. Again, I know that doesn't make any sense. I loved him but …

"I was still recovering from the birth when I walked into Joseph's room and—" My breath hitches at the horrible memory that will haunt all of my nights. My sweet angel, lying in his crib—a lifeless, ashen doll ascending to Heaven. The inescapable terror of the moment hits my stomach. "I tried everything to revive him; I opened the windows to get cold air, gently shook him while screaming in his ear, and threw cold water on him. Nothing worked. Joe rushed in to find me on my knees, hysterical and holding a soaked, lifeless infant." My stomach lurches, and I swallow hard and fast.

Peter sits next to me, hanging on my every word while looking as if he'd do anything to lend the tiniest of comfort. I swear tears are welling in his eyes.

My fingers push into the bridge of my nose, trying to press the horror away from my mind's eye. My mad river of tears won't stop as emotions bring forth words that sound as if I am pleading to God for understanding and forgiveness, because I am. "I still don't understand. He was happy and healthy when I put him to bed. Two beautiful weeks of life was all he had. Every moment I gave him the absolute best I could. I loved him so much it would sometimes hurt to look at him, but not looking at him was worse. Every night the three of us would lie on the bed and cuddle. Joseph would be sound asleep the entire time, but it was still wonderful to be next to him. Suddenly he was gone—stolen in a moment of my inadequacy without even the opportunity to whisper a prayer of a goodbye."

Damn it, Niles, do something! Please! Please don't let me live this alone again. I need someone to tell me it wasn't my fault. To tell me I didn't kill him like I know I did. Say something to show me a ray of hope somehow shines through my window in Hell.

Peter's gentle touch tingles on my knee. "It's all right, darling. We're here for you. Tell us what happened." I try to curl up to him, but much like Joe he's not really there. It makes the pain all the worse.

"Babies wake every few hours. Instinctively you shouldn't sleep through a quiet baby. A good mother gets her ass out of bed and checks on her child. She doesn't discover him dead after selfishly sleeping. Being exhausted from waking night after night due to a healthy, crying baby is absolutely no excuse. I should have known. I should have been there for him! I should never be allowed to sleep again!"

Peter does his best to wrap an arm around me. His eyes beg to help with such compassion I feel like even more horrible of a person for needing something tangible.

"He left. Joe abandoned us! People who love each other stick together through anything, right? How can anyone turn his back on his child the night before his funeral?"

My head collapses into my lap. My face is a burning mess

from unstoppable tears.

NILES

God, what do I do? When people cry you comfort them with love and words of encouragement. Holding someone is an offer to let the pain roll into you so you can replace it with love. I may have nothing to replace the pain with, but Peter does.

Shoving the box out of the way, I crawl to Rosalyn and basically sit on top of Peter who starts to leave. "No. We need you." Now is not the time for my pride to get in the way. Peter gives me a knowing nod and shadows my actions as I wipe away her tears. What do you tell people who are hurting? "I'm sorry you went through that. It wasn't your fault."

"Thank you," she says through a breath of relief. It's working. Can it always work? If I can persuade Rosalyn and Peter to live this way, it will be the three of us forever, and I'll never look back.

Great. Now encourage her by relating your own experiences. Your dog died when you were a kid. You were lonely until Mom bought another one. Work with that.

"Someday it will be better. Why don't you just have another child? It would solve everything."

"Niles!" Peter's shout is like a cold *snap*.

Rosalyn

My emotions freeze, yet my insides wildly quiver. My God, how could anyone say that? "Solve everything?" I barely choke out. "How would that solve anything at all?"

"Niles, don't you dare say another word!" Peter warns.

"You wouldn't be so sad anymore," Niles continues earnestly. "I can help you. It doesn't have to happen the old-fashioned way. If you need a donor—"

Peter jumps up and yells down at Niles. "Shut up! You are even more useless in this world than I am."

Finally I get enough of a grip to jump up and scream. The line Niles has crossed is so damn big that all my compassion has raced out of my soul. "You insensitive bastard! How can you possibly think for even a second I could replace the incredible gift that I carried inside me and loved with all that I had from the very moment I learned of his existence?"

Tears rain down my face, pouring onto a stack of Joseph's clothes and unforgivably soiling them with sorrow brought on by an outsider's ignorance. Oh God, how much worse can it get? Am I to suffer until all Joseph left behind is tainted?

Solemnly I turn to Niles. My face burns with the pain of wishing I could crawl into my baby boy's grave, curl him in my arms, and die. "The very moment that pink line showed on that pregnancy test I looked down at my stomach and marveled that someone sheltered inside was counting on me to do everything absolutely right. Now you've tarnished the last of the beauty he left behind." My voice turns threatening. "Get out! Get out of my life you sick, unfeeling ass!"

He stands to approach me, but his fabricated sensitivity has no place around my Joseph. I grab the blanket and lock it into my arms as I nearly growl at Niles. "Stay away from me!"

Jacqueline runs in. Upon seeing the contents of the opened box she screams, "What the hell have you done?"

My resolve falters, and an avalanche of horror crashes on top of me. I double over in a flurry of tears as my mind takes me back to the funeral, tossed over a sweet little gift from God in a casket while people try to restrain me, strung out on relaxants and sleeping pills that didn't work, crying, screaming, and wondering where the hell love and support were. Again I've been betrayed to suffer my hysteria alone. "How dare you invade my baby's privacy? You've killed him all over again!"

I curl into a fetal position as memories flood; that sweet smile Joseph had that filled me with love, the way he would curl his head into me when I held him, the big, trusting, brown eyes that stole my heart. That love can't be replaced. Not with anything in the heavens.

"Rosalyn, I'm sorry. I really only meant to help."

Jacqueline yanks Niles and pushes him toward the door. "Get out! Don't ever come back! Ever!"

Niles stops outside of the threshold. I can't face him—not now and maybe never again. "Rox, I swear I only wanted to help."

"Out!" Jacqueline screams, nearly shoving him down the stairs.

Peter wraps his arms around me, creating a halo of love. "I've got you, darling. Yell, punch, scream, and cry. Do all you need. I'll never abandon you." A sense of truth fills me. No other comfort has offered the right kind of love. The kind only someone who knows and loves you unconditionally on all levels can provide. "I can't make it better, but I can listen and be here for you."

Through the sobs I breathe slowly and smear away the tears. Peter tries to lend aid as I force myself to my feet. "Thanks, Jacqueline."

"I'll be right back," she says, "just as soon as I'm sure that ass is gone!"

Peter's comfort surrounds me as I lie on the bed. It's time to start facing everything in my life no matter how strange it may be. "Do you know what it's like for Joseph now? Is he okay?"

"I'm not allowed access over there anymore, but the other side is a wonderful place where everyone is happy, just like I will make you, Rosalyn. I promise."

Peter is a gift from God. He isn't a mere sign but absolute proof there is more beyond this plane than I will ever know while in this incarnation. Through this dead man I am finding life.

For the first time since Joseph's passing my thoughts of him are laced with hope. If Peter can return to Jane, I know someday in a world beyond my current one, Joseph will return to me.

Revenge

NILES

Well, asshole, this time you really did it.

The car's engine, whose roar Rosalyn loves so much, whimpers on her behalf. Please, Lord, have someone come out and stop me. My eyes float back to the front door and beg for it to open.

Stillness.

With the release of the parking brake the car meanders down the street. My attention is on the rearview mirror. I watch Rosalyn's walkway fade while praying for a miracle.

No one appears.

Finally my foot finds the gas pedal.

Niles, how stupid can you possibly be? You're supposedly so intelligent, yet you can't talk to a person with respect. What the hell is wrong with you? No more "it's not my fault" lies. No more placing the blame on psychobabble from the doctors. Accept the failure.

My phone vibrates in my pants pocket. Rosalyn? Please, Lord, let it be Rosalyn.

My hand fumbles behind me to grab the phone, only to I drop it between the seat and the console. I stretch my hand and slide it deep into the crack while swerving down the dark highway. Finally I retrieve it and check the caller ID.

Damn. A client.

The phone gets tossed onto the passenger seat. I'm pathetic.

Peter

Agh! I can't take how wretched this sod looks anymore.

It's time for sense to be knocked into him. I pop into his passenger's seat. "Are you done being a wallowing idiot and finally ready to listen?"

At the jitter of Niles's hand the car gives a swerve into the next lane and back. I twitch in fear, which is daft since I'm already dead.

"Jesus Christ on a pogo stick! Peter, what the hell! Do you want my blood on your hands, too?"

My, the boy is touchy. Do I really want him on my side? "You're useless to me should you perish. However, I'm sorry to say that your current state of desolation may be to my benefit. You're looking at this completely the wrong way. Stoddard goes down: we rise up. With your smarts and my generous heart, think of the team we'd make. Maybe you'll even get my talent and can cash in."

"I'm doing quite well on my own, thank you."

"I'd say tonight proves you are failing miserably." Seriously, how is it he could possibly think he still has the upper hand?

"You're forgetting something, Peter. I don't have a selfish bone in my body. You hoarded that one and screwed yourself, buddy."

Oh, yeah. That's how. "You just need a bit of perspective. Do you realize if you lose Rosalyn, you will continue to be alone for the rest of your life?"

"Maybe Rosalyn's just not the one."

I'm certain he got the memo on this, but did someone tape it to his back? "Remember, Rosalyn is Jane, and Jane is our soul mate. So, you either help me now and win her back, or you're going to be miserable until you and I reunite in the afterlife. Or maybe we won't. Maybe I'll decide to stay split apart and track Stoddard down five lives from now. Enjoy the next thousand years of suffering."

NILES

Geez, as if I wasn't depressed enough when I got in this car. If Peter's correct ... "I don't believe in that stuff."

"Yes, and I'm guessing a few weeks ago you didn't believe in ghosts either."

He has a point. As crazy as it is to think ghosts exist one sits beside me now. Since I know he's had a past life why wouldn't I believe he has a future one? Still …"I'm not doing it. There's a better way."

"And what might that be, oh great, super genius?"

Man, this guy is a bastard. Time to put on the old lawyer hat. "If we're split souls, won't we reunite when I die? If I off myself, all is solved."

Peter tugs on his brocade jacket and looks rather ill at ease. He'd make a terrible lawyer, let alone poker player. "Umm … There would definitely be a little problem in that."

Why am I not surprised? "Of course there is. I can't wait to hear how this one is botched."

"Not only would you be *dead*, and Rosalyn left alone, but if I don't settle all of this now, you and I are ever parted." Peter explains his "little dilemma" as he so delicately calls it. It sinks in on a deep level to where the core of my gut knows he speaks the truth. I don't have to be screwed for eternity—yet I am.

"So I help you kill someone, have a great life now, and then rot in Hell, or I go on this way forever?" This is nonsensical. "What was the exact agreement?"

Peter slinks back in his seat and let's his limbs loosen. He's forcing himself to believe what he is about to say is no big deal. "To get him to confess even if I have to hold a gun to his head. He needs to make some kind of irrevocable confession that can be made public." His voice is shaky. This is the behavior people exhibit when they know the goal they are driven towards is immoral, thus dividing them between the forces of love and hate.

"Do you have to be the one to make it public?"

"No, in fact I was given very strict orders to leave it for his wife."

"So the word kill was never used."

Tap, tap. Tap, tap. Peter is now rapping on the dash and

wildly bouncing his foot. "No, but if he writes out a confession, and there is no blood splattered on that paper, what's to stop him from saying it's forged?" His voice speeds through the words. Peter fears he is on the verge of losing, which means I have him over a barrel. It's moments like this I wish I could kiss my old counselor for teaching me this stuff.

"And what exactly happens once we accomplish this?"

"Per the agreement your body will act like a vacuum and suck me in as if I'm lint."

Given the beliefs expressed in most religious doctrines, Peter is being tested and is about to fail. In doing that he will hurt Jane who will in turn want nothing to do with him. "Okay, Peter. Our deal goes down on my terms. Since your only job is to deal out karma, nobody dies."

Peter jerks toward me, his hands going for my throat. While he is physically incapable of squeezing his radiating anger has me gagging. Slamming on the brakes brings us to a screeching halt. Is this how my anger would be if I were him, or is it amplified by the fact our emotions have been chopped and divided like slop in a soup kitchen?

"No!" he exclaims through gritted teeth. "We take the bastard down. We can't chance you being wrong."

Interesting. I thought I got all of the fear. I guess that five percent he kept for himself has him by the balls now that he realizes he may lose Jane forever. Perfect. When passion takes over mistakes are made.

"No deal." I calmly prepare to pull the car back out as if I'm completely unfazed by the life-threatening event. Now I could kiss my acting coach, except he's kind of big and gross.

Again Peter goes for my throat. This time I'm ready for him, my foot never having left the brake.

"My terms or not at all. The offer won't get any better."

Peter releases his grip.

Peter

Well, well, well. I've won the battle after all. Mr. BS is going down, but I won't risk Niles being wrong about not needing

to finish him off. "All right, Niles. You drive a hard bargain."
I extend my hand. Just as sure as when he goes for the grip
there's nothing there to grab, his smirk shows he doesn't
believe a word I say.

"Yeah, Peter, you're not really buying into this. Well, I've
got you there, buddy, because we're both aware if Stoddard
gets harmed, Rosalyn's going to know exactly who did it.
Thus, I am sure you see this was the best deal you could've
made."

Bollocks.

After The Fall

Rosalyn

My bedroom door flies open. Jacqueline marches in like I'm in deep trouble. "Out!" She points to the door while I flip the covers over my head. My precious, beautiful, little angel died, and his father, who I trusted implicitly, betrayed us both. Yesterday, another person whom I gave trust reminded me of that horror in a heartless way. My head is back in the nursery, holding a cold, wet baby, and losing him all over again. Trust is a game for fools.

The covers come flying off of me. "Up and out," Jacqueline commands, thrusting her thumb to Heaven. "No moping!"

I bring the covers back with a defiant yank. We have learned when I get into a funk over Joseph, Jacqueline needs to play Drill Sargent else I'm in bed for days. Usually I groan and agree. Today I hardly whimper as the tears return.

Jacqueline sits on the edge of the bed and slides down the sheet enough to expose my face. "You okay, Rox?" she asks softly. I shake my head. It hurts more this time. The pain of losing Joseph coupled with all I know about Niles and the need to never see him again dig too deeply. I had hope for my future. I even spoke to my parents again. Now all my gains are lost.

NILES

Dawn was barely breaking when I bolted into the office today.

I'm usually not one for determination. I do things because, well, usually I have nothing better to pull me away from work. However, today my nervous system races on a non-caffeine induced, caffeine-type high. Once I slipped on my lawyer hat last night, it became glued to my scalp. If there is a way to pull this stunt off, I'm finding it.

Doris waltzes up to her desk—like actually dancing—and *plops* down her purse with flair. She continues her dance into my office. This is one of the many reasons I hired her—that and the fact she's willing to come in on her day off because her boss is on a mad quest. She would have even done it if I hadn't offered three paid days off in exchange. "To what do I owe the honor of the very sweet and polite, surprise text I got on this beautiful Sunday morning?"

"I need you to pull everything you can possibly get your hands on regarding Benjamin Stoddard. He's a record producer out of England. He's also a crooked bastard who's attached to the mob, so don't trigger anything."

"Okay." Her hands clasp together with enthusiasm. "Just what exactly am I looking for?"

My nose stays to the grindstone. "You're looking for anything, and I mean absolutely anything, that can be held against him. Scratch that. I want all details no matter how small. If you find his shoe size, I want it."

Doris doesn't nod and leave as expected. Instead she stands before me and waits for me to finish typing. My eyes rise to find hers on the picture of Rosalyn. "You okay? You may be in full lawyer mode, but this is no ordinary case, is it?"

How is it she knows these things? Doris's understanding of people seems to make her actually experience life with them. Peter's right, I *need* to know what that's like. "No, Doris, I've never been okay, but some way, somehow, I am going to fix that."

Doris leaves the room while I resume my research of digging up everything I possibly can on Peter Lane and his wife, Jane.

Rosalyn

Shop bells chime as I enter through the door of my safe haven. Just inside I pause. God it is loud in here today. The lights are blinding, and the whole place reeks.

"Hey," Shane utters with a bop of his head. Nothing seems right here today. Nothing seems right anywhere.

Shane stops his reading, then actually bothers to put down his ancient issue of Cream Magazine and rights himself from slouching over the counter. I hoped coming here would help. It doesn't. Nothing does. Instead, tears beg for release as I brave facing the world.

"Where's your traveling sideshow?" Shane asks.

God, already? That's the cue to start flipping through the nearest bin facing away from Shane while I swallow the urge to break down. "Get anything good in over the last couple of days?" My voice cracks as I say it.

"Yeah, some geezer must've conked. There's a butt load of vinyl in the corner no one wants to sort. It's got a ton of old crap you'd probably like."

"Sure way to make a sale." The grumble in my voice is reminiscent of tires on gravel. A Runaways album grabs my attention. Niles loves these girls. I shake my head at the wording of my thought. How should I say it? Niles *enjoys* them? The tears start to trail their way down my face.

"Hey, are you okay?" Shane asks while on the approach. "You seem to have the symptoms of a bad breakup."

"Epically. I'm sorry. I never should've come in here." My feet make for the door. If I cry here then nothing is sacred.

Shane touches my shoulders. His eyes narrow, and a little *huff* of concern tells me the feelings I've shown for Niles must have been obvious. "Stick around a while. Help me sort those albums. You know that era way better than I do." He goes behind the counter and returns with a tissue he nearly smacks into my hand with a squeeze. "Don't tell Rob, and you can have your choice of one out of each box as a salary for helping. If you take two, I'll suddenly forget how to count, okay? You *need* it."

He's right. I need to get past my association of Niles with my love of music. I can't let my passion get soiled. "You do know I'm totally gonna bogart the most expensive ones, right?" I say with a forced smile.

"I expect nothing less."

As we head off for the boxes I catch a glimpse of Peter watching from across the room. He shakes his head before hanging it and disappearing.

Long after the store has closed the listening booth blasts a treasure from a dead man's stash. Shane and I sit surrounded by records, beer bottles, and takeout boxes. The flipping from album to album and allowing myself to feel the beat of one happy song after another has the despair in my gut dissipating. I'm even nibbling on food. The real shocker though is Shane has me smiling. He was right. I needed a night of music with a comrade. "Why was I born so late? I have the same taste as a teenager, circa nineteen sixty-seven. Hell, even my two favorite books, *The Outsiders* and *Valley of the Dolls* are from that era. Why couldn't I have existed then and loved the times for all they were worth?"

"There was a ton of crap on the radio back then, too. Now you get to hone in by artists and genre on the Internet instead of being stuck with what the deejay plays."

I grab another stack of albums to sort by sub-genre and stare at a copy of The Chocolate Watchband's *The Inner Mystique*. The multitude of images and implication of a brain exploding reflect how I envision myself. "Yeah, but remember when you were a kid and how excited you were to hear a new single? It's completely different from coming into a store and exploring. I missed out by being a walking freak show." The album gets moved to the garage rock stack, and I find a familiar image underneath where it once was. "Peter

Lane," I utter. My being Jane would explain so much about who I am and what I love. He's right. I *am* her—which means I'm a living ghost who is married to a dead one.

God, my life is a train wreck!

"Dude." Shane's tone implies a warning. "Don't say that name around me. I'm still in trouble for that mishap."

"Huh?"

"That signed album you bought. Apparently my habit of tapping on the note pad bit me in my skinny ass. I accidentally popped in a decimal point and screwed the store out of five hundred and ninety-four bucks. I'm an idiot for not knowing better, but if it's not my genre I kinda don't give a rat's ass who they are. If I didn't have an investment in this place, I'd have gotten the axe up my butt."

And I would never have bought it. Meaning I never would have met Peter. Fate is a freaky dance partner. "Investment? You part own this place?"

"Yeah," he says, shrugging. "Smartest decision I ever made was living off of unemployment while working in exchange for a stake in the place. Anywho, I'm done dealing with this for tonight. I was serious about helping yourself to some albums."

Well, that's a drag. Going home now is not what I want, but I had a great diversion while it lasted. Shane walks me to my car. Thanks to him and our musical journey my love affair with music is shiningly intact. Maybe heading home to no one but Jacqueline isn't so bad.

"Hey, Rox, how about I take you to dinner Saturday night as a thank you?"

Maybe I'll get even a touch of sleep.

"Rox? Dinner Saturday night? Where would you like to go?"

"Anywhere. Anywhere at all sounds great."

Driving off, a debate over whether or not to call Niles bounces in my head. He feels bad. He has to. But I can't brush aside what he said. No one is allowed to talk about my baby that way.

Wait. Did I just make a date with Shane?

I Don't Like Mondays

Rosalyn

Coffee.

The exaggerated weight I feel from this plastic container of cookies, along with the clouds that swirl in my head, signal the need for more coffee.

No. The pitiful truth is there is no simple cure for the hollowness in my chest, and I'd still be crying in bed if Jacqueline hadn't again played Drill Sergeant. I swing the lobby door at work open and force myself forward. "Happy Monday, Darla!" In my mind, my flipping off the container's lid looks like film played at half-speed.

"Ah, insomnia strikes again, eh?" Darla helps herself to a sugary boost while my eyes blur over her.

"What's the word around the water cooler this morning?" God, did I really ask that?

Darla abandons her cookie to give my hands an assuring squeeze. "How about we stop playing games and you let me tell you I'm sorry you are hurting. Is there anything that I can do?"

I hang my head and shake it. Niles returning to my thoughts turns my stomach. I fear now my mind will always connect him and Joseph in a horrible way.

"Want me to go kick his ass? I can take him, you know?"

I actually chuckle, not because it's funny, but because it is true.

Darla tightens her grip. "I'm here for you. Whatever you need," she assures. Her phone rings, and I start to head off to the elevator. "Rox, hold up." With a few clicks of some buttons she sends all incoming calls to voice mail. Dashing to me she covertly whispers, "Come on. Let's go sneak out on the line and steal some jelly beans out of the hopper." She starts to head off like a spy who is leading me astray. Suddenly she drops the act and high-tails me in the other direction. "What the hell am I thinking? No one should eat the crap we make here. Someone left Oliver a Starbuck's gift card. Let's make sure it works."

MILES

Twenty-four hours into my search and I've barely slept. Slowly but surely Doris has uncovered information on Benjamin Stoddard. Her findings were speculative until she slammed her heels into the ground and kept digging on a quest for middle earth. The guy's guilty of just about everything, yet his rap sheet is spotless.

For decades England's Serious Organized Crime Agency has been on to his ways, however the local police departments leave him alone and quickly dismiss all charges. Everything Stoddard does is unethical but also legal. The guy has his grubby little fingers in everything and is double and triple dipping all around. Since he happens to own all of the businesses, he's got complete control and is technically entitled. I have to admit the man knows what he's doing.

Damn.

Forever Afternoon (Tuesday?)

MILES

After three days without a word from Rosalyn my lawyer hat has become a king's crown in the game of chess that plays in my mind. It's the only way to combat my regret. Nothing interferes.

Nothing.

Not even sleep.

Doris keeps running into slammed doors, but every now and then one creeps open. So far she hasn't found anything dramatic, but I have to believe the breadcrumbs she's uncovering will form a trail that leads to my salvation.

Doris tosses another stack of papers on my desk. "What did you find this time?" I ask.

"A *friend* across the pond pulled a bunch of documents. Included are all of Stoddard's vital records and marriage licenses along with the added bonus of his prenup, which is so lovely it got me checking for birth certificates listing him as the father. No such luck. All of this isn't much, but it shows I am getting somewhere with someone. Give me a little more time."

There's nothing out of the ordinary in the prenup except the guy's a big douche bag who wants to scarf his cake while guzzling fine champagne. The infidelity clause states he's allowed to have affairs left and right while the wife has to act like Mother Teresa. All is well on his end as long as he doesn't let the swimmers catch their prey. If that happens, the wife gets half of everything in a speedy divorce settlement. What kind of woman would sign this? He's got something on her. "Hey, Doris—"

"I'm already on it," she calls out on her way back to her

desk. "Nothing on her yet, but if something's out there, I'll find it."

Of course you will. There's not a doubt in my mind.

The alarm on my phone sends it buzzing against the desk. With briefcase in hand I head off to face my day in court, fighting someone else's battle.

Seven exhausting hours later I return to the office. While I was victorious in my case I'm far from winning my war for salvation. Doris is long gone, but she's left her legacy on my desk. The stack of personal information on Stoddard has grown, as have other stacks on his business ventures. It's going to take a lot of dot connecting to find something I can pin on this guy. That's okay. I have all night. Actually, I have my entire life, because if I fail with this, there's nothing else worth working on.

Why would a manor-born woman sign such a brutal prenup? Maybe a lack of birth control and a shotgun were involved. Maybe they just wanted a fancy party and to shack-up without shame.

Shacks, like in the B-52's song. Every time they talk about that tin roof I want ice cream. No, no, no. I need lobster. Can you eat Rock lobster? Maybe someone will deliver one. What time is it?

The hit of my phone's button reveals that it's 3 A.M. on Wednesday. Seems I should know since I check it every ten minutes in case I miss a call from Rosalyn.

Inside the break room I groan in disappointment it hasn't magically restocked itself within the last six hours. A bag of dry Malt-O-Meal goes into a cup of yogurt and breakfast is served. Just the smell of coffee brewing enlivens my senses. The last of the yogurt gets gulped down with the aid of warm, nutty, liquid salvation. "Ahhh, black coffee."

I need to listen to some Humble Pie. No one sings "Black

Coffee" better than Steve Marriott. I wonder if he drank his coffee black. Did he drink coffee at all? Do the English drink anything other than tea?

This is bad. My brain is meandering into casual mode. I grab another coffee pod and pop it into the machine before finishing the first cup.

"Still insist on doing things your way?" Peter's voice comes from behind. I'm too tired to jump at the surprise.

"It's only been a few days. I'm hardly giving up yet." Geez, the man doesn't let up. I'm more like him than it is desirable to admit.

"Really? Because you look as if you've resigned yourself to death and have been torn up by hawks. You're starting to smell like it too." Peter's nose crinkles as he waves his hand past his face while shaking his head at my allegedly rotting corpse. Great, the death of me is another commonality for us.

"Cut me some slack. I'm deep in over my head with Stoddard research, and I'm due in court this afternoon with real work—you know, the stuff that pays me." The last bit of coffee is guzzled. Time for more—like a gallon more. Tomorrow I'm hiring us a twenty-four hour, on-call barista.

I wonder how well Peter would sing "Black Coffee?" If he's gonna hang around, I'm making him entertain me.

Wow. I really need to pull my head together.

"Which is precisely why your methods are bloody ridiculous. That Shane chap is jumping on Rosalyn—I mean, jumping on opportunity. They already spent too much time together Sunday night."

While Peter sees it as a threat, he's no idea that for me this is a common occurrence I got used to years ago. This time though... This time it hurts. "Maybe I don't mean much to her after all. Why am I even bothering?"

"Quite the contrary. Apparently she's rather broken up over the whole debacle." Grabbing the fresh cup, I make my way back to the office. "What is all this?" Peter asks, swiping up a stack of papers.

With a yank I *smack* them back onto the desk. "*Do not*, I

repeat, *do not*, shuffle *anything*. Put *everything* back in the *exact* order in which you picked it up, okay?"

"My, you get nasty when in need of coffee. You should bring that device in here and make a lorry full." Peter *plops* on the sofa and flips through documents while grumbling about how screwed he was. *Robbed, blah, blah, blah. Swindled, blah, blah, blah. Hurting people, blah, blah, blah.* "Personnel records?" he asks of the stack in his hands. "That yob had some luscious secretaries. They were always young, fresh, and willing to do *anything* he needed. It was downright disgustin'!"

Peter's humming brings welcome relief from his yammering. Where was I with all of this? Right, the wife. Doris found she came from a wealthy family and signed that prenup just three months after turning eighteen.

"Jenny Reed," Peter says. His evil laugh is almost a cheerful melody. "A real right one she was. Just as we were starting out, BS sent her to the apartment we all shared to have us sign some papers. I answered the door wearing nothing but a towel. Since I was half ready to go I asked if she fancied a shag. Her little mouth dropped open, so in turn I dropped the towel." He laughs. "That was the last I saw of her. Pity."

"Peter, you done yet? Really need to focus here." The wife. Her parents divorced when she was young, leaving her and her twin in the full custody of their mother.

"Fine." He drops the stack back on my desk so the papers become wonky. The compulsion to straighten them further impedes my ability to focus. "Boy, I really screwed you over didn't I? Seems I got all of the fun parts of our personality." Peter sticks his tongue out, crosses his eyes, and disappears. If what he says about us being the same person is true, I may become an ass when this is over. If he doesn't get off of my case immediately, it's gonna happen even sooner.

Time Is Passing

NILES

Every moment dedicated to our cause is a losing one. Peter didn't exaggerate a thing about Stoddard being a snake. He was also right in another little fact. I reek like spoiled apples. The point of how long I have been here is driven home at seven-thirty when Doris arrives with a sympathetic smile, a jumbo cup of coffee, a knife, and a white paper bag with grease seeping through. Yes! Old-fashioned donuts. Doris never lets me have junk food. If I reach for it when no one is around, she'll literally slap my hand, just like my mother.

Both hands jet out for the bag, waving in a "gimme" motion. "Oh, thank God." There's no time to properly open the bag. Instead—*rip!*

"Due to my waking to an encyclopedia's worth of emails from you I anticipated your desire for comfort food. But if you even think for a hot second I'm going home tonight before you do, you have absolutely lost your marbles."

I slice the bottoms off of both a chocolate and a maple-glazed donut and press the two tops together, reforming the fried delight.

"Niles, you have now hit your fourth day of obsessing, and I'm not going to let you hit a fifth."

The chocolaty, mapley, greasy goodness hits my mouth and my eyes close off the world as sticky sugar is savored. "Sorry to disappoint you," I mumble while chewing. Closing my heavy lids was a mistake. "I'm getting absolutely nowhere. I shudder to think what you'll bring me on day seven."

"That won't happen because by day six either you will have

collapsed from exhaustion or it'll be funny farm time for you. Your choice." She gives me a wink and a smile. Man, I must be half dead. I swear Doris looks as if a couple of years have been knocked off overnight.

"Hey—" Don't ask about it! You'll screw it up and need a new paralegal.

Umm … Seriously, this donut is amazing.

"So I had a bit of a revelation last night," Doris tells. "I suspect that Mrs. Stoddard may have been a rebound relationship. Remember how there were two marriage licenses? Shortly after the first one was issued, the now former fiancée married the son of a very wealthy ambassador. A few months shy of a year later that prenup was signed."

Doris's words cause a light bulb to illuminate in my brain. "So you suspect that Stoddard became a shrewd bastard out of jealousy?"

She takes a seat across from me. Her legs slowly cross while her face gently scrunches in an expression of thought. When she tilts her head, the way the light hits her hair changes. She's dyed it a slightly different color. "It may go much deeper than that. Niles, people don't always make the best decisions when their heart hurts. That horrible prenup may have been his way of guarding against more pain. He may have felt the only way Mrs. Stoddard would leave is if she found someone richer."

"If that's true, then the more he felt someone to be a threat, the worse they would be treated. Still, why do you think Mrs. Stoddard was willing to effectively get paid to be the only permanent member of a harem?" I take another chomp of the donut. Man, this is tasty!

Oh, tasty, like The Good Rats song…

Niles! Back on target!

"Well, she was only eighteen when she signed it. People do foolish things when they are young and in love or in need of it. Maybe she was in a similar situation."

Alice Cooper's "Eighteen" starts playing in my brain. When I was eighteen all my head thought about was college.

All my dick thought about was girls. My God, Sarah Thompson and her taunting rack. Too bad her nose was always in a book. Then again, none of us cared about her nose.

I miss Rosalyn's cute, little nose.

"Doris, when you were eighteen, what were your concerns?" I toss the last bit of donut in my mouth and lick some chocolate off of my thumb. Heaven.

"I was lucky. The only real one I had was what college to go to. Money was tight, but my parents covered all of my basics."

Neglecting the unglazed donut halves I dive in for a new set. Doris was lucky her parents stayed together. At least Mrs. Stoddard's mom received child support. My dad couldn't be bothered to remember to pay. Mom should have had plenty of help until at least the day I turned eighteen. Even then …

The Godfather of Shock Rock still screams in my head about being eighteen and wanting to escape his world. Ah, you can only do that if you have the cash. When Mrs. Stoddard turned eighteen, the child support money would have stopped. Marrying Stoddard ensured her lifestyle continued. She may have also really been in love with him, thus explaining why she was so shortsighted. If she is still emotionally attached, it could pose a problem.

"Doris, do we have any reason to believe Mrs. Stoddard wants out of the marriage?" I take another bite of chocolaty, mapley goodness. This time not while closing my eyes.

"You mean, other than the fact that she spends a good chunk of her free time traipsing around the world without her husband? Sounds like a tumultuous relationship to me."

Tumultuous. That word sounds ominous. My ninth-grade English teacher used it a lot. She was a happy person until her bastard husband left her for a woman twenty years younger. God, we men are pricks. No wonder why women are always fussing with their hair and makeup.

My proverbial shovel just hit a treasure chest!

"Doris, we're looking at this affair thing the wrong way. We know he's snuggling up with other women, but get surveillance on Stoddard ASAP and find out who they are. I'll settle for any pictures implying he has had an affair within the last, say, ten years. I just might be onto something."

Instead of heading off, Doris leans in and stares me dead in the eyes. "Only on one condition. For the sake of the entire planet, go home immediately and shower."

Out of court settlements are supposed to be a way to find middle ground. Realistically, no one wants that, thus making them a boring tennis match. One person serves, the other lobs back, then back again, then back again—each swing a quickly calculated retort in an effort to get the other party to screw up and miss the return shot. My key to winning is time and patience. Eventually the other party grows tired of my cool demeanor, gets emotional, and blows it. It makes winning easy.

The guy across the table lobs another shot. I stick out my racket and don't even swing. The ball bounces off and nearly bops him on the head. If Joy Perfume Industries didn't already pay this firm so much, I'd increase their rate. We are twenty-minutes past when this meeting should have wrapped. Surely we all have places to be, yet my opponent leans back in his chair. He stretches out his legs and tries to act cool. However, I know he's sweating on the inside over how much of his reputation he has to lose because of this frivolous lawsuit regarding his client's alleged allergy. That's okay, I have endless patience.

It's too bad that today my determination outweighs it. Or maybe it's not bad at all. The day is almost over and Doris has a big fat nothing to show for it, which means I need a new angle.

My opponent takes another shot. This time he knocks an insignificant ball out of the court so far I don't even glance at it. Out of sight, out of mind—like a hot foreign band that has a big hit then returns to their homeland and is never heard from again. If Love Machine had been in America's face from the beginning, their success would have been different. Instead—

If Stoddard had contacts here, his secretaries did as well. It's time for a surprise maneuver.

"Ladies, gentlemen, since we are failing to progress I must excuse myself for another appointment."

My opponent rights himself and loses all traces of cockiness. He stammers to stop me, but I'm out the door and already on my phone. "Doris, check birth records in other countries, starting with America."

On Thursday morning I'm barely out the elevator when my expertly sneaky partner in crime dashes up to me with her hair bouncing, her hips swaying, and her smile dazzling. She's struck gold. "Guess what I found in Reno." She grabs my arm and rushes me into my office. "Not only did a former secretary have a child within seven months after leaving Stoddard's employment, Stoddard is actually named as the father on the birth certificate."

Excellent. If the wife wants out of that marriage, I'll soon have the backing for her to get a tidy settlement. All I need is for the kid to submit to a DNA sample. I'll sell it to the wife for my modest legal fees, plus a hefty favor. It's shady but above board, just like Stoddard's slimy tactics. "Great! Where's the kid now?"

Doris rubs the back of her neck. She must not want to share the next bit of news. "Actually, Niles, I found the information through death records. He lost a battle with cancer a few years ago."

"Doesn't matter. I just need cells. Did he have any kids?"

Doris closes her eyes to me. "Lord, give me strength."

Damn. Mr. Insensitive strikes again. Stupid jerk.

"No, Niles, he didn't. However, his mother is still alive. *Someone* might want to try talking to her."

My butt hits my chair. I'm so tired of being a vile ass and watching people hurt. Protocol says to apologize and move on which makes zero sense. Doris isn't the one who lost the child. Shouldn't I apologize to the mother? But she's not here, which means she doesn't know. So why should I— "I'm sorry, Doris. That was horrible of me."

Doris nods and takes a seat. It's my sign to move on with the conversation.

Okay, if I were Stoddard, I'd either pay the lady off or remove the threat. "Doris, if you got pregnant by some guy and feared you could become a mob target, would you list the father's name on the birth certificate?"

"I guess in the end I wouldn't for the sake of the child, but ... but the reality is it would depend on both my inner strength and my feelings toward the relationship. Since the baby was born out of the country she probably thought it to be safe."

"So she might be willing to talk." Okay, yes, this is totally insensitive, but the woman has to be at least pushing seventy and her son is gone. She may feel she has little to lose at this point.

Doris shrugs her shoulders and vacates her seat. "With women, Niles, you can never tell. Hearts take a long time to heal, and the deeper the cut, the longer the healing time. However, if she's ballsy enough to list the dad she may be ballsy enough to talk."

"Where are you going?" I call as she strolls out.

"To see what else I can clear off of both of our calendars so I can buy two, first-class tickets to Reno."

"I assume you'll book us in the most expensive hotel with a spa day for yourself?"

"Damn right!"

Strange Movies

Rosalyn

Lo and behold, I didn't imagine it. At six o'clock on Saturday, Shane's car pulls up to pick me up for our … our … date.

Seriously, is this really a date?

Jacqueline steps up from behind as I peer out the curtain. "Wow. What an odd universe we live in. Are you sure about this? You've been off since that blow out with Niles, and I'm not just talking about how it relates to Joseph."

"It's fine." No, it's not. It's weird. "It's an innocent little date I wasn't even aware that I was making. Other than the shock I'm not even fazed by it."

Jacqueline plops herself on the sofa, looking all kinds of cozy in her flannel jammies that she wears instead of turning to food for comfort. "That's the issue. You didn't know what you were doing, which concerns me about what you may do next. Sometimes our judgment gets all funkified when we're on the rebound. Admit it or not Niles got to you."

I try to soothe my mother hens, both Jacqueline and the one inside who is nagging me to call Niles and try to find the forgiveness I know he wants. "Don't worry. I neglected to shave my legs. Not only does it keep me from caving, it also keeps me away from alcohol for fear I'll lose all inhibitions only to be doubly mortified in the morning."

"That's my Rox! Now head out there so he doesn't try to come in, just in case he's casing the place."

Shane looks pretty much like he always does except his jeans don't have holes and his ratty Chucks have been traded in for boots. He's actually wearing a button-down shirt that's—Wow, his shirt has been pressed. Truthfully, it's the most elegant I've ever seen him. However, I put little thought into the matter. I grabbed a white mini-skirt and pink turtleneck and then whipped a white belt around it. Instantly I was done and feeling totally at ease.

Shane drives his freshly vacuumed, late nineties Toyota Camry to Canter's. It may be just a deli, but to people like us it's like dining in Buckingham Palace while the queen is away. Pretty much all of our idols have eaten here.

Shane and I have only ever talked about music. My eyes circle the room in search of the perfect ice-breaking question. "Tell me a little about you," is the best I can come up with.

He looks lost, then a bit embarrassed. He shrugs with a confessional expression that he doesn't have much to offer to the conversation. "What's to tell? I work in a record store where you can see what I do every day. That's pretty much about it."

"Any hobbies?"

He throws one arm over the top of the booth to counter balance his weight so he can slump more without sliding. I think he's trying to look casual, not lazy. The poor guy is failing. "Working in a record store is sort of a job/hobby combo package."

Geez, help a girl out here. "Do you ever read any rock bios?"

"Nah, just the magazines we have in the store."

"Those things? Those are so outdated my grandmother could appreciate them."

He shrugs. "I go to movies sometimes."

Oh, thank God. "What kind of movies do you like?"

"Pretty much anything that comes out as long as it's got a lot of action in it."

Oh, seriously? He's such a total guy. "So just modern action films? No classics?"

He rights himself, suddenly aware of his posture and that he's on a date.

Are we really on a date?

"You say it like it's a bad thing. Really, Rosalyn, I'm exactly like you in that I know what I like. Color film was a big deal for a reason. I'd rather watch something colorized than anything in black-and-white."

Is this guy freakin' crazy? This is a test, right? Maybe Niles paid Shane to make me miss him. "Really? You would dis a movie just because it's in black-and-white?"

"If there's no color, I fall asleep. It's never failed. Not even once."

"Really? Have you seen *Psycho*?"

"Slept through it."

"How about *Some Like It Hot*?"

"Best nap of my life."

"Geez! *A Hard Days Night*?"

"That I actually made it in about twenty minutes before nodding off when The Beatles got on the train."

"Sorry, Charlie. They get on the train at the end of the opening credits, so you lasted about three minutes."

His shoulders dip in disappointment. "At least I woke up for the music at the end. Now *Magical Mystery Tour* I can do. No problem."

Seriously, what am I doing here? "*Magical Mystery Tour*? Without the music it's a bore fest. The Beatles can barely save it."

Shane shrugs. "What can I say? It looks beautiful. I have an affinity for beautiful things." He gives me an embarrassed slip of a smile before diverting his eyes. Did Shane just call me beautiful? Warmth coats my cheeks. "See? That's exactly why I'll take color over black-and-white any day."

My fingers start making little tears along the side of my napkin. Okay, so he may be totally wrong for me, but that was sweet. He also looked really cute when he smiled. How have I never noticed his dimples before?

Now I feel totally awkward. He must too because he barely peeks up to talk to me. "So, uh, there's a two week rock film festival going on at The Egyptian. Wanna check it out?"

Yeah, I'm painfully aware I was supposed to be there every night this week with Niles. "That'd be a gas. Wait. What's playing? Not anything in black-and-white, right?"

Shane chuckles. "You know what I like about you, Rosalyn? The fact that you use words like gas."

"You know what I like about you Shane? The fact that I can use words like gas and you don't call me grandma."

Shane's touch is sweet yet firm as he takes my hand while guiding me to our seats. The lights dim, and I'm bathed in a glow—the glow of a black-and-white newsreel. Shane groans. I chuckle. He barely makes it through the five-minute short before salvation in the form of a cartoon covers the screen in color. "See," he whispers, "don't you get absorbed in the excitement color brings? It's like being resurrected from the dead."

Peter and the darkness into which he was banished come to mind. Never have I compared how Niles is forced to live to Peter's incarceration. Even if I can push the image of Niles living in a cold, empty darkness out of my mind, I can't push the sorrow it brings out of my heart.

Shane pulls his car up in front of my house and puts on the parking brake. "I had a really nice night," he tells as the engine runs.

"Me too."

He pauses a moment then actually face-palms. "I'm sorry." He shuts off the car before running around to get my door and walks me to the porch.

I should have made a break for it while I had the chance by getting out of the car with a simple thank you and saying that I appreciate his friendship. I don't want to be cold, but I can't be with anyone until I clear my head. Shane is the perfect comrade, and even if he were boyfriend material, I certainly couldn't give him a proper chance now.

A smirk pops on to Shane's face, and he goes in for a hug. "Hang in there. You'll find the right guy someday. Call me any time you want to hang out, or just drop by and harass me. You always make my day, even if you are like my annoying little sister."

Oh, thank God this wasn't a date.

I playfully punch his arm and nudge him toward his car. He watches me get safely inside before driving off.

Jacqueline reclines on the sofa with her nose still in her book. I don't think she's moved a millimeter. "I take it from that lack of a passionate display outside that you could have shaved your legs after all."

"My *non*-date was very nice. How was your evening?"

"Peaceful. After the last few disasters I needed a break." The book meets the coffee table with a thumping skid. "You know, you're already kind of like a boyfriend, only better because you don't make me feel guilty for spending time with my friends. We go out on dates. We finish each other's sentences. Lord knows we hug each other enough. I'm even your emergency contact. Maybe I'm just not ready to see anybody else."

"Yeah, and there are more pictures of us on your phone than of your family."

"Not to mention when I went to that party without you the other night everyone wanted to know where you were. Janis and Catie asked, completely independently of each other, if we were fighting."

"Did you miss me?" I bat my eyelashes.

"Maybe just a little." She sends me an air kiss.

"Yeah, we're totally dating."

"So it was okay, huh?"

"Yeah. It really was."

"Good. I'd put out, but you didn't shave your legs." Jacqueline strolls off, wiggling as she goes. With moistened lips she turns and eyes me. You'd think I was a chocolate bar wrapped in solid gold. "However, if you go shave them, I may or may not have left my door unlocked."

"Tease!"

Flight 505

MILES

An emergency suit. Two extra shirts. Where the heck is my neck pillow? This suitcase is too small. Damn, where did I put the files for the Aoyagi case?

"Skipping town?" Peter suddenly appears next to my suitcase, and my feet stammer at the surprise. Now I know how Major Nelson felt. Why couldn't Peter be a cute genie who grants wishes?

"Hardly, Peter. For once your timing is perfect. If all goes well tomorrow, we're going to make Anne Stoddard one hell of a happy woman." Those files are key to that case. If I lost them—Oh! I put them by the door with my keys so I wouldn't forget them. Crap, I've turned into my mother.

"Well, I'm certain Annie hasn't had a good shagging in a long time, though I hardly thought her to be your type."

Eww, that's vile! "I'm not touching his wife, Peter. However, I am going to make it so that she can get the quote *shagging of her life* by someone else, if that is what she chooses. Now I just need your help in finding out when the best time and place is to get her alone. Preferably not anywhere near the house, because I'm assuming a guy like this has cameras and guards everywhere." Damn, I forgot to pack underwear.

"And what exactly will you be doing in the meantime?"

Six, maybe seven, days. A pair each day. Blue to go with the blue shirt, green to go ... Where are my green—screw it, just grab all black. "The breathing can't travel as quickly as you, Peter. I'm off to Reno for the day. I'll be back for court tomorrow before hopping on a red eye for England. Meet me at The Village Green Hotel in Dunchurch on Tuesday afternoon."

"Dunchurch? That's nowhere near—"

"Exactly. If all goes haywire, no one will think to look for me there. Besides, *Village Green Preservation Society* is one of The Kinks' most brilliant albums. Be prepared to have the information as to where I can find the wife, alone. Meanwhile, can you contact people who have completely crossed over?"

"Like sit down and have a chitchat? Hardly. I couldn't get over here until Rosalyn yanked me. Getting back won't be easy, unless you die. In which case I'm ghost." Peter does a little soft shoe to punctuate his minuscule slang play. Lord, if this works, please let me keep my own sense of humor.

"Don't they provide some type of liaison?"

"Like a crossing guard at a primary school? Oh, sure. Instead of a big red Stop sign they carry one that says 'Hold Please', oh so politely. Are you barmy?"

"I wonder if my friend could help us." At the thought I start humming "Ain't That a Shame." Why didn't I think of Steven before?

Peter

Niles has just answered my question. He is indeed nuts. "You want to call a psychic?"

"No, Steven's a dead, seven-year-old kid who used to play with me. Every now and again he still visits."

Steven? No, it's not poss— "Tell me more about this Steven. And why are you humming that song?"

"Steven hums it all the time. He told me hearing it was the only thing that made him happy while he was sick."

Yes, and entertaining him during his illness is the reason I started singing. "Would that Internet device have pictures of me at his age?" Niles gives me a funny look. Did he drink spoiled milk?

"It might. Why?" I motion the slow lad to the computer. He goes to some colorful site with a funny name and types, *Peter Lane childhood photo*. A bunch of snaps pop up. Niles may be unfazed by me, but now it looks as if he's seen a ghost. "How the heck?"

"Steven is my twin brother. He used to watch out for me. If he's doing the same for you, he probably knows what's going on. How do you reach him?"

"Sometimes he appears when I think about him a lot. I'll try to reach him. Meanwhile, pop in on Rosalyn and make sure she's okay. Tell her I miss—Don't tell her what's going on. If all this fails, I don't want to hurt her all over again."

Rosalyn

Warm water sprays down on me, washing away a fraction of my pain. So many sleepless nights have taken their toll that even the simplest task leaves me fatigued. Joseph's birthday is fast approaching, making me an emotional wreck.

With the push of the knob, the water halts. Purple Egyptian cotton embraces me, and a memory of Joe helping me out of the shower the day I went into labor hits. I miss what we had—the rat bastard. With the force of anger my hands *smack* the shower door open. I *shriek* in surprise as I step out and literally walk in to Peter. The towel falls, causing my nerves to frazzle while I scramble to cover myself. "Damn it, Peter! You have a talent for picking the worst times." I don't know if I'm more embarrassed or frustrated.

"Sorry. I'm depressed." Without the slightest reaction to my peep show his butt *plops* onto the toilet seat.

I quickly tighten the towel around me. "What's got you so worked up?"

"Since I've time on my hands I went to one of those big department stores and looked at the new electronic doodads. I expected to be overjoyed by my findings."

The towel stays tightly wrapped as I slip on my bathrobe. God, I'm so embarrassed! At least when he walked in on me with the vibrator he was clueless as to what I was doing and didn't see anything. There is nothing like a man discovering you naked to make you forget your woes and feel fat. "You weren't impressed by the technological advancements of the last fifty years?"

"That part was amazing. It's what I saw on those enormous TVs that's got me." His elbow hits his thigh at the *smack* of his chin into his palm. "I can't believe we've been so foolish as to get ourselves into yet another war. Also, did you know they're poisoning your food? They claim it's to help end hunger, which makes perfect sense because in doing so they'll kill everyone off."

My words groan out. "Thanks. I needed that dose of cheer."

"I take it you're rightfully still upset from the other day."

The water that sprays behind me as I brush my hair has a perkiness I can't even dream of. I blot my damp tips, then watch the towel as it sags from my fingers and drops onto the counter. Its bleak drape mocks me. "I know Niles didn't mean it, still ... Add in that I miss yet another guy who hurt me, and that I can't seem to take more than a baby step forward at a time, and I'm more disappointed in myself than him."

Peter's gaze races toward me. "Really? You actually miss him? So you're not seeing that Shane fellow again?"

"With all of the madness in my life it's kind of nice to have someone to hang out with." I take a good long look in the still steamy mirror while hating the facts of my existence. "I need to move forward at some point."

"What exactly does that mean?"

Great question. "Peter, I need to get ready for work. Would you mind?" I nod towards the door.

Peter drags himself off of his seat. His lips are pressed together tightly, not in a pucker but more like in a sign of annoyed concern. "Promise me you'll be careful, okay?"

His image fades at my nodding. I bend over to grab my hair dryer out of the cabinet. "That's a rather lovely view," his voice calls out from behind. "I was hoping you would've lost the robe by now."

"Damn it, Peter! Get out!"

"Enjoy your day." As his voice trails off, I chuckle along

with him.

MILES

The shine of my shoes blends with the sheen of an oil slick on the pavement. Was coming dressed like I am prepared for a day in court a wise move? What looks scarier to a woman who has spent nearly fifty years in hiding, a ratty thug or a man in a well-tailored suit? Doris puts a hand to my shoulder. "Slow your pace." She's right. Fast clicking heels sound threatening.

The house is small with a yard free of clutter, yet a broken gutter hangs off the roof. Lively, classical piano music floats through the windows. Except for the dry, desert heat, the setting is unassuming enough to be tucked in the backwoods of Anytown, USA.

"Remember what we discussed on the flight." Doris's hushed tone contains the firmness of a warning. We have one shot, and lately I've been striking out in the tact department.

Surprisingly, my knock is readily answered. Since people in hiding are generally cautious when opening a door, I scan her for a gun. Instead, a German Shepard sits attentively at her feet. Don't dogs usually bark when strangers approach? Still, he's right by her side, licking his chops and ready to eat me for dinner if so instructed. This woman is cautious, but she's hardly paranoid.

Ms. Mills is comfortably dressed in un-tattered jeans and a soft-blue blouse. Her silvery-blonde hair is neatly clipped, thus exposing a face that's lightly made-up. She appears to want to look respectable, even if it's only for a walk around the block. Our business cards are already in my hand so she doesn't have to wonder why I'm reaching into a pocket. "Ms. Mills?"

"No, you have the wrong address." It's said flatly and without the slightest trace of an accent. How odd that she has yet to shut the door.

I brave it up and try not to sound like I completely don't believe her while exhibiting camaraderie. "My name is Niles Barton. This is my associate, Mrs. Doris Clayburn. We work for a legal firm in California." I offer our cards, yet Ms. Mills stays in her fortress. She looks at Doris like she's an odd part of a complex equation. "We're here on a personal matter. A friend was caused great financial damage by a former employer of Ms. Mills and is trying to recover his losses. Do you know anyone who ever worked in England for—"

The door flies open, and I'm yanked inside the house. Quickly she shuts the door behind Doris and I. The dog, whose teeth are now quite visible, begins sniffing me in the most uncomfortable of places. "How did you find me?" Ms. Mills demands while still gripping my arm. A *growl* occurs so close to my crotch that my balls are warmed by dog breath. Cautiously I raise my open hands while looking into the eyes of Rin Tin Tin's evil twin.

"Through desperation. I wouldn't trouble you if this wasn't something that I felt to be important."

"Take off your coats," she demands.

Doris and I obey by handing over our jackets then slowly turning so she can see we don't have weapons. With my hands still signing a request to keep the dog at bay, I lift my pant legs to reveal nothing but shoes and socks. Ms. Mills pats our coats before flipping them over her arm. "Your card claims you are a paralegal. Isn't that like a secretary? Why are you here?" she asks Doris as if her presence is a crime.

"I came to assist Niles."

I continue Doris's display that, unlike the prior boss of Ms. Mills, I have a respectful relationship with my employees. "Mrs. Clayburn is a valuable asset to my work. She often provides insight I am incapable of finding."

Doris gets eyed over. "Well, aren't you a lucky one. Go on." We are motioned toward a worn, yet clean, tan sofa that sits in front of a window with frilly curtains inside a light grayish-green living room. Numerous happy moments in the form of family photos cover the walls. I sit farthest away from the chair in which Ms. Mills sits, thus lessening my threat. Regardless, as soon as the dog takes a seat next to his master, his eyes are right back on me. He's salivating as if I'm a raw steak.

I dive into my story. I try not to sound rushed, but I have to move forward before Ms. Mills gets scared and tosses us out. Her face contorts through a myriad of emotions over how my friend was robbed and basically left to starve. I leave out the little detail that he was also killed.

"Who's your friend? Maybe I know him."

Idiot! You spent so much time developing your character you forgot to learn your lines. Just mash two celebrities together. Use, uh, Ray Davies and that cute girl from *Here We Go Round the Mulberry Bush*. "Ray Geeson. He's a musician who was promised the moon and back."

"Doesn't surprise me in the least. Ben would screw anyone, one way or another. He even screwed the only tailor that could properly fit his sloppy gut. Ben's a weasel. If you tracked me down, you're well aware of what he did."

My eyes meet those of Doris, and I get a nod to proceed. We have an agreement. If Doris starts talking, my trap gets locked shut. "Honestly, I don't have proof of anything, but I'm assuming he did something to make it easier for you to leave than stay. I only hope he didn't threaten you like he did others."

Doris gives me a subtle thumbs up. Whew.

"Oh, he threatened me all right. I thought I had the stomach flu, but that little snake recognized my pregnancy signs before I did. Ben was conveniently called out of the country while my replacement handed me a substantially sized severance check. A visitor then greeted me at my apartment. He wanted to be sure that I never contacted Ben again, regardless of the reason. His eyes were on my stomach the entire time as he said, 'Well, lady, you got what you wanted. You can go get that problem fixed now.' I know damn well Ben gave me that check because he dared to think that getting an abortion and cashing out was my end goal. That's how he sees women."

Now is a great time for this male to lock his lips. With a single look I request Doris chime in. "Ms. Mills, I can only begin to imagine what that must have been like. You showed great strength in having his child. If you felt strongly about the man, I'm sure it hurt all the more. I'm very sorry that happened to you. No woman should go through that."

"Thank you, but it taught me I could either wallow in misery or move on in strength. I never even cashed the bastard's check." She points to a frame on the wall, and I pop up to take a closer look, forgetting about the sharp canine teeth that long to devour me. Sure enough, it's a check made out to Harriet Mills for five thousand pounds, signed by Stoddard himself. That was a hell of a lot of money in nineteen sixty-six. To think she relocated thousands of miles away and had a child, all without cashing that check. The strength this woman has shown is unfathomable.

"Good for you, Ms. Mills." Doris beams as if the pride is her own. "I can't even begin to tell you how much respect I have for you."

"Thank you. Please call me Harriet. You're very lucky to have a boss who values you enough to let you speak."

Excellent. Keep keeping your trap shut, Niles.

"And how are you now, Harriet? You seem to be without need."

"That's far from true. I need to see that horse's ass burn in Hell, which is the root of why you're here. What is it you want?"

Doris wipes off her sympathetic smile and brings on a braver, proud woman face. "Ms. Mills, would you be willing to make a statement saying you had an affair with Mr. Stoddard and he is the same person listed on the birth certificate? Without that statement, if his wife divorces him, she won't get a penny. She's either stuck with him or out on the street."

"Are you kidding? I was a slave to working and raising a

child for years by myself because of that asshole. David's father should've helped our son through his life. That coward needs to burn."

Niles, you are a real dirt bag for betraying Rosalyn's trust in such a blatant fashion. Steven has got to help Peter with that contact. What you're doing now just isn't enough.

When Angels Sing

Peter

This is rubbish. How is it Niles is able to contact my brother but I can't? If I'm meeting with an angel, or a ghost, or whatever Steve is now, why am I on a street corner in El Segundo?

I lean on a lamppost and wonder what all the mystery is about. It's been ages since I've seen Steve. I've missed the guy. Is he still a boy or has he grown?

A tug comes on my sleeve. Excitement hits me in the gut as I spin around and give what looks like a mirror's reflection of myself a hug. Finally I'm able to make some type of physical contact with another being. "Steve, how I've missed ya! How are ya?"

He rubs my arms then pats them heartily. All the while his smile brings back happy childhood memories. That is, until he swallows heavily, and concern blankets his face. "I'm good, but you're not. All I can do now is push you in the right direction before I finally move on. You made a shady deal with the dark part of the other side, and it's biting you in the bum. Niles is right. Stop falling for trickery. Stoddard has earned his place in the pits of the afterlife, but your desire to right a wrong could earn you yours." He points to a shop across the road with a big red and green sign. "Head that way. Goodbye, Pete."

Is he kidding? After all these years I get a brush off. "Wait, Steve. There is so much I want to say. So much I want to hear."

"I love you, mate. Mum and Dad have moved on and are great. Now it's my turn. Everyone is great, except you. Go make us proud." Steve fades away. With a heavy sense of defeat and anger toward myself I head off to the 7-Eleven.

MILES

Damn it, Peter, you were supposed to meet me here yesterday afternoon. Why is it you pop in at the most annoying times yet when I need you—

I catch a glimpse of the hotel room clock. Crap! It's 10 A.M. already. Asking Peter to chat with the other side was stupid. If he got trapped, I'm screwed and ... and I can't bring myself to think about the rest, other than he's gonna be pissed off as hell if this mission doesn't get completed.

Screw it! I'm off to Stoddard's place without him.

The lovely manor in Henley-on-Thames is unapologetically built like a fortress. Cameras around the perimeter boldly announce it is under heavy surveillance. Add in the fact it's tucked up on a hill and it's one tough place to watch discretely.

I'm parked halfway down the road with my surveillance gear pointing out the back window. I'll be barely able to catch warning if someone leaves Stoddard's house. My jittering stomach makes the ham sandwich I nibble tough to choke down, but I'm attempting to look like a random guy on a lunch break.

The monitor in the seat next to me shows a big guy on the approach. My inclination is to race off, but that will raise even more flags. Instead I hang fire and use a remote to re-aim my camera so it's looking at the house down the hill. As the big man with the dark sunglasses steps up I roll down the window, slip him a smile, and raise my hand in a wave. "Hey."

"I'm part of the neighborhood watch program. Mind telling me what you're doing here? You're making the neighborhood a little nervous."

"I am?" I ask oh-so-innocently. "Sorry. I'm visiting from America and got a little lost. The countryside looked lovely so—"

"So you decided to drive out here of all places?"

"I was raised a country boy."

The big guy looks at my designer suit and curls up a side of his lip into his nose. His arms cross, and I'm reminded of a roadblock.

"Okay, you got me. Isn't this where a bunch of big rock stars live? You wouldn't happen to know where George Harrison's estate is, would you?"

His eyes go off of me and catch a glimpse of the monitor. The cool steel of a gun barrel gets pressed against my temple. "Out!" he demands. So much for respecting England's gun laws. Slowly I reach one hand down to open the door while the other stays in his view. I slide out with cautious movements. My hands are placed against the side of the car before being asked. With the gun still aimed at my head his free hand searches me. "Okay, mate. What's the real story?"

A good lawyer always comes prepared with the truth and an angle. A great schemer prepares like a lying lawyer. "I'm a lawyer from The States doing some research for a client. My business card is in my left jacket pocket. I'm investigating Lionel Jones who lives down the block."

"Since when do lawyers get their hands dirty? I thought only detectives did stuff like that."

Damn it. I'm jittering. Look at his eyes, not at the gun. "I'm a corporate lawyer. My client never buys anything without knowing who they are buying from. You know how paranoid Americans are, which is why I don't trust investigators."

Backup arrives and begins searching the car. With a *smash* and a *stomp* my equipment is destroyed, thus increasing my bill for services rendered. The new guy digs under the seat. If they find the slit cut in the carpet where the affidavit is stored, I'll be seeing Peter on the other side.

He comes up empty and heads for the trunk where he

finds the decoy—my briefcase containing papers that show Lionel Jones is interested in selling some American-based assets. Doris's hourly rate just doubled.

The gun-toting big guy practically shoves me back inside the car. "You'll be on your way now."

I don't argue.

Heads I Win, Tails You Lose

Peter

Some things never change. Stoddard's tactics are so old I swear the same goons still work for him.

Once he's had a chance to steady his pulse I pop in on Niles. "Well, that was foolish! You could have been killed." The car swerves. You'd think this chest-clutching bloke would be used to me by now. "Do you have a medical condition?"

Niles pants while saying, "You are so, so lucky that you got *most* of the anger. When you didn't show I feared the worst and tried to implement the plan anyway."

"Aw, you'd do that for me? Makes me all toasty inside. Thanks, mate." I pat the old boy on the back and his shoulder bounces forth a tad with each tap. "Anyway, I just spent a spell watching the old broad get ready for a lunch appointment." I shiver at the memory of how she looks like a shriveled old piece of chicken skin. "She's not the right bird she used to be! Anyway, stay on this road a spell, and we can join her. We need to grab her while—"

Niles's eyes shift toward his shoulder and then back at me. It's about bloody time he caught on.

NILES

Either I've gone off the deep end or there's been a major turn of events. "Waiiiit a minute. Did you just …"

Peter fades, but this voice carries through. "While I was off taking care of your little request, I learned a few things." The glove box appears to open without help. The car's rental agreement flies out and rips in two. Each half then flips aside.

"You're fully functional!"

201

"I've something else." Peter reappears, rolls down his window, and catcalls a girl crossing the street. She checks out her admirer only to watch him vaporize before her very eyes. Her mouth goes agape.

"Amazing!"

"Don't get too excited. I can only stay visible briefly. However, my new abilities do mean I don't need your help. I can simply stroll my ghostly self into Stoddard's place, knock out one of his goons, and borrow his gun. However …" Peter taps his fingers on the door. Could it be he has come to the conclusion he has been tangoing with Hell?

"However you've come to learn that Rosalyn means more to you than any crazy revenge you have deluded yourself into thinking is insurance?"

"Yeah, this odd division of emotions has me acting like the female of the species on special, monthly occasions. It's now so clear I only need to be as close to my true self as possible and all will fall into place."

I have to wonder what Peter's true self really is. Once more, "Peter, after all this happens, will I be more like you or will I stay like me?"

A moment passes while Peter ponders the question that seems to perplex us both. "I don't know, really. Jane's not much different from before in that the same things make her heart sing. Whether you and I care to admit it we're already very much alike—determined to be happy, get what we deserve, and take care of Jane. The only difference is I have love on my side. I figure that's the only part of you that will really change when I die." Peter's voice chokes. "When I die… ," he mutters softly. "Make a right at the corner. Mrs. Stoddard is due at Badgemore Park any moment."

"Yes, and you'd better make ghostlike so only I can see you, else you may cause a scene—especially in those clothes. Men haven't worn brocade and frills for nearly half a century."

Peter eyes his swanky jacket and fluffs the frills on his sleeves. Outside the window stands a guy in a tattered grey hoodie and cut-offs that slide down to his hips, thus exposing the plaid glory of his boxers. "Damn pity. If I'd known what crimes I'd be exposed to under the guise of fashion, I may have very well stayed dead."

Inside the restaurant I request a corner table so we can watch the entire room. When Mrs. Stoddard arrives she's guided straight to where a friend awaits her arrival. Damn.

Twenty minutes and two glasses of champagne later her friend finally makes for the powder room. Thankfully we are in an expensive place so the women don't feel the need for safety in numbers. I slip into the recently vacated seat. "Mrs. Stoddard?"

"Yes," she says hesitantly. A wicked, pink-painted smile blooms as her eyes run up and down me. Her teeth capture her lip so hard I expect to see blood. "May I help you?" This time Peter did exaggerate. The skin of the perfectly made-up woman is tight for her age, presumably from plastic surgery. This tells me a lot about her ego and bodes well if I need to resort to using my insurance policy.

"I'm sorry to trouble you, but I need to speak to you about your husband."

Her gaze sours. "If you're here to see if I will give my husband a demo recording of your little brother's band, forget it. Ben got out of that part of the business a long time ago."

I slide her my business card. "Actually, my presence here is intended to benefit you. I've caught wind of some nasty rumors about your husband's behavior over the years. I also know you signed a very strict prenup. I have a way to get you around it, if you are interested."

Her head cocks to the side, and her grey-blue eyes narrow. She's summing me up. Her eyes then widen and get a little bit of a gleam. "You have my attention. Please, carry on." Before she can blink, a copy of the affidavit is slid under her nose with all of the key points highlighted. "Harriet Mills? I always wondered what happened to her." Her eyes float back and forth several times before she flips to the last page and sees that it is unsigned. After a beat of thought her head pops up for our eyes to meet. "You must take me for a fool. This can't possibly be real." Her glare at me intensifies. I remain expressionless. Her eyes dart back to the first page, and she resumes her reading.

"The signed version of the affidavit is notarized. Also, here is a recorded confession stating all of the information is true." I pull out my phone along with a headset and play a video of Ms. Mills boldly revealing everything.

Mrs. Stoddard's features appear to have locked. Her mouth barely moves as she speaks. "My God, that is Harriet. She was such a fantastic secretary. I knew when my asshole husband let her go something was up." Mrs. Stoddard's eyes rise to mine, her features softened in respectful disbelief. "And she never cashed that check? That would have been a fortune to her." Her harsh expression returns. "What do you want in exchange for the signed copy?"

"Normally, my fee would be five hundred dollars, plus travel time, airfare and accommodations. To make a legitimate business deal I only need to charge for the affidavit. However, I have to ask you for an additional five hundred and seventy-eight thousand, eight hundred and twenty-three pounds in cash."

The paper gets tossed down and her defenses go back on the rise. "That is one very odd, and surprisingly low, number given my husband's wealth. What is the significance, and what are the hidden requirements?"

I pull up my sleeves and the backs of my hands hit the table. My palms open in an expression of showing there is nothing hidden. "Two things." I raise an index finger. "It is believed your husband made some deals that had negative impacts on my friend's life. Though he's entitled to far more, that sum would be enough to recover from a major loss. I seek that sum and not a penny more." Frankly, I don't care about the money. It's a bargaining chip, and that odd number is getting the attention I intended.

Mrs. Stoddard's fire is quelled by my straightforwardness. Still she gives nothing away. "Who is your friend?"

I try to out poker face her. "It is for the estate of Peter

Lane."

Her eyes tick open just enough for me to register her shock. Clearly she knows the story. "Yes," she says, hesitantly. "My husband definitely did know Mr. Lane. His untimely death was tragic." Remorse rings in her voice. She seems to be confessing on her husband's behalf.

"Lastly," I say, adding a second finger to stress my two points, "you need to get Mr. Stoddard to confess being involved in Mr. Lane's murder while I record it. You will immediately receive the only copy."

Mrs. Stoddard laughs so hard it draws attention. "And how do you propose I do that? My husband may be somewhat vocal about his business dealings, but he would never confess, let alone allow you to record it, unless there's a gun to his head. You'd better pull the trigger because he'd never let you get away with it."

I keep my poker face on, which is difficult because I am far from fearless, and I'm about to get really ballsy. "In order to tap into your home surveillance system all I need is for you to slip me an IP address, the type of software used, and the password. Unless the data is being backed up to a cloud, I can easily be in and out without detection. The recording will go straight to a flash drive, which is yours to sit on or use to strike a deal with the government. You can give them the recording in exchange for immunity."

"It would never hold up in court."

I hold my ground with the addition of giving a devilish grin. "How is you accessing your own surveillance system not legal? Even if it got dismissed, it will make Mr. Stoddard's life hell. Isn't that actually better?"

Her little grin shows it sounds appealing, but she's tapping her foot. Nerves are kicking in. "How do I know you won't keep a copy and turn it in before I can?"

"You don't, except for the fact I'm acting under a code of ethics. The small amount of money I am requesting reflects it. It goes to a deserving person and the drive goes to you. Besides, I suggest you just mention Peter. Your husband's ego will probably take care of the rest. Can Mr. Stoddard prove that you know he's responsible for the deaths of Mr. and Mrs. Lane?"

"He's never let me anywhere near anything to do with his business. He probably assumes I'm too stupid to connect the dots, but frankly, I'm not sure the payoff is worth the risk. Young man, you have no idea who you are dealing with— who *I* am dealing with. Besides, my life is rather cozy. If you'll excuse me …"

She stands to leave. Time to whip out the insurance policy. "What if I showed you just how cozy his life is?" I slide a picture of Stoddard and a girl nearly fifty years younger right under her nose. "Mrs. Stoddard, meet Natasha Borskev, twenty-seven years old, five-foot-ten, one hundred and—"

Her butt hits the chair. "Stop! I especially don't need to know the last part. Why that little snake! We have a granddaughter that age!"

She stares at the girl in the photo who is snuggled up to Stoddard as they step into a cab. An umbrella in his hand shelters her from the elements. "He used to do that for me. I've spent the last forty years waiting for it to happen again while he's paraded around town as if I don't exist. I never wanted my life to be a game of cat and mouse. As much as I needed the money I did once love him. Love can only survive so much, and his deceit broke us." Her eyes hide behind hooded lids. "So Harriet gets nothing out of this?"

"All she wants is for you to break free like she did."

"If I were strong enough to break free like she did I wouldn't need her affidavit, and I certainly would not have signed a document supposedly only to help my husband maintain the image of a rock and roll lifestyle."

Yep, stay cool and calm and the slam dunk always follows. "Off the record, Mrs. Stoddard. I suggest you settle your divorce before going public with the recording, if you so choose. This way if his assets are frozen, you're already in the clear."

Mrs. Stoddard laughs. "Now wouldn't that be a double

whammy. Actually, let's take these negotiations a little further and make it a triple." Under the table, a foot slides up my leg and into my most private of areas. She's kidding, right?

As if she could hear my thoughts, her eyes give me a good once over—twice—while licking her lips. Her painted-on eyebrows cock, showing me that she is serious. I just about gulp my tongue down my throat. "But what about your prenup?"

"What about it? To Ben it's just a game to make me work harder. The only thing that prenup does is keep this ring glued onto my finger and my personal bank account dry. You came prepared, so I am betting that you are desperate. We can either finalize this deal elsewhere, or we can part ways right now. What shall it be?"

Oh, dear God.

This Wheel's on Fire

NILES

In my efforts to become normal I have done a lot of stupid things. One time I read about a guy who was so tired of being lonely he took a razor blade to his arm. He said when he saw the blood he realized that he loved life, so I put in a couple of gashes to see if it would wake me up inside.

It didn't.

What I am about to do now may be less dangerous, but it's about as ridiculous. Mrs. Stoddard slinks out of the bathroom and eyes me like I'm dessert with a double helping of chocolate sauce. Her updo has been let down, revealing long, blonde locks that obscure much of her face, thus making her not half bad ... for pushing seventy.

Not half-bad? Niles, are you crazy?

I hand her a glass of champagne and toast to her health, leaving out the part we are doing it because I fear she'll soon have a heart attack and our vile fling will make the papers. I sip along with her, then turn my back and down the glass while reaching for a refill. Mrs. Stoddard takes a seat on the bed and pats the spot next to her. I gulp more bubbly to push down the sick.

Maybe it'll help if I stop thinking of her as Mrs. Stoddard. I was on to something with the hair. Who else has hair that color? Courtney Stodden? No, she's too plastic, which makes her kind of gross. What non-gross actress does Mrs. Stoddard look like? Glenn Close? No-ho-ho-ho-ho, still not gonna do that.

I loosen my noose of a tie, down the second glass of champagne, and take a seat next to her while forcing a smile and trying to hide the wince that accompanies it. Okay, try again, and make her British in case she talks, else the illusion will be broken.

A blonde, British actress who's a little older ... Joanna Lumley from *Absolutely Fabulous*. I can handle Joanna Lumley, especially if we are talking about when she was in *Sapphire & Steel* with the fake Russian dude from *Man From U.N.C.L.E.* Okay, look only at her hair and think she's Joanna Lumley, circa nineteen seventy-nine.

Joanna Lumley grabs me by the collar and yanks me down on top of her. She wraps her legs around my waist and slams her crotch against mine with a *growl*. My eyes widen in fear as my tie gets ripped off without shame or pretense, nearly strangling me in the fervor. With lightning-fast movements she rips at my shirt, sending its buttons flying. One steals my attention as it *pings* off of the wall. Her fingers claw at my chest, and I'm reminded of a woman jumping into a lake after she hasn't bathed for months.

Dear Lord, help me!

Joanna reaches around the back of my head and yanks so our lips smack together. I'm grateful that I sprung for the swanky hotel because she tastes of mouthwash from the little samples they leave in the bathroom. Mercifully, she releases some of the pressure and her lips soften. Her tongue finds mine in a surprisingly sensual kiss.

You know, this situation could be a lot worse. If she keeps this up ...

Maybe I am looking at this the wrong way. Maybe I can learn something from this woman. Okay, this is a training mission with Joanna Lumley, nineteen seventy-nine, who tastes of mouthwash and kisses like a goddess.

With a surprising amount of force she rolls me onto my back and straddles me, pressing her crotch against mine with strokes that are long and carnal. She's already moaning. I hate to admit it, but if this really were Joanna Lumley, nineteen seventy-nine, it would be hot as Hell.

Joanna's lips leave. As she pushes herself off of my chest

I get a good look at Mrs. Stoddard, and reality slips down my stomach and churns it. Her long, pink nails claw at my skin, leaving a trail of red. She goes for my belt as if she's in a race against her own mortality. The way the light hits her face tells mortality may be winning. What kind of hell have I gotten myself into?

What will I tell Rosalyn when she asks what we did to take care of Stoddard? What if leaving out the part about banging a fake Joanna Lumley, nineteen seventy-nine, comes back to haunt me? Rosalyn may be going out with Shane now, but damn it, I feel like I'm cheating on her. I'm so capable of guilt that I should turn Catholic.

With a swift unzip Joanna's hands go for my underwear. She's not concerned I still have pants on. Dear God, please help!

Kisses hit my navel, followed by a tongue that slinks down the trail that leads to my—oh God, she's already got her hand on my crotch! It's nineteen seventy-nine and Joanna Lumley has her hand on my crotch. It's nineteen seventy-nine and Joanna Lumley is yanking down my pants. It's nineteen seventy-nine and Joanna Lumley is cupping my balls. It's nineteen seventy-nine and Joanna Lumley's lips are about to—

Wetness touches my manhood, and everything inside me silently screams, "Gah!"

Click.

"Hello, Annie. Missed me?" Joanna Lumley looks up, and I'm barely able to cup my hand over her mouth in time to stop her from screaming at Peter who hovers above while holding my phone. "Well, isn't this quite the ghastly sight? I thought a pesky little prenup would prevent this from happening."

Joanna Lumley jumps up from the bed and grabs her blouse that I didn't even realize she had ripped off. She holds it against her chest, suddenly very embarrassed while Peter types on the phone and the *swoosh* of an email being sent rings through the air. I wipe the spit off of me and smear it onto my pants. I zip them so quickly my boxers get caught. Joanna

Lumley, nineteen seventy-nine, makes for the door.

"Please," Peter says, "don't let me interrupt your business deal. I believe the two of you were about ready to reach," he clears his throat, "an agreement. In fact, I am certain you were just about to tell my friend here that you would be absolutely delighted to assist him in his *needs*."

Peter's pathetic efforts at rubbing this in have my lips pursing and my fists tightening in a desire to let him have it. It's pretty impressive. No one has ever gotten my feathers ruffled.

"Let me out of here!" She reaches for the doorknob.

"Aw, don't break up the party on my account, Annie. Then again, I'm sure we'll see each other very, very soon."

"We most certainly will not!"

"I wouldn't count on that. Oh, how I love the technology of this modern world. You see, the snap I just took on this little device was sent off for safe keeping. Since I'm kind of stuck on this side of the rainbow until your assistance comes through, while my friend is deciding what to do next with the photograph, I'll just keep paying you visits at the most unsightly of times until you either assist him or he turns that photo public. Stoddard will have no choice than leave you behind without a pence."

As much as I kind of want to smack Peter with every drop of that five percent of our anger I have I'm pretty damned grateful for what he's done. I just wish he had arrived a few minutes sooner. I hand Mrs. Stoddard the address and room number of the hotel where we're staying. "Within twenty-four hours, drop all of the information along with the time that you will have Mr. Stoddard in his office to get the confession. After that's done, simply pick up the drive and the signed affidavit. I'll delete all copies of the picture, and you will never hear from us again."

"And if he fails to talk?"

I shrug, oh so innocently. "A picture is worth a thousand words, or several million pounds, depending how you look at it."

Mrs. Stoddard rips the card with the information out of my hand and flees toward the door. She stops shy of turning the knob, adjusts her skirt, holds her head high and gives her hair a shake before heading off and shutting the door with dignity.

"Gah!" I cringe all over, repeatedly stomping my foot to shake off the heebee jeebies. "Where were you? I want to rip off my clothes and burn them while soaking my body in alcohol!"

Peter flings the phone at me. I catch it as it smacks into my gut. "Since it was clear you were failing miserably I went back to Stoddard's place to see if I could mess with the system. I figured I could try to spook the information out of him by doing a little of the old, now you see me, now you don't, but I didn't have any luck. I'd no choice but to return and watch that disgusting display until you, or rather, she finally sucked it up."

"You were here the whole time?" I squirm again. With how my arms are flailing I must look like a six-year-old girl. "Couldn't you have taken that photo when she first kissed me?"

"Why, yes, I *could* have. Are we leaving now or are you staying to dream of what romance may have bloomed?"

Swiping the bottle of champagne, I guzzle while heading for the elevator.

Now we wait.

Tired of Waiting for You

Peter

Aren't we supposed to find peace when we die? I've spent the last few decades completely on edge and wondering when everything will come to fruition. Today that feeling has reached the highest of highs.

My thumbs twiddle, my feet pace, and then my arse bounces on the bed. I'm doing anything I can to pass the time. Niles continues to shoot me silent glares, implying I've put him on the verge of madness. Yet he just lies there reading a book on some electronic doodad. Every now and again he mumbles something at it like, "I can't believe you did that!" or "What the hell is wrong with you?"

"Dear God, man. What is it you're reading?"

"*Out Of The Box.*" His eyes stay intently on the thing.

"Is that one of those silly, self-help books?"

"No, it's a romance novel."

"A what? Like the ladies read?"

He nods without giving himself the trouble of looking up at me. "I always read romance novels."

"That's just blooming crazy."

"Not at all. The guys in these things are always screwing up, thus showing me how not to act. Romance novels have saved my ass many a time."

"Not recently they haven't."

A big, red 3 A.M. glows on the nightstand's clock. Someone is bound to show soon. Annie Stoddard wouldn't be stupid enough to send the information to Niles's phone, would she? Apparently it's "traceable." I've half a mind to nab it and check myself.

"You know, we have scarcely three days until the weekend.

Rosalyn's been talking of moving forward and probably has another date. Maybe I should do something to—"

"Stop reminding me, Peter. I'm concerned about that date she had with Shane, too. Girls like Rosalyn don't often give second chances. If I'm going to persuade her to forgive me, I've got to go in armed for battle. Disregard your emotions else we may fail. Just ask my opponents in court who can't hold it together."

I really blew it with this guy when I kept most of the anxiety. I thought that would play out in my favor so I'd never waste time. Little did I know it would chap my bum.

Finally, the light that shines through the bottom crack of the door is obstructed and an envelope is slid underneath. I jump for it, but Niles puts out a hand and *shhs* me silent.

NILES

Feet rush down the hallway. With the envelope in hand I resume my position on the bed. Since the delivery guy wanted to get away quickly I grant him a respectful moment to do so. Meanwhile, Peter stands so close to me that personal space is nonexistent.

Mrs. Stoddard came through with every piece of information requested. They're using StarFire Security's well-known program. IP address 160.13.245.98. Username is Emily. Passcode is WOT121067. Below that is the time of 10 A.M., Friday—as in more than twenty-four hours from now.

"Not a peep out of you," I warn Peter. With the flick of the bedspread to cover me, my eyes close off the world, yet the sound of Peter's impatience kills my quest for slumber. What if he's right about Rosalyn? Will my fate be like that of *The Graduate*, running into a chapel to stop her from marrying the wrong guy? Would she run off with me only for us to get those same looks on our faces that Elaine and Benjamin do, thus signaling that once the battle is over the thrill is gone?

Peter's gaze on me seems to penetrate through the darkness. He says he and I act in extremes because we don't have the necessary tools to counterbalance our emotions.

When all this goes down, how balanced will I be? "Hey, Peter. Why didn't you kill Stoddard while you were alive?"

My body tilts slightly to the right in response to a sudden dip in the bed. Peter takes pause before responding. "You know, the thought never occurred to me. When I had Jane and my music, even if all else was going to hell I was pretty happy. Then I only wanted justice. Jane would be so disappointed in me now."

"Don't worry, Peter. We'll make her proud. Meanwhile, I want to hear all of your stories from the time you were signed onward, especially if they involve Jane."

Poet's Problem

Rosalyn

A guy who looks like Mr. Clean asks, "And what do you do, Jacqueline? You must be some type of model or actress, right?"

Why did we do this to ourselves? We thought if we came to Mulligan's on a Thursday we could focus on quality conversation.

We were wrong.

"I'm on the marketing team for STN," Jacqueline says to the man with the muscles bulging under his tight, black T-shirt. Every now and again he gives them a little flex and winks at her. Creepy! I'm surprised he hasn't kissed them yet.

"Really? Sporting Today Network? I bet that means you know a lot about what men like." His hand goes to her knee. I cringe on her behalf while she stays cool and continues to look him in the eye like she doesn't notice his advance.

"Actually, I'm head of marketing for women, so it doesn't matter what the big dumb jocks like. However, I can tell you everything the ladies like." Jacqueline leans over and puts her head on my shoulder, then gazes up at me like we are the Dynamic Duo of Sex Goddesses. Poor Darla is so entertained she nearly sprays her drink out of her mouth. Much to Jacqueline's dismay, her will-never-be-suitor doesn't seem to get the hint.

"So, uh, there's a party at my place tomorrow night. Maybe you'd like to come by." His eyes leer at my tits as he asks. Wow. As if the deal hadn't already been sealed that he is out of luck, he's now taken out an insurance policy.

"I'm sorry. I'll be busy with my *friend*." Jacqueline makes a show of giving my hand a squeeze, thus messing with the clueless man.

"Well, I'm sure there is room enough for both of you."

Gross!

Touching our foreheads together, her eyes stare into mine. In their own way they burst with laughter. "Nah. Have a nice night," she tells him. He strolls off, trying to hide his walk of shame.

As soon as he is out of sight Jacqueline's jovial grin fades. With the dip of her finger into her glass she swipes some of the chocolate ganache off of the inside of her Mayan Chocolate Martini and stares before sucking it off. "Why is it so hard to find decent men who appreciate us?" Her solemn tone reflects the darker side of romance. "I know we are just as guilty as they are of checking out the hot ones, but even if a guy who I wasn't attracted to approached me in a genuine fashion, I would at least ask his name and talk to him. Instead, all we get are the creepy freaks who just want to get us in bed."

"Wanna hear something dumb?" Darla says. "I'm depressed because Chris left poetry on my windshield this morning."

"Was it that bad?" I ask.

"Terrible, but in a very sweet way, which is the problem. If he's willing to leave me bad poetry he wrote himself it means he really cares." The ice in Darla's glass crunches as she smacks her straw into it. "He's a great guy. So great I'm scared it's all going to fall apart, you know?"

"All too well," Jacqueline says. "You know what though? Someday that risk will have been worth taking. I know it seems I'll date anyone who comes along, but the truth is I want what my parents have. I want to wake up next to a great guy each morning so we can both complain about how cold it is and try to bribe the other to get up and make coffee. When we are old, I want to be the one who helps him up the stairs while he teases me about my false teeth. And I want kids with him, even if we adopt." She halts to dab the water welling in her eyes. Her voice gets a little shaky. I wish I could do something to give her relief from loneliness. "And when I die, I want be buried next to him after giving him the absolute best I could each and every day. I'm never, ever going to find that if I don't keep taking risks. Believe me, he is out there, and I *will* find him."

I squeeze Jacqueline's hand with the deepest of love and sincerity. "You're right. You will find him. I know you will."

Darla puts down her drink and braves to face her own concerns. "How many of these have I had?"

"Just one that I know of."

"Good, then my resolve is real." Darla rises and grabs her cell phone. "I'm off to make a call. There's someone who illuminated my day, and I'm going to tell him I don't want to wait until Saturday to see him again."

Everyone around me is trudging forward. Darla is daring to hope for her future. No matter how many times she falls on her face Jacqueline refuses to stop looking for Mr. Right. Niles uses his lack of emotions as a reason to be a better person. Meanwhile I get lost in my heart and flail.

Through my foolishness a few things have become abundantly clear. There are no short cuts to healing, but I have to stop dragging my feet. Niles is a beautiful man that I want in my life. He shows strength by attempting to tackle adversity whether it's with his perplexing emotions or by building houses of sugar packets. Deep in my heart I know I can find trust in him. Niles in any capacity is a gift, and I will kick my own ass so I can be a gift to him as well.

Communication Breakdown

NILES

Quarter of ten on Friday morning finally rolls around. Peter hovers over my shoulder. He reads the passcode aloud as I type and then verifies I've tapped the proper keys. My jittery finger hits a three instead of a two and we both jump like it's the end of the ever loving world. What happened to Niles, the cool cucumber?

After entering the last digit I take a deep breath and hit the return key. A seemingly innocuous red message appears.

Invalid login.

Crap!

We begin the process again, hunting and pecking keys to be sure the right ones are hit, calling out the characters as they are tapped, and verifying each one.

Invalid login.

Crap!

"Have we been duped?" Peter asks.

"Slip into the hallway. Check any place where someone could be waiting for us. Also, make sure no door is cracked open where somebody could be watching our door from their room."

My attention turns back to the password. Each character is clearly written, including the distinct line through the zero to show it is not an O. This is exactly what was entered, twice. A third time will end with a system lockout and Stoddard getting a breach of security message. Why would she hand over the wrong code instead of standing me up?

She wouldn't. It wouldn't be worth the risk of getting caught. Either she grabbed a decoy password or this one is encoded.

Peter reappears, his face stern. "The hall is dead. No one in the elevator. Nobody suspicious looking in the lobby. We've been had, haven't we?"

"No. She's got the wrong password, and we've only got fifteen minutes to figure the right one out."

Peter

Figure it out? He's barmy. Either I'll find it myself or it's time for plan B—whatever that is. "Don't go anywhere," I warn Niles. I pop into Stoddard's stodgy office. Somewhere here is the password. He probably left that phony one in a drawer, which likely means there's a safe containing the real one somewhere.

It being in the wall seems too obvious, so I forgo the notion of having a solid body and drop myself halfway down the floor with my feet in the room below and my head still in the office. I look for changes in the structure that feels like muck as I pass through it. Everything seems the same until I reach the area just under Stoddard's desk. Under the floorboards sits a box with enough cash to end hunger in Africa. With the exception of needing a good vacuuming, the floor is clean. However, a piece of paper is taped under the desk drawer, and it has all of his passwords. This can't be real. Stoddard is not that stupid. The fact it shows the same password that Niles has proves it's a decoy. This means Annie's planning on having Mr. BS in here pronto.

I make for the walls, pulling off gold record after gold record, searching for a safe, a list of passwords, or anything of use. The first record has a series of numbers on the back. Could I have gotten so lucky?

No, I'm Peter Lane, and I'm up against Ben Stoddard. Luck does not exist. He makes sure of it.

Each award has writing on the back. Usually it's a bunch of numbers. The one given to Love Machine flares my nostrils. What does seven two seven five eight three mean? If one of these holds the code to that system, how can we tell which one it is?

Anger builds. He doesn't deserve this award, and he doesn't get to keep it. I'll smash it down on the desk and shatter it to bits, hoping the bastard will cut himself while picking up the pieces.

I raise it in preparation for the smash, but something shifts inside and pops out from under the loose backing that was clearly once removed and reattached. A knot hits my stomach as I slide out several photos. The first shows my old flat ablaze. The second is of emergency services pulling out a cloth-covered stretcher with a body on it. Jane sits on a curb, huddled over and screaming.

Oh, my darling, Jane. I'm so very sorry for getting tied up in this mess. I was only trying to stand up for us.

The final photo makes my throat clench. If I had a stomach, I'd be retching. It's a snap of a car on fire in a ditch. I'm barely able to make out the blood-splattered body in the front seat as Jane's. This is what the two guys who were seen walking away from the wreckage were doing. This was their proof that they got her. That sick creep, Stoddard, is keeping trophies!

See Emily Play

MILES

Where the hell is Peter? We're running out of time.

"Out of Time," like The Stones song. I begin humming.

Who could Emily be? The girl he's having an affair with is Natasha. Maybe Emily is code to enter the name of whomever he is seeing at the time.

I begin typing, *N-A-T-A*

Stop. Risking being locked out on an unfounded hunch is mission suicide. Rapidly the keystrokes are deleted and my hands slid under my lap and away from making a foolish move. My humming resumes.

Emily isn't a kid, a grandchild, the wife, his mom, or any of the former secretaries that we came across. A dog? Childhood sweetheart? His version of Rosebud? Was the Rosebud thing really about playing with a sled?

Huh, playing …

Pink Floyd did "See Emily Play." The Zombies did "A Rose For Emily." The Moody Blues had "Emily's Song." What was the other song that had Emily in it? Wasn't there one with some weird name?

I do a quick web search. "Look to the Rainbow (Emily)" by The Airwaves Of Time pops up. That sounds right. My humming changes tune as I lean back.

A click resounds in my head, almost as if I hear it. It sends me popping up to surf to a Wikipedia entry on the band out of Nottingham who just happens to have been produced by Ben Stoddard! Robin Hood may have come to my rescue.

On YouTube I find an old promo shot of the band as they recorded the hit. It starts off with a clapboard with information that smacks my head. *Date: October 12, 1967.* 101267 or, as the English would write it, 121067. This is where the passcode came from. Meaning the leading characters are not WOT, they are AOT, like the band name. He changed a single character so it would be easy to remember.

Take the risk Niles—slowly. Use hunt, peck, and verify.

And ... Deep breath ... Enter.

No lock out message! I'm in!

Leaning back in my chair with a stretch and the crack of my knuckles I shout, "Take that high school jerks who made fun of my music. Loo-sers!"

On my monitor, framed objects float off of the wall, flip about, then return to their places. Peter has to get out of there before Stoddard catches him.

Okay, that's stupid. The guy's a ghost and generally invisible, so why worry?

Because it's Peter, and he gets a little crazy at times. Besides, someone's got to occasionally monitor these feeds, so if I can see those pictures moving, so can they.

Peter

Nothing. I keep coming up with a big nothing as far as a safe goes. However, what I'm finding behind these records is damned depressing. How the hell can we tip off the authorities without it looking like a set up? Besides, when you get right down to it, they prove nothing other than the fact that Stoddard is one sick, creepy little monkey.

Footsteps are on the approach. They sound heavy and determined. The door flies open and a goon bursts in. He sees the award seemingly suspended in the air and snatches it out of my invisible hands. Comically he looks to the ceiling. His brow scrunches as if thinking wires surely must be attached to the frame. I audibly laugh, and he spins around as his search intensifies. "Who's there?" he calls out with a hint of treble in his voice. For once, little old me is the one frightening the big guns. I laugh again. All things do come in good time.

After closing my eyes, because it somehow seems to help, I pop back to the hotel room to find Niles watching Stoddard on his computer monitor. *"What are you doing with that picture?"* Stoddard asks the goon.

"You did it!" I exclaim with a delighted stomp of my foot. "You bloody well did it! How'd you manage?"

The guard says to Stoddard, *"I, uh—it looked like it was about to fall, so I was just—"*

"Get out of here!" Stoddard shouts back. *"It's bad enough I have to deal with my wife in a few minutes."*

"It was actually pretty simple," Niles tells. "The coding system he uses isn't unique."

Stoddard yanks the record out of the goon's hands. The pictures start to slide out of the backing. He shoves them back in. Good, now I know they have his prints on them, but all that does is prove he knows they are there. *"Peter Lane,"* Stoddard says, shaking his head while reattaching the record, *"you are still a pain in the ass."*

"How did he code it?"

"Wait, wait, wait," Niles says, waving a hand to me and drawing himself closer to the monitor.

"Sometimes I wonder if that seven hundred and twenty-seven thousand, five hundred and eighty-three, post-tax pounds I've made off of you from this album alone has been worth it."

So that's what those numbers mean. That filthy little prick!

Stoddard plants his hands on his hips, steps back, and snickers, *"Apparently lighting a guy on fire doesn't lead to true death. I spent far too much money making sure you and your girlie were silenced to have to deal with you again, yet you haunt me anyway. Well, good for you, Mr. Lane. I'm certain I would do the same if you were responsible for my demise. Who knows where things would've gone had it not been for my boy, Pritchard, starting that little fire. Then again, sometimes a dead legend is worth more than a live wire. No one cares about the old and living, but the young and dead—now that gets people to shell out nostalgia money. Thanks for the cash flow."*

"That ruthless bastard!" My hands grip into a mock strangle. "I ought to go back over there and—"

"Peter, wait a second." Niles jumps out of his seat. For the first time I feel true enthusiasm from him. "Didn't you hear? We got it! We got our confession! Mrs. Stoddard could completely fail us, and it won't matter. Pop on over and tell her we are switching to the hotel across the street as a precaution. As soon as I hand her the drive, I'm off to claim Rosalyn whether the merger between you and I happens or not." He holds his hands up to the heavens as if in thanks. The grin on his face is like he's struck gold. "It's always satisfying to win a case but this, this is different. Never before have I won a personal battle. I feel—I *feel* amazing!"

My Mind's Eye

Peter

The bitter reality hits. I'm about to die.

Niles won't have my memories, and our evolution will not allow him to see the world in quite the way I do. The next time my memories will surface is when he passes on. At that point Niles, myself, and all those we have been before will be resurrected. When you die, and the memories of your past lives return, you become the only guest at a family reunion.

It's all lovely and well, but no matter how you look at all the rubbish in the can, with Niles out fooling around with Mrs. Stoddard, doing his business and giving her the hard drive, there's not much longer to write my own epitaph.

Stoddard kept a small fortune under the floorboards. He doesn't need it, but I know a few blokes who are worthy. Given what Stoddard said my old band mates are not likely to be living high on the hog. Like the unkillable spirit that I am, I play Robin Hood by strolling into Stoddard's place and helping myself to the filthy lucre in the floorboards. I laugh while waltzing out the front door. Not only am I liberating part of Stoddard's fortune, I'm well aware if anybody walks by, they'll see a floating bag of cash like in one of those cartoons the kiddies used to watch before the matinee.

After three stops, Peter Lane and his memories can disappear. I went through so much with these guys only to be torn apart by the wicked money machine. We all deserved so much better.

My feet get planted in front of a modest house. The inside is warm and inviting—light tan walls, cozy furniture—yet it's as simple as the outside. Sadly, I've come while Bobby is away. I've missed the old fellow.

Photos grab my attention as I head down the hall. Bobby's managed to have quite the family. At least one of us got that. Farther down is a platinum album—his version of the one Stoddard has on my behalf. Two more reside next to it—the one awarded to John, our drummer, along with mine. Has Johnny passed on? That web doodad of Rosalyn's showed him as alive and living reclusively. How odd.

Where to leave the money? Maybe I should spread it out on the bed so he and the Mrs. can enjoy a tasty romp. Better yet, Bobby always did love a good laugh.

Inside the sun-filled kitchen I create a piece of art. The money gets spread into a circle before I squish a tomato on top, and then finish it with a hunk of cheese. "You can't make pizza without dough, mate. Hope you don't try to bake it."

My core gets tugged from the inside. Niles must have finished with Mrs. Stoddard. Time's ticking away.

Bernie, our keyboard player, passed on a few years back, but his wife is still kicking. Inside a flat somewhere outside of London, a senior-aged woman in a waitress uniform puts on her jacket and tosses her purse over her shoulder before heading to the mantle. With a kiss to her fingertips she touches them to an urn and smiles despite her sad eyes. "Bye, honey. I'll be home in a few hours. Love you." In my mind she turns into a senior version of the Jane that could have been. Life can be so wrong. Everyone deserves someone to stand by their side so they don't have to shed their tears alone.

While standing at attention before the mantle, pain resides heavily in my heart as I salute and solemnly utter, "See you on the other side soon, mate."

My humorous spirit now seems lost, yet I move forward with placing his third of the cash in the produce drawer of the refrigerator. I force a smile and hope his wife will remember how Bern used to refer to money as cabbage.

Now, why does Bobby have Johnny's platinum record?

My thoughts take me to the other side of London. I land in a seedy alley you only ever want to see in films and you certainly don't want to smell. Piss and puke bake in the sun

227

along with sweat from derelicts. Every other time I have tried to come to a person, no matter how odd the path has been, I've been guided in the proper direction. This does not bode well for my old friend.

Trudging onward, my feet seem to step into mud. On the pavement lies an old man, curled on the ground, asleep, and wearing a tattered, old, wool trench coat. His hand barely holds a needle. My friend is nearly unrecognizable, not merely from age and self-abuse, but also from a hearty coating of swill. "Johnny, old boy." I do my best to rattle him awake. "Hey, Johnny. Wake up, it's Pete."

He scarcely moves.

"Hey, Johnny, come on. It's Peter. Peter Lane. Remember me?" Johnny starts to come to. His mouth parts as if in awe of seeing an angel.

"Pe ... Pete?" His voice sounds paved with gravel.

"Yeah, Johnny Boy. It's me."

"I didn't think you'd be the one to greet me in Hell." He groans and rolls back into a fetal position.

Again I rattle him. "Johnny, you're not dead. You need help."

"I'm not?" He sounds disappointed at the fortune of living to see the day.

"Why does Bobby have your award?"

Johnny's brow crinkles as if he hasn't a clue what I'm saying. He then shakes his head and smacks his lips like there's a bad taste in his mouth. "He won't let me have it. What's it really worth to us anyway?"

Why was everything so hard for us? We didn't get what we deserved and nobody wanted to talk about it—not anyone in the industry and certainly none of the authorities. That computer thing Rosalyn has tells people claim the only problem with that last album was it was ahead of its time. What rubbish. Releasing something the world's not ready for only shows everybody else is behind. Sadly, you can't make society catch up to where you are.

Somewhere in there the real lesson lies. My life fell apart

because others weren't ready to hear what I had to say, whether it was musically or regarding the industry's shady ways. People don't want to step outside the comfort of their homes and put themselves on the line by saying anything in the defense of others because the world shuns those who are different. Every now and again someone manages to slip through the cracks of normalcy in a way that gets them heralded as a genius, which generally happens after they've died. Not respecting someone while they are alive is a perverse way of showing respect for the dead. What's so wrong with respect for the living? The lessons we teach our children are abominable.

My generation thought we were destined to change the world. Instead this world hasn't changed a dammed bit. If anything, it's gotten worse. There are ridiculous wars that nobody wants, widespread hunger, and laws still prohibit people from marrying whomever they want. It's damn disgusting, and somehow I need to be a part of change.

The tug toward Niles deepens as my time to act shortens. "Come on, Johnny. Let's get you to the bus. I'm taking you to a friend."

"No." His voice is barely audible. "The only friend I want to see is our father."

"Johnny, come on. Get up and follow me." I try to shake him awake, but I'm fading. I have to get this cash to Bobby along with a note to help Johnny before it's too late.

When I arrive, Bobby stands in the kitchen musing over the pizza. "Bobby? Bobby can you hear me?" Bobby's eyes glance around the room and find nothing unusual. He rattles his noggin. "Bobby, it's Pete. I left the money."

Again he eyes the room in wonder. "Great. Now I'm hearing things. Decades later, all that acid has finally caught up to me."

"Bobby, Johnny really needs you."

"Well," he says, sounding resigned. "At least the voices are friendly. I miss you, Pete."

"Bobby, try to listen. Johnny needs help."

He scoffs. "The Johnny I have thrown into rehab twice to the tune of tens of thousands of dollars? The Johnny who won't come clean? The Johnny whose platinum record I have because I basically stole it from him so that he couldn't sell it for drugs." Shackles seem to weigh his voice. "We were given this great honor, and we all should've been there. Instead it was just me and Stoddard. Now I'm hearing voices. *Humph.* It figures. Nothing ever added up with the four of us."

Bobby's feet *stomp* as he walks out the back door. Outside the kitchen window the flicker of his lighter's flame brings me a shudder, and my eyes slam closed. He's right. We should have all been there. Worse, Johnny could have been, if he cared enough about himself. What can you do when someone doesn't want to be helped? You can only put yourself out there so many times before …

After tossing another handful of cash on the counter, I pop back to Bernie's house and leave the remainder of the money next to his urn. "One more for the road, mate." With the scribble of a note on a scrap off of an old magazine I head back to Niles—home where I belong.

Today Your Love,
Tomorrow The World

NILES

My Camaro races up the hill, its tires screeching with urgency at every turn. My knees jittered the entire flight home, causing me to spend a small fortune on little bottles of alcohol just to keep my sanity. I should have insisted Peter pop in on Rosalyn and tell her I'm on my way with big news. What if I'm too late? What if I never really had a chance? I may have a nice car, beautiful home, and high salary, but when it comes right down to it, Shane has so much more to offer.

But not for much longer.

Tires squeal as I swerve, barely missing a squirrel. After being stuck in L.A. freeway traffic residential streets feel liberating. Finally her house stands before me.

The *click, clomp* of my boots hitting the pavement matches the pounding of my heart as I run to her door. Please be home. Don't be out doing something stupid with Shane.

No, this is Rosalyn. She's not that kind of girl. There's nothing to worry about. Right?

Bam! Bam! Bam! My fist hits the door. If anyone's home, they're going to kill me for running up like the block is about to combust. Footsteps race up to the other side of the barrier that flies open to reveal Jacqueline. "Niles? What the hell?"

"I need to see Rosalyn."

Jacqueline shakes her head like I'm a hopeless case that won't go away. "She's out."

Damn it. Where would Shane take her? They are probably at the movies, but how many theaters are there in Los Angeles? My fingers snap. "The movies ... I was supposed to take Rosalyn to that film festival ending tonight. That's where they went."

Jacqueline's voice halts me as I reach the bottom porch step. "Niles, please don't try to track her down. Why don't you give her a call in the morning?"

Don't give up. Keep running.

No. Jacqueline's her best friend. Win her over.

But how? This isn't a jury. Juries require professional decorum laced with anything resembling compassion, but women need the real deal.

I'm screwed. I've no Rosalyn, no Peter, and no magical transformation into a prince. I return to the porch and lean against the post so it can take the burden of my weight. Peter said I could only process about five percent of a normal person's capacity to love. Right now that five percent is giving me chest pains. "I know I screwed up, but I'm about to fix myself, and I want her to be there when it happens."

Jacqueline's brows scrunch. "What the hell are you talking about?"

"Rosalyn belongs with me, and I need to stop her before … What if she actually loves being with him and I've already lost my chance?"

My head bounces back against the post. It hardly knocks sense into me. "Screw it, I'm finding her."

"Niles, wait. I don't understand a word you are saying, but … Rox is in her room. She's been having a rough time, so please watch what you say to her."

In a flash, I'm through the door and nearly mowing over Jacqueline. My feet rumble up the steps like the lead-in to an earthquake. I touch the cool knob then jerk back my hand. Remember, Niles, people like privacy. Don't screw this up before you even plead your case.

Knock. Beat. *Knock*. Beat. *Knock*.

Breathe.

"Hey, that new dress may—" Rosalyn's door flies open. Her pale skin peeks out under a black bra and panty set. She's delicious, beautiful, and sexy as hell as she shocks me.

Gasp! She slams the door. "Just a minute!"

This is nothing. She probably always dresses this way. It has nothing to do with her dating Shane.

The hell she does! Damn it, Peter, where the crap are you?

Slowly the door reopens. Rosalyn keeps her chin to her chest with her eyes barely peering at me. Her flesh is covered in a soft pink satin robe that accents rosy cheeks. She looks so damn beautiful. "Hi."

"Hi. Have uh—Have you seen Peter?" And what the hell is up with the take-me-now outfit?

She draws the robe tightly across her, looking totally embarrassed and absolutely adorable. "Not since Wednesday. Everything okay?"

"No. Nothing is okay. Rosalyn, I can't retract my words, but please know I had the best of intentions when I related to the situation the only way I knew how. I will never, ever forgive myself, and I don't expect you to either. Please, stay here with me tonight. Give me one last chance to try to make everything better. I can't promise you the romance you deserve, but I can promise to stand by you no matter where life takes you."

Rosalyn's eyes go to the ground. She has that look people get when they are about to say something that will bring forth pain. How can I stop her from dumping me again? Girls like Rosalyn deserve better than to give people who hurt them another chance. I'm too late.

Her mouth begins to open, and my eyes close her off. With the grab of a breath I brace myself for the inevitable.

"Niles, how can I not give you a chance when there is so much about you to love?"

Slowly my eyes open to her soft and gentle features that are braving an awkward glow. What I can only describe as an ache of hope drifts across my face, filling my breath and gripping my throat. She's taking a chance. She's taking a chance on me! Me, the Niles of old. The Niles who wronged her. Not the person I hope to become, but the person I've always been. The one called unlovable by almost everyone.

No matter what lies ahead for Peter and I, the Niles of the last thirty-one years just found life.

Tears fall from my eyes. They are not streams of loneliness but rivers of hope. I did it. I found acceptance. For the first time I am real to someone other than me.

Rosalyn gives me an eager nod that tells me I've found someone who will stand by me through the madness of my world. She steps into my arms, and all I want to do is hold her for as long as she will allow.

"So why were you asking about Peter?" Rox asks, still wrapped in my embrace. "He's been suspiciously absent. Is everything all right?"

"Honestly, I don't know. I expected to see him when I got off the plane. It couldn't have happened already. I don't feel any different. Something's wrong."

Wait. I've been running around like a madman. Did I immediately start pulling Peter in once I gave Mrs. Stoddard the drive? If not and this turns out to be one of those things where the magic was already inside me and I just needed to find the catalyst, I'm gonna be pissed! I hate that crap!

Rosalyn pulls back. "The plane?"

"We did it, Rox. We took care of Stoddard. It's just a matter of time until I am fixed." My hands fly in the air like I'm in an episode of *Bewitched* and have turned into Darren, screaming for Samantha to appear. Actually, with Peter it's more like waiting for Endora. I walk into the middle of Rox's room and scream, "Damn it, Peter, where are you?"

Rosalyn pushes me toward the door. "What do you mean, you *took care of Stoddard?* You need to leave." She thinks I killed him like a remorseless sociopath would.

"No, Peter had it all wrong. We got Stoddard to confess to Peter and Jane's and murders. We also got the wife enough information so that she can invalidate the prenup she signed fifty years ago and finally have a real life."

Jacqueline cracks open the door and slips inside. "Rox, are you all right?"

"Stoddard is still alive? You didn't have to—" Her look of

fear becomes one of hope. "So, you're waiting on Peter to—"

A bloodcurdling shriek comes from Jacqueline. Finally Peter has appeared, looking very ghostly and nearly drooped over in a weakened state. "Where the hell have you been?"

He rights himself with a deep breath that seems to pull in energy instead of air, making him appear whole again. "If you were about to disappear for eternity, what would you be doing? I had some important business to tend to. Trust me, I've been feeling your pesky pull. Now hold on. I've one more dying wish."

Peter

I approach the glorious woman with whom I have traveled through the ages for more centuries than man has recorded. She is, and always shall be, the love of all of my lives. My fading hand cups her silken cheek, and I keep willing with all I have left to be seen, to be felt, so that the lips of Peter Lane can touch hers one final time. I never got to say goodbye to Jane, and now God has blessed me with the chance. "Please promise you will always remember me. Without you holding on to what we've had I'll be lost. Everything I've done has always been for you."

My eyes take in the world and land on Rosalyn's replica of Jane's sketch. We never die. We just change.

As I step toward Niles I slip a note into his hand, and the magic of our soul sealing sizzles through us. Good-bye, world—for now.

Afterglow (Of Your Love)

MILES

Sweat builds under my collar. I'm crazy to allow this without understanding more of what I am getting into. Peter has always driven me a little nuts. Does this mean that I'll drive myself batty? Oh, God. I'm going to be like Gollum from *Lord of the Rings* and get what I seek only to fall victim to a horrifying death.

Peter slips me a piece of paper. The touch nearly paralyzes me as his hand fades into mine. What if he is stealing my body like in *Skeleton Key* where the ghost runs off in another body— a young lawyer's body!

I'm screwed.

Peter steps forward. Pressure builds in my throat as my tongue pushes against the roof of my mouth, absorbing my emotional stress that is amplified by the electronic hum growing in my ears. Something silent and without physical sensation sizzles inside me. Suddenly the chaos comes to a grinding halt.

And then …

All of my life I have felt as if I were drowning—struggling toward an unreachable surface for a gasp of fresh air. I'm no longer deep in a vicious ocean. Instead I feel the peace of standing in a warm pool with the water stopping just below my neck.

My eyes slowly open to deep sable locks cascading in a frame of swirls around the face of an angel. Her eyes are of copper and gold, the colors of autumn's glitter. I want to get lost in those eyes.

My fingers glide through the glorious threads of silk upon

her head. Her lips are so plump and pink, baited with moisture and calling me to taste them. She smells of berries and flowers on a warm, spring day. This is my Rosalyn. Could I be worthy of someone so lovely?

My lips touch hers, and my body enlivens as every cell becomes rejuvenated. However, it's the soaring of my heart that causes me to take pause. Dear God, this feeling, this all-consuming euphoria, this is what I was missing.

Rosalyn

With a tender touch of his lips to mine, my heart longs to surrender. My grip around him tightens in fear that once we stop kissing the feeling will forever fade, yet I'm tempted to temporarily break away so I can enjoy the sensation of our lips meeting again. This is what I always wanted, and I wanted it with Niles. My hope for us someday finding it kept me from letting him go.

Niles pulls back, but the tingle still sparks on my lips. His eyes—now so alive and bursting with emotions that refuse to be tamed—joyously scream his life just changed in a heartbeat. Never before have I noticed their glimmer of emerald.

A sound of happiness, like a hint of a laugh, passes through his lips. He yanks me to his chest, and his lips again grace mine. The tingle returns.

"Rox?" Jacqueline sounds shell shocked. "Rox, what is going on? Is—Is everything okay?"

No, everything is far beyond the realm of okay. I pull back and look at Niles again, utterly spellbound. "It's wonderful, Jacqueline. Wonderful beyond dreams."

"Rox, what just happened?"

My dumbstruck best friend is forced to wait as the need for Niles's lips on mine again overwhelms me. The poor girl. I have a whole lot of explaining to do.

Niles pulls back and his eyes again lock into mine. Dear God, there is something about him that radiates amazingness. The tears come harder than ever, for both of us.

NILES

So this is what everybody raves about. Lord, I can't blame them, but it poses a question. If being near someone overwhelms you with love, why wouldn't you tell her how she has given you a precious gift? We have this ridiculous notion that it is fine to have sex on the third date, yet we're supposed to take months to say I love you. We have it all backwards. This woman right here in my arms, the one who tried to stand by me, the one for whom I risked my life because she drove me to better myself—she is my reason for going on, and I will not shy from telling her. If everyone follows the rule of never being the one to say it first, the most important words in the world would never be said.

"I love you, Rosalyn."

Rosalyn

My God. Such strong words, and so soon.

No, with what Niles and I have been through it's not soon at all. This man has shown me so much. He makes me want to overcome my obstacles so that I can be like him. As I begin to say the words my voice cracks. "I love you, too, Niles, and I love you, Peter. Thank you for giving me faith in love again, and thank you for preserving us."

Fresh Air

MILES

What else about me has changed?

With reluctance, my view pulls away from Rosalyn's beauty so that I can take in the room. Swing-era wood dressers, a marble trinket box, perfume bottles in a myriad of shapes, and books on music and film surround us, but it's her desk that draws me towards it. A waterless vase holds brittle flowers—flowers from me. She saved them—every last one. What really gets me is the drawing she did of me with M&M's. I look like a lost little boy. Do I still appear that way now?

The sketch of Peter fills me with both love and loss. Jane, you must be somewhere in my memory. Why can't I remember the color of your eyes, the smell of your hair, or the sound of your voice? This sketch proves if Rosalyn's memories of Peter live within her then you're within me, somewhere.

The scrap of paper Peter placed in my hand reveals his final introspection, reduced to a scribble of ink.

Use your intelligence and passion like a magic wand. Change the world.

Rosalyn tugs my hand. "You okay?" Her other hand dabs away my tears. They emit sparks of love that warm my entire being. This is what Peter gave us by leaving his memories of Jane behind.

I can't change the world if I've never experienced it. "Pack your bags. We have big things ahead of us."

The chill of the salty breeze. The golden sun glowing among cloud-dotted azure. The fresh air that wafts over me. The rumble of the Muni. This is the real San Francisco.

"Come on," Rosalyn says while pulling on my hand. We head down Haight, past all of the little shops, both ancient and trendy, on our way to a place of magic. "This way. Just a few more blocks."

Rosalyn's green and yellow paisley dress billows in the breeze. She perfectly looks the part. My beautiful girl with the beads around her neck and buttercups in her hair. Their glow reflects off of her cheeks that have been kissed by the sun.

Artful painted ladies of brilliant colors surround us as we stroll to the tune of a street musician playing drums made of plastic tubs. The physical beat vibrates in my chest while the power behind it brings my senses to life. Does this man know the control he possesses over my emotions?

All of the sights and sounds paint my heart and fill my ears, but what rings in my head is Quicksilver Messenger Service with John Cipollina's guitar and Dino Valenti crooning the lyrics to "Fresh Air." Its sound reflects a moment in time, a unique drop of life on this tiny planet.

Finally, the three-story palace stands proudly before us, and we take seats on the curb across from seven ten Ashbury Street. I should be kneeling. The deep purple, lavender, rose, and metallic gold of The Grateful Dead House enliven my spirit.

I pull Rosalyn's head onto my shoulder while dreaming of the music that once poured out of the turn-of-the-century home and into the streets. "Of all the things we've said to each other, the night you first came to my house and we talked about this place stayed with me. You described San Francisco by the way it felt, and I realized I had never really been here, or anywhere for that matter." I hand an earbud to Rosalyn. With the press of my iPod's button, *Workingman's Dead* begins. We sit—listening, staring, and dreaming.

The spot takes on a new dimension when "Uncle John's

Band" begins. I imagine the sound coming from inside. My mind seeks to see what once was and the hopes of those who walked up those stairs. Did they know that in some way they were changing the world? Did they have any idea how many lives would be altered because of the music pouring out of those orange-trimmed windows? Not just the lives of the musicians, but also those of the followers—the people who traveled the world supposedly just to see a band play. But it meant so much more. It was the birth of a peaceful community that experienced the world instead of sitting behind a desk.

Never before has Uncle John's message of taking his children home to peace spoken to me. This is what Peter was trying to tell me with that note. I'm in the wrong kind of law. I should be helping people enjoy the precious things this world has to offer. "I'm going to uphold Peter's wishes—my wishes—and change my focus to civil rights. I don't care if it means less pay or if I'm an old dog who now needs to learn new tricks. Peter has shown me I can't be detached any more. It's time to grow." Rosalyn's eyes well with pride. They do that every time I mention how I've changed. "You okay with this?"

She smiles, and the water streams down her cheeks. "Of course I am. I want anything that makes you happy. I'm by your side the entire way."

Faithful

Rosalyn

"Hmm ..." Niles moans. "We've been curled up so much I'm losing track of the days."

Though it has been a week of bliss I'm all too aware of what day tomorrow is for a very solemn reason, meaning "Today is Friday, honey."

"Riiight. Two days in San Francisco followed by three days in court, followed with I don't have to be anywhere until ten so stay in bed with me and show up late for work."

"You've forgotten about the six nights I've spent in your arms."

"I don't dare forget a thing. Peter taught me to cherish every memory. Lord knows I have enough bad ones from the stupid stuff I've done, so I'm clinging to the now."

I wish my quest for self-forgiveness would bring me as much success. However, I'm now daring myself to blow away the layer of darkness added on by Niles. I don't really want to talk about this, but we've agreed to lay the foundation for the best relationship possible.

"I need to let something go, but it won't happen without your help." I pause and brace myself. While the answer is kind of water under the bridge anything related to Joseph rips at my heart. "Why did you open that box in my closet?"

Niles rolls onto his back. His face contorts with a cringe that leads into a gulp. Does he think I'll hate him?

His eyes start to close, but he forces himself to face me. "It's kind of complex, but truthfully—" he rolls onto his back again, "this is so lame." He sucks it up and faces me. "I was desperate to find a way to win you over. With the box being under your lingerie, I thought maybe something in there held the key to keeping you around until I could figure everything out."

After spending the last few months learning who Niles really is I find his untypical, typical guy move to be hysterical. "You mean you wanted to lure me into a relationship with kinky sex?"

A cringe *hisses* through his teeth. "Sorry. I still feel dirty about it."

His sincerity is touching. If he had said this a week ago, it might be different, but now ... Yeah, I can move past this. "Well, maybe it would've worked if you had looked in the right place. I keep all that stuff in the nightstand."

Niles bolts up. The sheet falls to his waist as he yanks open the drawer. His eyes grow wide in response to the contents as mine grow wide at the beautiful specimen in my bed. This trim yet beveled sculpture was forged by a master and then coated in golden silk.

Okay, truthfully, he's a little thin, but I'm good.

"What the hell is all this? Dear God, did you rob a porn store?"

"They are called adult book stores, and no, I didn't rob one. I happen to appreciate a variety of men and it would be disrespectful if each one didn't have his own symbol of the place he holds in my heart, or rather, in my body."

"These all represent different guys? Dear Lord, there are like three dozen in here."

I'm dying to hold up a mirror so he can see his expression. I also wish he'd stop staring at my flushing face. "There are only seven. I'm not exactly a harlot."

Niles laughs. With a touch as soft as a cloud he raises my chin so our lips touch. It removes some of my reddening. "Should I pretend I didn't see those?"

"Nah, it's fine." I'm fine too. At least I am as far as this is concerned.

"Okay, in that case, I'm asking." He grabs a vibrator. "Who does this represent?"

I throw the cover over my face and mutter, "Jerry Only."

"That creepy guy from The Misfits?"

Rapidly I nod. My face is still buried in shame while my insides are laughing.

"What about this red one?"

I peek out. "It's not red, it's cherry. There's your clue."

"Huh?"

No! Don't tell me the merger fried the most important part of his mind. "Think, 'Cherry Bomb.' "

"Last I checked, The Runaways were all women, so which one is—"

I lose the makeshift mask of the sheet. "Niles, do not make me explain myself!"

"Lord!" Niles tosses the vibrator back in the drawer. I love this diversion of happiness he brings me. "All right, who gets the honor of being the bad ass this gargantuan one is named after? Geez, does this thing even fit?"

"Aren't you done yet? This game has gone on long enough." I yank the black bad boy from him and slam it in the drawer before burying myself back in the bed.

"Oh, no." He opens the drawer and points to the mammoth thing. "Who is that one?"

"Led Zeppelin."

"All *four* of them?"

"Hey, we all have our fantasies. Do you have any that you would like to share?" Niles shuts the drawer and crawls back under the covers. "Yeah, I thought so."

His arms wrap around me, brightening the darkness of the cloud hanging above. "I really wish you'd let me stay with you tonight."

"I can't, Niles. With all that's gone on I need to step back and absorb everything. Tomorrow is going to be a tough day, and …" and we won't recover if he blows it again. "I'm just going to shut myself away until it's over."

It's sweet that Jacqueline is trying to disguise the fact she has called to check up on me, but it would be so much better if I could crawl into a hole of isolation for a few days.

"It's not that it's bad," she says, "it's that I'm unfulfilled and not seeing any room for advancement. My chances would be better if I were in the same position elsewhere."

The tone in Jacqueline's voice translates stronger than her words. I totally get it. We are both wasting away in our current jobs. The fact I am again rebooting my computer that keeps locking up reinforces that. "It's the same here. I love the people I work with, but this isn't the life I want."

"Then let's go on a quest to start our own business. With your degree in business and mine in marketing we are already part of the way there. Let's start saving money with the plan that the moment we find the right avenue, we hop on it! Are you with me?"

This pep talk is a little on the much side even for my Drill Sargent. "Jacqueline, this isn't some crazy idea to get my mind off of everything, is it?" Darla dashes in while waiving a piece of paper and motioning me to cover my mouthpiece.

"No, Rox. I am dead serious," Jacqueline continues as Darla smacks the paper on my desk. "We're always talking about taking chances. Frankly, this isn't just to boost you, it's to boost me as well. We've spent decades growing up together. Let's not stop now."

"Guess who is here completing his employee orientation package," Darla whispers. She points to the résumé for the hot guy who came in here a few weeks ago—the one she held on to just in case he was *needed*. "Think Jacqueline would like him?"

I nod with gusto. With all the stability on that résumé and his desire to move forward, yeah, there's a damn good chance she would. Darla is brilliant!

Something in my brain clicks. No, Darla's not brilliant, she's ingenious! Maybe my current mental state is clouding my sense of good judgment, but she and Jacqueline may have planted a seed for our futures.

My computer finally does something definitive in the form of presenting me with the blue screen of death. Omens surround me, and I'd be a fool not to get my head out of my butt and act. I look to Darla while speaking to both her and Jacqueline. "Okay, I'm in. Start dreaming."

Five o'clock creeps its way into the day, and what is the kick-off to two days of fun for the rest of the world is the moment that deepens my suffering. Once I leave work there's not much to keep me from thinking about tomorrow.

I've been so intent on staying busy that my desk is nearly spotless. I head down the hall while practically begging for someone to give me a reason to stay, but everyone is leaving, and being here seems futile.

Existing seems futile.

Witnessing all of the Friday enthusiasm that others display while exiting the building is salt in my wounds. I've been that happy before. I've been that happy all week. In fact, since Niles returned my life has become a carnival filled with cotton candy and lineless thrill rides. Right now though, happiness seems wrong, not just for me but for everyone. Don't they know that two years ago the sweetest little angel was brought into the world only to be ripped from it two short weeks later? Everyone should have witnessed his beauty.

The *click* of my heels echoes in the desolate hallway. It's sterile-looking walls seem the perfect reflection of the inside of my heart—the perfect place to sit and cry alone. Regardless, I move on exactly I promised myself I would.

My drive home is spent in silent mourning. Music means life, and because of my negligence someone's life ended.

Jacqueline sits on my bed with my most colorful dress sitting in her lap. "You're late!"

"Late for what?"

"Okay, you're not really late, but I know you're going to try to wuss out of going tonight. Darla and I have decided you don't have a choice. I've already pulled out one of your favorite outfits, and the second you get done putting on all that crazy eyeliner you wear with this thing, we're off to Mulligan's."

"I don't want to go out right now. I'd just cry off my eyeliner and people will think I'm Alice Cooper. Besides, with the mood I'm in I'm not so sure I should be drinking."

She pops up and tosses me the dress. "All the more reason not to cry. If you want to stay sober, I'll do it with you. Besides, I've barely seen you since that weirdness with Niles happened which, by the way, I still can't get my head around no matter how many times you wackadoodles describe it to me."

"Jacqueline, I really don't know about this."

Her features soften as my Drill Sargent is replaced by the best friend anyone will ever have. She takes my hands, and her expression conveys the understanding that only she can have. "Knock it off, Rox. Tomorrow I'll stand by you each and every second and help you dry every single tear that I'll shed right along with you. However," she swallows back her own pain over losing her Godchild, "you were the best damn Mom in the universe, even if it only was for two weeks. Just know that, okay?" She heads out the door, sniffling away sorrow as she goes. "Five minutes!"

Inside Mulligan's, Darla and Jacqueline do all they can to take my mind off the pain that won't lessen. They get me to check out guys, to laugh, to generally suck it up—and it's all a joke. Every bit of my participation is faked more for the sake of my friends than for myself.

Jacqueline looks to Darla. "Why do you keep looking around the bar? Are you expecting someone?"

"Nope, just checking out the scenery."

"Why? I thought you were happy. You're not giving up on Chris already, are you?"

"Nah, everything is great. In fact, there really is something to this thing about allowing yourself to be happy."

Jacqueline puts her hand on her friend's arm and squeezes. "I'm really happy for you."

While honesty shines in her eyes I can also tell that Jacqueline's wishing she could get so lucky. We all wish it for her. Of all the people who deserve someone special in their life, Jacqueline is at the top of the list.

Now that it has been mentioned, I'm also noticing how Darla keeps eyeing the place. I softly kick her under the table and shoot her a look asking what she is up to. With a demure wink she slurps her drink.

Laughter fills the room as a group of guys enter. It's a bunch from the warehouse and the new hottie is right among the pack. Out of the corner of her eye Darla catches a glimpse and then shoots me a "don't say anything" glare. "Hey, Rox, did you hear about the latest pranks Oliver and I played on each other?"

I play into it. "Lord, what now? You didn't follow through on your threat to exchange sweetener packets with salt in them for the ones he uses in his coffee, did you?"

"God, what is it with you two?" Jacqueline asks.

Darla's eyes subtly follow the guys. Casually she pulls her purse off of the back of her chair and rummages out a tube of lipstick. She dives back in, presumably for a compact, while her eyes keep roaming upward. "Well, I had to come up with something clever after he gave me—" Her hand slams onto the table, and with a hearty shove, the spider doll sails toward Jacqueline. It looks like a tarantula flying into her lap. Jacqueline jumps up with a shriek, accidentally shoving her chair back and cutting off the guy passing behind her. The act also lands her in his arms. "Are you okay?" the cute new warehouse guy asks.

Jacqueline's eyes dart up to him while she's still in shock over the freakish doll. Her expression of terror dissipates only to be replaced by something entirely different—something that says, "My God, who are you?" The moment has them so captivated I feel I am witnessing the mysteries of the universe unraveling before me.

"Hi," he says, his eyes locked and gleaming into hers.

"Hi." She sounds a tad winded.

More of our co-workers stop to see what the ruckus is about, and the jig is up. "You all work together?" Jacqueline ask.

"Yeah," Darla says. "I asked a few people to join us. I figured we all needed a little party."

Jacqueline's posture softens as she caves to the fact she's been set up. However, that doesn't matter anymore because she's had that moment—that magical, elusive place in time that, if this works out, she can gush about to their grandkids. Every great love story should start with a thrill. Jacqueline's is off to a hell of a start.

Fly to the Angels

MILES

Today is a critical day in our relationship. My impending actions will hopefully help Rosalyn heal, but in doing so they may rip us apart. I understand that she wanted to be alone last night, but I pray to God she lets me be there for her today.

Jacqueline answers the door. Her cool-blue eyes look itchy and dry after a long night of support for her best friend. Even though Rosalyn has insisted on not having visitors today, Jacqueline has agreed to my plan.

Rosalyn sits on her bed, staring out the window and clinging to the blanket from Joseph's box. "Let me go in first," Jacqueline says.

Jacqueline whispers to Rosalyn while putting an arm around her and smoothing back her hair. Rosalyn shakes her head. Her eyes squeeze shut in an attempt to remove the dam from the river of tears that have long run dry. Jacqueline continues her whispers then kisses Rosalyn's forehead before leaving the room. "I hope you're right about this. For what it's worth, while I want her happy regardless of what it takes, I hope she decides you're what's best for her."

I kneel before my best friend who's also the only love I'll ever need. Swollen eyes and patches of red skin reflect she holds more pain than anyone should endure. Her silken hair is a ratted mess. The poor girl has probably been trying to pull it out all night. "Come on, sweetie. I have some place to take you."

"I don't want to go anywhere. I only want to crawl up in a ball and cry."

Her sniffle sounds dry, yet I reach for a tissue while

running the risk of letting my newfound emotions lead the way. "I really think I know something that can help ease the pain. I'm sure trusting me isn't easy, but just know I'm aware I'm taking a huge personal risk by doing it."

Rosalyn spends our entire drive staring out her window. Occasionally I force a smile towards her, but her eyes and mind are understandably elsewhere. The best I can do is keep my hand on her arm. How would it feel to carry a child, let alone love and lose one? I fight back the tears that come with envisioning my angel's moment of terror.

Rosalyn

I've accepted we are going to the home of my nightmares. The only thing at the end of this long and winding road is the cemetery. Niles is right. I need to be here. I can't leave my little boy alone today. But if Niles says something stupid, we won't recover, and I don't know if I will either.

The entire trip I've been anesthetized because I haven't allowed anything but the grey of the road to enter my mind. The bile in my stomach splashes as the car pulls onto a gravelly path. "Pull over here," I mutter when we're close. Niles shuts off the engine, and I hate the fact I find relief in his sorrow. As we walk towards the grave I cling onto his arm for dear life. The love that radiates in his eyes and through his touch is the only thing keeping my emotions stable.

I delay looking at our destination by focusing on the ground. Walking like this adds to the dizziness that has been seeping in along with my guilt. Once we stop, I have to stare at my shoes a moment before I can brave looking upward.

My eyes rise with hesitation only to have my fear replaced with the awe of God smiling before me. Beautiful, baby blue carnations and white daisies carpet the ground where Joseph's casket lies. Across the headstone a small banner reads, "I love you, Mom."

My knees hit the ground, my body crumpling along with my emotions. Niles kneels beside me and holds me in tight comfort. "Flowers spring out of love and hope. Those are from Peter and I. The words on the banner came directly from Joseph." I shake my head in disbelief at the little game. If only it were true.

Niles looks me straight in the eyes and seems to pull up a hearty dose of strength from the pit of his heart. "Peter took a huge risk, but he came back with a very important message. Joseph said, 'Tell Mom that God called, and I answered. Her parents are so very proud of her, but they wish their Rose would talk to them more. Most of all, tell her I love her. I could not have asked for a better mom.'"

My river of tears becomes a gusher. Never have I told anyone Mom used to call me her Rose. Not even Jacqueline.

"Rosalyn, I'll never understand the depth of your loss, but at least now I have some idea how much you hurt. Please forgive yourself. It was never your fault."

Niles wipes away my tears and then looks up at a man with long, blond hair who casts a shadow over us. For the first time in two years, the father of my child stands next to me. "Please don't be angry, but you two need to talk this through." Niles helps me to my feet and touches his lips to my cheek before walking away. A few steps later he turns to mouth, "I love you," and visibly swallows before walking on.

Joe's hazel eyes are surrounded in red and frozen on the grave in regret. "Hi, Rosalyn," he says on a deep exhale, still staring downward. "How have you been?"

I want to scream for him to go to Hell and never dare show his face around me again, but Niles is right. I need some kind of closure, and if I flip out, I'll never hear why he left somebody he supposedly loved so much when the chips were down.

"I'm good. As good as I can be." Instead of politely returning the inquiry I wait for him to take the lead. I won't ask any flowery questions to help him stall for time or give him an excuse to leave before saying his piece, but if he walks away without another word, so help me God, he's gonna loose his balls.

Joe stands with his shoulders and hips slightly crooked,

like something inside him hurts and he can't right himself. "All of it is my fault. You wanted a SIDS monitor, and I thought it was a waste. Less than one hundred dollars could have saved his life." Joe halts short of wiping his tears on his sleeve. Good, he deserves to feel the burn. "I felt so guilty I deluded myself into thinking if I didn't see the coffin, maybe the whole thing never happened. Maybe you and I never met in the first place. Foolish idiot! I've been trying to figure out how to come back and tell you I'm sorry. Every time I pick up the phone I get to the last digit and then hang up like a coward."

Anger builds, but the pain of the moment keeps me calm. "Why are you here now?"

"Yesterday I got a call from some guy saying if I ever loved you at all, I needed to help you move on with your life. He also said if I wanted you back, this was my last chance to plead my case. After that he was never, ever taking the risk of losing you again. Everybody I know has tried to talk me into doing the right thing, but two minutes on the phone with that guy and I understood my guilt was no reason for you to suffer. Just who is he?"

Niles sits two rows over, looking up and seemingly talking to God. He fiddles with blades of grass, but his calm expression shows he is at peace with himself. Suddenly the reason for a chunk of my pain becomes clear. "I'll never understand why Joseph was taken from me, but Niles is the reason you and I never got married. For once I'm grateful you left. The saga of Niles and I is crazy and complex, but he's changed how I see the world. Once your world view changes there is no going back."

Accepting that my innocent, little boy's body lies under the blooms of love seems a little less horrible now. My darling angel is not dead. He's more alive than ever. "Thank you, my sweet prince. Again you've found a way to bring me joy. I love you, Joseph, and I love you, Mom and Dad. I *will* see you all again. Meanwhile, we'll talk more often. I promise."

Picking up the banner and clutching it to my heart, I go to Niles. If anything here is dead, it's Joe and I. My child is off thriving. Now it's my turn.

In the distance, the sound of dogs barking is music to my ears. I smile at Niles, take his hand, and start running—not a run of escape, but one towards the hope of all our bright tomorrows.

Wasted on the Way

MILES

Precedents, precedents, and yet more precedents. How did I ever survive law school?

As I brush up for a case where my client was wrongfully accused in a blatant display of discrimination, the need for food suddenly strikes. Hmm ... French fries. No, too starchy. Still, I want something fried, but it needs to be lighter. Zucchini? No ... Fried pickles! Man, that sounds good.

"Oh my God!" Rosalyn rushes in and nearly trips over the clusters of boxes and bags in her way. The sight sends me jumping out of my desk chair to catch her fall.

Our bedroom is an disaster while she finishes moving in. The media room is by far worse. On the flight to San Francisco, nearly three months ago, we started debating if we would merge our music collections. We decided not to, not for fear of breaking up and having to remember who owned what, but because neither one of us wanted to deal with remembering if we put her *Kids From C.A.P.E.R.* album alphabetically under TV Soundtracks (her system) or C for crap (my system for stuff absolutely no one should own but I can't bring myself to part with). The chaos drives me a little crazy. However, I wouldn't exchange all of the trips, falls, and toe jabs for anything.

"Oh my God! Oh my God! Oh my God! You have *got* to see this!" Rosalyn's locks cascade over her nineteen sixties' chartreuse sweater with a zipper in the back as she takes over my computer. How I long to inch that zipper down and inhale her scent that makes my senses go haywire. Tomorrow I'm calling Joy Perfume Industries to have them bottle it to help me through moments where nothing seems right because I am without her.

Rosalyn's autumnal eyes are aglow as she types in a URL with such excitement she keeps making mistakes due to her bouncing. I laugh and place a peck of a kiss on her bicep as she hits return. I draw Rosalyn onto my lap and into my arms, inhaling her luxurious perfume and just being damn overjoyed at the happiness she brings.

A blonde, female newscaster with a lovely English accent reveals, "This morning in Henley, music mogul Benjamin Stoddard was arrested on murder charges in the nineteen sixty-eight deaths of former rock star Peter Lane and his wife Jane."

She did it! I figured she'd go for the divorce, but I dared hoped that she'd go for the gold.

"Isn't that fantastic?"

I take pause. How do I really feel about this? For months I've avoided pondering Stoddard and his impact on Peter's, and now my, existence. Peter's deep love carries through me towards Rosalyn, but what about the hate?

The broadcaster goes on to tell how Anne Stoddard was recently granted an impressive divorce settlement. The remainder of Stoddard's assets have since been seized, pending criminal investigations.

My anger flares when they show our footage of Stoddard confessing his involvement in Peter's murder. That bastard took so much away from so many people. Even if they had caught him when everything initially happened nearly fifty years ago, life in prison still wouldn't be payment enough. He should be forced to come face-to-face with the damage he has done, putting him on the streets and praying for death.

The broadcast ends, and my girl twists in my lap. The warmth of her lips on my cheek is a reminder from above how Peter triumphed in the end. That, and my love for this beautiful creature, are all that matter now.

"Yeah, Rox, it is fantastic." And everything truly is.

"I have to get back to work. In just a few minutes,

Jacqueline and I will sign the final documents making Cupid's Stardust a bona fide business. We have everything in place to do the background checks, and I think we've hammered out the best way to verify letters of recommendation from friends and significant others. Oh! We've also created a post-date questionnaire so we can track how well each party represented themselves along with other vital information, such as if they know not to keep you waiting while they text a former conquest." She pops up from my lap with a bounce. "This is so exciting! I can't wait to see the look on people's faces when Darla, Oliver, and I all resign on the same day!"

With a sweet smack on my lips, she skips off.

"Hey, come back." I motion her over and she plops back into my lap. "I've been thinking about our future."

"Three kids!" Her legs start swaying, her feet wiggling with excitement. "And a dog! Wait, make that two kids for sure, and once we see how that goes I reserve the right to badger you for a third."

God, I am such a lucky guy. Please don't ever let me be so foolish as to lose sight of it. "Remember how the seed money for your business came from what of Peter's money I was able to recover from Mrs. Stoddard? Well, there's a lot left. We could move into someplace bigger—"

"Oh, but I love it here so much, and you put so much work into it."

"Or we could add on another floor and buy this." A click on a bookmarked link brings up a real estate page for a quaint cottage in the country. A field with wildflowers grows behind it.

"Is that—Oh, my God, it is, isn't it?"

"It's the place Peter wanted to buy for Jane. When I asked for the money this was the end goal. It would be kind of unreasonable to have such a small place here yet have a summer home across the pond but—"

"But it's perfect! Let's reclaim it. Do we have enough to buy it outright so no one can take it from us? I feel the need to pay him and Jane back for what they gave us. Is that weird?"

"No, I totally agree. We can make sure no one ever touches it."

"Knock, knock," Jacqueline calls as the front door swings open.

"We're in the bedroom," Rosalyn calls back. "You have to come see this!"

Just shy of Jacqueline reaching the door I ask Rosalyn, "You did warn her about our no clothes in the house rule, right?"

"Ha, ha. Very clever, *Peter.*"

Jacqueline enters the room, and Rosalyn motions her over. "Come here and look at what we're buying with the rest of the money! It's the house Peter wanted to buy Jane. Isn't it perfect?"

Jacqueline shakes her head at the screen. "That Peter story is so wacky that I question the level of sanity around me." She hands Rox an envelope. "Here. Every freaking time I see Mom she goes on about what to get you for a wedding present and asks when Davion and I are getting engaged. I decided to spare you another blender and me some of my sanity by putting in a request for this." Rosalyn opens the envelope as Jacqueline continues, "Dad said to give it to you now so Mom will zip her trap. I told him that was nuts because now she won't want to come to the wedding empty handed."

Rosalyn's hand goes to her mouth as she gasps. Her eyes express amazement as she hands me a notarized Transfer Of Ownership document. Effective on the date of our marriage, Rosalyn and I will own the rights to three songs penned by Peter Lane. My gratitude is expressed in what almost sounds like laughter. Soon I'll own the rights to songs I've always loved—songs I actually wrote. "How?"

"My grandfather left them to my dad. Apparently he took a pretty underhanded risk and won them in a poker game. Gramps always hated how so many artists got screwed. He made Dad promise when he inherited the songs he wouldn't allow them to be used in diaper commercials."

A little something inside of me—a voice I can't hear, a vibration I can't feel—something nearly indiscernible—gives me a nudge and a wink. *You didn't let me down, Vince. I knew you'd come through in the end.* It's a moment of satisfaction made possible by a part of me that was, and always will be, Peter Lane.

"You know, Niles, despite all you two have said, one thing still nags at me. You took some pretty big risks by thinking of Rox as your girlfriend, let alone all the ways the situation with Stoddard could have played out, and that Peter could have been screwing with you. Why were you willing to put yourself on the line?"

I point to the framed sheet out of Peter's notebook that once hung in my sanctuary. Now it's a crown over the bed where Rosalyn and I sleep away the darkness while in the comfort of each other's arms. "Steven popped in while I was considering the purchase of that and told me to always take advantage of opportunities. It took until after I got home the night we met for it to hit me, but Rosalyn's introduction brought those lyrics to life. Once I learned Steven was Peter's brother, there was no turning back."

Jacqueline steps to the treasure. "Dear, Lord. Rox, this whole thing reads like an omen, starting with the text and ending with the dress you were wearing. Your entire story is right here."

Rosalyn

One day I walked into a record store, and I met both my future and my past. I had been praying for a way to put the past behind me and have the doors to the future reveal endless possibilities. Never did I dream those doors were the ones that opened into Warped Records.

When I thought I foolishly spent some hard-earned cash on a luxury, I not only changed my life, but also the lives of others. How many times has one simple action altered so much and I have never been privy to the results?

I give Niles a sweet and simple kiss and then another for

Peter. My heart sends a third to my son. He'll be back with me. Maybe I'll find him when I die, or maybe he will be the nurse that befriends me in a rest home when I am old and frail, or maybe he will come back the next time I see a plus sign on a pregnancy test. All I know is that we will be together again, and no matter what happens in this crazy life, or in any of the ones to follow, I will always have my Niles.

"All I ever wanted was someone to smile with. Someday, when our worlds collide, my soul will be complete. Until then I await your simple hello and the colors of pink and purple that will forever flower my world."
- Peter Lane, July 1966

Playlist

"Scary Monsters [and Super Creeps]" - David Bowie
"Have a Cigar" - Pink Floyd
"Friday on My Mind" - The Easybeats
"I've Just Seen a Face" - The Beatles
"Spill The Wine" - Eric Burdon & War
"I'm Not Like Everybody Else" - The Chocolate Watchband
"Biff Bang Pow!" - The Creation
"I'm Into Something Good" - Herman's Hermits
"The Job That Ate My Brain" - The Ramones
"The Last Rock Show" - Bowling For Soup
"Proud Mary" - Ike & Tina Turner
"All Sold Out" - The Rolling Stones
"I Can't Control Myself" - The Troggs
"I Wanna Take You Higher" - Sly & The Family Stone
"Can't Find My Way Home" - Blind Faith
"Bless The Wings (That Bring You Back To Me)" - The Moody Blues
"Freak of the Week" - Marvelous 3
"Wedding Ring" - The Substitutes
"Oliver's Army" - Elvis Costello & The Attractions
"The Great Rock 'n' Roll Swindle" - The Sex Pistols
"Stupid Jerk" - The Muffs
"A Million Miles Away" - The Plimsouls
"Money, Money" - The Moments
"Who Do You Love" - Quicksilver Messenger Service
"Broke Down and Busted" - Todd Rundgren
"Boris the Spider" - The Who
"The Threat" - Skid Row
"Up in Her Room" - The Seeds
"The Ghost Of Change" - Mercyful Fate
"I Can Remember" - The Raspberries
"Him Or Me (What's It Gonna Be?)" - Paul Revere & The Raiders

"I Don't Know How To Be Your Friend" - Redd Kross
"The Element: Fire (Mrs. O'Leary's Cow)" - The Beach Boys
"Beautiful Child" - Fleetwood Mac
"Revenge" - The Others
"After The Fall" - Ray Davies
"I Don't Like Mondays" - The Boomtown Rats
"Forever Afternoon (Tuesday?)" - The Moody Blues
"Time Is Passing" - The Who
"Strange Movies" - The Troggs
"Flight 505" - The Rolling Stones
"When Angels Sing" - Social Distortion
"Heads I Win, Tails You Lose" - RATT
"This Wheel's on Fire" - Julie Driscoll & Brian Auger
"Tired of Waiting for You" - The Kinks
"Poet's Problem" - Blondie
"Communication Breakdown" - Led Zeppelin
"See Emily Play" - Pink Floyd
"My Mind's Eye" - Small Faces
"Today Your Love, Tomorrow The World" - The Ramones
"Afterglow (Of Your Love)" - Small Faces
"Fresh Air" - Quicksilver Messenger Service
"Faithful" - Julian Lennon
"Fly to the Angels" - Slaughter
"Wasted on the Way" - Crosby, Stills & Nash

More by Diane Rinella

The Rock and Roll Fantasy Collection

It's A Marshmallow World
Queen Midas in Reverse
Voices Carry
Moonlight Serenade

Something to Dream On

The Forbidden Flower Series

Love's Forbidden Flower
Time's Forbidden Flower

About the Author

Enjoying San Francisco as a backdrop, the ghosts in USA Today Bestselling Author Diane Rinella's 150-year old Victorian home augment the chorus in her head. With insomnia as their catalyst, these voices have become multifarious characters that haunt her well into the sun's crowning hours, refusing to let go until they have manipulated her into succumbing to their whims. Her experiences as an actress, business owner, artisan cake designer, software project manager, Internet radio disc jockey, vintage rock n' roll journalist/fan girl, and lover of dark and quirky personalities influence her idiosyncratic writing.

You can visit her website at www.dianerinellaauthor.com and on Facebook at https://www.facebook.com/DianeRinellaAuthor/